DEMPSEY'S GRILL

by Bryan J. Fagan

Foundations Book Publishing Company
Brandon, MS 39047
www.foundationsbooks.net

**Dempsey's Grill
By Bryan J. Fagan**

Cover by Dawne Dominique
Edited by Steve Soderquist
Copyright 2019© Bryan Fagan

Published in the United States of America
Worldwide Electronic & Digital Rights
Worldwide English Language Print Rights

This is a work of fiction. Names, characters, businesses, places, events, and incidents are either the products of the author's imagination or used in a fictitious manner. Any resemblance to actual persons, living or dead, or actual events is purely coincidental.

All rights reserved. No part of this book may be reproduced, scanned or distributed in any form, including digital and electronic or mechanical, including photocopying, recording, or by any information storage and retrieval system, without the prior written consent of the Publisher, except for brief quotes for use in reviews.

ISBN: 978-1-64583-005-4

Acknowledgements

First, to my wife and two daughters for their love and support.

To my team: Jo Pemmant and M.K. Martin.

Jo: You took a rambling mess of a first draft and somehow found the story that I was trying to tell. You chopped away all the gunk and brought these characters to life. You gave them a heart and a soul.

M.K.: You took Jo's work and raised Dempsey's Grill to the highest level. You loved these characters as much as I did. You demanded the best out of me and somehow I was able to succeed.

My grandmother always said that a man needs a smart woman in his life. To create *Dempsey's Grill* I had two. I am an author because of you two, but most of all I am happy to call you my friend.

To Steve Soderquist and Laura Ranger of Foundations Books. You gave an unknown author a chance and I will never forget that. Words cannot express the true thanks that I have for you and your team at Foundations Books.

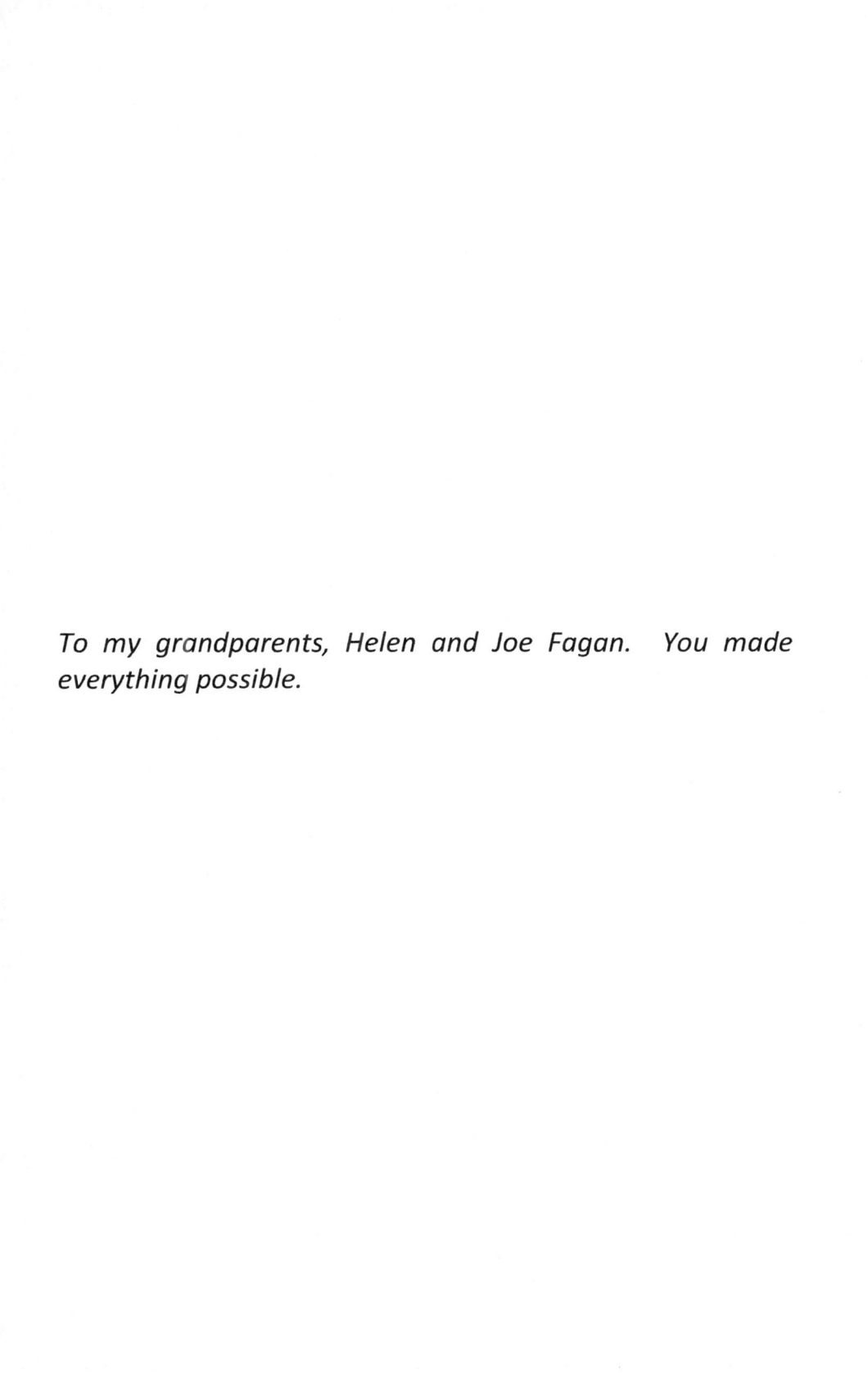

To my grandparents, Helen and Joe Fagan. You made everything possible.

Table of Contents

Chapter One: *Seattle and Lourdes and Homeless, Oh MY!* 10

Chapter Two: *Tail Between My Legs* 15

Chapter Three: *Prodigal Son* 18

Chapter Four: *Hope Has a Plan for Your Life, Sinner* 21

Chapter Five: *Good Morning, Dempsey* 25

Chapter Six: *A Shit Jam Sandwich* 27

Chapter Seven: *A Man, A Plan, A Restaurant?* 31

Chapter Eight: *An Invitation with Consequences* 35

Chapter Nine: *Your Former Bedroom* 39

Chapter Ten: *The Hand I Held* 49

Chapter Eleven: *Clothes Make the Man* 54

Chapter Twelve: *Dangerous Furniture* 56

Chapter Thirteen: *A Needed Embrace* 60

Chapter Fourteen: *A Stand-Up Guy* 64

Chapter Fifteen: *Duct Tape is Not Enough* 71

Chapter Sixteen: *Friends Like This* 74

Chapter Seventeen: *William's Grill* 78

Chapter Eighteen: *Scouting for an Outhouse* 81

Chapter Nineteen: *En Morpheno Veritas* 89

Chapter Twenty: *I Hate Lemonade* 95

Chapter Twenty-One: *So-Called Friends* 100

Chapter Twenty-Two: *Enjoyable Wrecks* 105

Chapter Twenty-Three: *Ice Cream from Former East Germany* 111

Chapter Twenty-Four: *The Trouble of Love* 126

Chapter Twenty-Five: *Running Away* 130

Chapter Twenty-Six: *We're Getting the Band Back Together* 135

Chapter Twenty-Seven: *The Biggest Boy on the Block* 139

Chapter Twenty-Eight: *Arms Waving, Running About* 148

Chapter Twenty-Nine: *Trigger-Happy Hicks* 154

Chapter Thirty: *Speak to the Trees* 157

Chapter Thirty-One: *TMI* 162

Chapter Thirty-Two: *Of Cops and Corndogs* 165

Chapter Thirty-Three: *New Blood* 170

Chapter Thirty-Four: *Happiness is an Empty House* 177

Chapter Thirty-Five: *Smelly with Disgusting Hair* 180

Chapter Thirty-Six: *A Polite Kidnapping* 183

Chapter Thirty-Seven: *I'm In* 186

Chapter Thirty-Eight: *Claire* 188

Chapter Thirty-Nine: *Hope Saves the Day* 195

Chapter Forty: *Risk Takers* 199

Chapter Forty-One: *Eager to Help* 202

Chapter Forty-Two: *Palaver at Picalo's* 205

Chapter Forty-Three: *Life Coach* 209

Chapter Forty-Four: *The Great Escape* 215

Chapter Forty-Five: *Walk with Me* 219

Chapter Forty-Six: *Our Rock* 221

Chapter Forty-Seven: *Unavoidable* 224

Chapter Forty-Eight: *Cold Ice Cream and Hot Housewives* ... 229

Chapter Forty-Nine: *A Promise Kept* 233

Chapter Fifty: *The Only Sport in Town* 238

Chapter Fifty-One: *Falling Apart in the Rain* 241

Chapter Fifty-Two: *Burning Desire* 246

Chapter Fifty-Three: *Stairs to Heaven* 252

Chapter Fifty-Four: *Table Your Remorse* 255

Chapter Fifty-Five: *A Dream of Waking* 259

Chapter Fifty-Six: *Enough Silence* 261

Chapter Fifty-Seven: *Seattle Calling* 265

Chapter Fifty-Eight: *The Rainy-Day Shirt* 270

Chapter Fifty-Nine: *Here to Help* 278

Chapter Sixty: *Opening Night* 281

Chapter Sixty-One: *The New Hope* 284

Chapter Sixty-Two: *A Family Dinner* 291

Chapter Sixty-Three: *The Lonely Stake Fry* 296

Chapter Sixty-Four: *An Overdue Farewell* 299

Chapter Sixty-Five: *Unexpected Homecoming* 304

Chapter Sixty-Six: *Breaking and Entering* 308

Epilogue: 324

About the Author 327

More from Foundations Book Publishing 328

Chapter One

Seattle and Lourdes and Homeless, Oh MY!

Everyone's life has a defining moment. For the longest time I thought mine was the crash of 2008. I was wrong.

It was only the beginning.

I always wanted to be a teacher. That is, until I taught. How messed up is that? It was the final day at Queen Rainer High School in Seattle, Washington when I was informed my contract would not be renewed. The crash hit hard and that included the Seattle school district budget. While my fellow teachers stared off into space as their careers took a nosedive, I was secretly doing cartwheels and popping champagne. After all, I had picked the wrong career. But I wasn't worried; I had a roof over my heard and a lady in my life.

Her name was Lourdes. At the beginning I thought our relationship was perfect. Ideal, even. Seven months and four days to be exact. Lourdes liked things just so, and I tried to be the perfect, considerate boyfriend. I learned to tiptoe before she woke, served her favorite tea, and watched TV on mute thanks to subtitles until she finished reading.

We lived in her father's rental. Lourdes kept a busy social calendar what with her friends always dropping by. She was always on some diet fad or another, so I couldn't remember if this week we were eating Paleo or vegan; low carb or gluton free, so Lourdes controlled our menu. It was an ideal life until it wasn't.

As I exited Queen Rainer High School for a final time, I came up with a brilliant plan — Pizza. I stopped at Gino's and bought two specials. One for her, one for me. I'd break the news, have lunch, and search for a new job in the morning. Life was simpler back then.

I double-checked her pizza. If one item was forgotten, it was Trash City. Carefully, I opened the box. Three mushrooms, four sliced bell peppers, six cherry tomatoes, a mixture of tamari, and dried herb blend. Perfect!

You might be wondering how we met. Trust me, it's a cool story. We bumped into one another at a Halloween party. I had gone as Frankenstein's monster, and when Lourdes arrived dressed up as a mad but oh-so-sexy scientist, I took it as a sign. With our costumes a perfect match, we figured so were we. We dated over the holidays and by January, I moved in. Sure, us crazy kids may have been rushing it and maybe I should've seen the red flags when she ditched all my clothes in favor of ones she preferred, but life was good. Why rock the boat?

I entered the house in my customary silence. Once I'd accidentally woken Lourdes from a nap and can honestly say I saw a glimpse of hell. But on that weird day, she opened the door before I had a chance and stormed away. She paced from the kitchen to the bedroom to the deck, her phone pressed against her ear the whole time. She listened while glaring at me. Her silence made me uneasy. When it came to conversations Lourdes was the dominant one, always talking, but not today.

Lourdes stood near the window with her back to me. It was a sunny day, but the clouds were moving in and a raindrop or two would probably find its way to earth eventually. *Why couldn't we enjoy the*

Dempsey's Grill

moment? I wanted to scream. Looking back, I wonder what would have happened if I did.

Lourdes's head slowly turned until her eyes caught mine. I didn't notice the luggage by the door or that our pizzas were getting cold. Something was wrong.

"Yes, Daddy. I agree." She speaks!

Lourdes placed her phone in her pocket and gave me a long, measuring glare. I had grown used her looks, but the, "Yes, Daddy" part gave me a chill.

"You lost your job." It wasn't a question. Her voice was steady, her eyes were mean.

The sound of her voice made me happy. Maybe it was because she was always angry. Maybe, deep down, there was this beautiful person hidden underneath this mountain of disgust and disdain. Or maybe I was a typical horny guy and I didn't care. Good old angry sex, that's my motto. Maybe that's why her voice made me happy.

"How the hell did you get fired?"

I tried to explain. "I didn't get fired, I was laid off. The budget collapsed."

But I already knew there was no point in contradicting her. She didn't care if her facts were right. I may have loved the sound of her voice, but I hated the look in her eyes. They always carried the same message...disappointment.

"I don't care how it happened, I'm not going to support a freeloader. I'm not your Sugar Mama. I will not live with an unemployed man."

"Huh?" It was slowly sinking in. My afternoon wasn't going as planned. "Wait. How did you find out?"

"Daddy knows everybody on the school board. They said you were the only one who didn't cry. You wanted to leave!" She stabbed an accusatory finger in my direction.

I can fix this! my panicked mind gibbered. I never wanted to be a teacher. I hated teaching. I hated high school kids, grade school kids, preschool. I needed somebody to blame for getting me into this mess. I had an idea. How about Mom and Dad? Of course!

It was at that moment that I should have held her, or at least tried. Maybe if I promised we'd get through this, or I'll find another job, one that I actually liked, the day might have turned out different. But this was me we're talking about, and I said the only thing that made sense at the time.

"Would you like some pizza?"

"*Fuck the pizza!*" Her voice slammed against the walls and echoed down the street. I pictured this giant gray glob pushing its way through town, destroying everything in its path.

"Okay," I mumbled.

"Gibson, you lost your job. Daddy is mad and I want you out."

"Why?" It was about this time I noticed the luggage.

Lourdes rose to her feet and walked to the window. Her long fingernails tapped against her thigh. "This shouldn't come as a surprise," she sighed. "We've been drifting apart."

We had, I later admitted, but at that moment I was convinced everything was fine. *There's no drifting!* I wanted to shout. *I didn't see this coming! Don't do this.* I wanted to say all of this. At least *something*.

"I want you out of here. Daddy wants his keys." She turned and walked out the front door, leaving it open. I listened helplessly as her car door first slam then as she sped away. I wouldn't see her again for a long time.

I sat alone in the house we rented from her father. All I could do was stare at the door she had left open. How many times had we walked through that door together? Two horny love birds ,ready for an evening of endless fun. She was exciting and I blew it. I didn't blow it by losing my job, I blew it by simply being me.

Lourdes, she loved the taste of fine wine. I on the other hand, thought it smelled. She loved to dance. I never saw the point. She loved loud music, TV, her voice, anything. I enjoyed the silence. It allowed me to think about how much I hated teaching.

How is it possible that a twenty-nine-year-old got dragged into a profession he hated? And worse, I have no training for anything else. I suppose I could always pump gas or work drive-thru.

Yes, ma'am. The number two special comes with fries.

"Oh, good God!" I bolted to the door and ran outside. I could still smell her perfume and the exhaust from her car.

I stood alone on the empty street, a part of me convinced she would calm down and come back. She will come back, I told myself, and she will hear my side of the story. We're a team, we are one. This is a game. A silly little game, that's all.

Would you like fries with that?

Most twenty-nine-year-olds are in a career they hate, she'll say once she cools off. I will support you; I'll be by your side until you discover what you want. We are together in this, you and me, Gibson, and a team never quits on one another.

"That's great. I knew I could count on you," I said to no one.

Chapter Two

Tail Between My Legs

By the time I reached the bus station I was wet, hungry, and in dire need of my couch. As I would never see that couch again I made the best of what I could out of the nearest wooden bench. The bus station matched my mood on every level. Cold to the touch, dampness in the air, and echoes of another lost soul throwing up in the nearest bathroom.

I had to call home and warn them I was on my way, beg them to take me in but a huge chunk of my brain demanded I wait. The moment I called was the moment it became real. I was five months shy of my thirtieth birthday. I had no job, no money, and at the moment, no home. I was calling my parents to ask if I could move into my old room. The one with the Spiderman posters and Marvel comic books. Trust me, Mom kept everything.

My parents still lived in Eugene, Oregon. I checked the schedule. The next bus to Eugene left tomorrow at 6:45 am. Or, I could wait two hours and take the bus as far as Portland. On top of everything else, I

Dempsey's Grill

would need someone to drive two hours up to Portland and pick me up. The only bright spot in all this was that my older sister, Hope, had moved out, so I wouldn't have to face her when I got home.

I removed my finger from the speed dial. I needed this moment. I had to remind myself why I was here before I shared it with someone else. I deserved this. The dim lights flickered above my head. The smell of diesel blended with the afternoon air. Near the door, a homeless couple was fist-fighting. The woman was winning, in case you were curious.

I had a chance of making this relationship work but deep down, I knew this was where I'd end up. Maybe that's why it was so easy to leave, or maybe it had something to do with her father being twice my size. Whatever it was, quitting was easy. I was good at it.

I fought back another anxiety attack and made the call. I kept it quick and to the point. Mom cried and Dad said nothing. Mom put the phone on speaker so he could join in. I always found that funny. Dad and I never talked. I told them when my bus would arrive in Portland and asked if Dad could pick me up. Mom agreed. Dad was silent.

After I hung up I took a deep breath. *Now* It was officially real.

I spent the trip in a fitful sleep, trying to ignore the reek of potheads in front of me and stale urine from the tiny bathroom in the back. To end the day on a perfect note, my bus arrived in Portland an hour late. I was worried Dad would have given up and left, but when I exited the bus, there he was, sitting on a bench. My dad was sixty-five years old. Retired exactly one year after putting in forty-five years for the railroad. We were strangers and I was pretty sure he liked it that way.

Whenever I thought of Dad, I thought of brown. In the spring and summer, he wore a combination of solid brown shirts or white shirts with brown stripes. In the winter it was brown flannel all the way. From the waist down it was brown slacks or jeans with brown cowboy boots and brown socks to finish it off. He also had brown eyes. By now, you're getting a good visual of Dad. A guy who liked brown and had very little to say.

I can count on one hand – actually one finger – the only time Dad made a joke. He stood 5'7". Mom was 5'3", while I grew to 6'. I once heard him laugh with a neighbor when asked how I got my height. "Long road trips," he answered, still chuckling.

I saw very little of my dad growing up. His job as an engineer for the railroad meant long hours away from home. When he was home, he was on call. So even then his mind was elsewhere while his ears were listening for that call.

Growing up I never knew what he liked, what he hated, who he voted for, or what kind of music made him smile. I often wondered what my mom saw in him. Maybe he was different when she met him. He might have told jokes, shared his wisdom, and spoken of the future with eyes full of excitement and curiosity. To me, he was just Dad, a distant man dressed in brown clothes.

At the curb of the Portland bus terminal our conversation began and ended in one sentence. I was hoping for some curiosity or an argument, anything to get my mind off what had just happened, but this was Dad we're talking about.

"Need help with your bag?" he asked.

"I've got it. Thanks."

He turned and walked away, and I followed.

Our ride home was silent. No radio, no small talk, no stopping for gas, and no pee break. Dad just drove.

I knew if I started a conversation, he would nod his head up and down, but no words would be spoken. I didn't even try.

I closed my eyes and tried to relax but my mind kept flashing back to Lourdes's face. I saw a face full of disappointment and anger. Would that be the face I always saw when I thought of her?

Chapter Three

Prodigal Son

I dozed off at some point on the way home. I was jolted awake by a half dozen railroad tracks Dad failed to slow down for. I raised my head to look around and discovered I had been transported back to Eugene, Oregon.

Dad gave me a quick glance and turned away. For a moment I thought I saw disappointment in his eyes, but I quickly convinced myself it was my imagination.

The first thing I saw when we arrived home was Hope's car parked out front. Mom stood behind the front room window, biting her nails. I hadn't been home in over a year. Seattle and Eugene were not that far apart, but I had reasons for staying away. I suddenly became an eight-year-old the moment I stepped inside.

I was raised in a home straight out of the 1950s. A two-story house, complete with attic and basement, an oversized backyard with a workshop, a huge kitchen, a large dining room used only during the holidays, a large front room that nobody sat in, four medium-sized bedrooms and a large walk-in hall closet that once served as a perfect hiding place when I was a kid.

Mom gave me a hug and started to cry. Hope stood in the entryway examining me, waiting for the right moment to pounce on her injured prey. I was an undersized, dying lamb and I had just made my way into the lion's den.

Dad dropped my bag at the door and headed out to his shop. He spent most of his time out there, I was told, during one of Mom's phone calls.

"Hi Mom, I'm home."

I had to pry Mom away from my shoulder. She would stop crying long enough to collect herself, take another look at me and start all over again. I glanced over to Hope, wondering what to do. Normally, Mom had one good cry in her and that was it, but not today. This was a full-blown thunderstorm.

Hope dealt with the situation by shrugging and disappearing into the kitchen. After Mom's tears dried up, she gave me the same rundown she has given me since I moved away. She's getting fat, Dad doesn't eat, Hope works too hard, and I look sick. I have always looked sick to Mom.

Growing up in that environment set the foundation for my adulthood. By the time I was a teenager, I had convinced myself I would die in my twenties. I was still waiting for that one to happen and while I waited, I had this feeling of doom that my thirties would be the decade of failure and mishap. As I looked over my current situation, death seemed almost inviting.

Mom pushed me into the kitchen and sat me down at the table. It was the same table I'd sat at when Hope and I were children. In fact, everything in the kitchen had a life span longer than either of us. I used to wonder what would happen if a sparkling new butter knife was suddenly introduced to the others. Would a butter knife hit be ordered? I cringed at the thought.

"You need a home-cooked meal," Mom said, wiping her final tears away. I couldn't tell if they were tears of joy for being home or tears of worry for my future. To be honest, I was afraid to ask. "After that, everything will be better. You're home, and we're all going to

Dempsey's Grill

help you through this mess. This family sticks together. Don't feel for one second you are alone, honey."

Hope glanced at Mom, sighed, and joined me at the table. Eating had always been a huge event in our family. If there was ever an artist in the family, it was Mom. Give her a slice of dried-up ham, a half jar of mayo and a cup of brown sugar, and Mom would produce a legendary dish not to be outdone by the finest chefs in Europe. Nobody could touch her talents in the kitchen, and nobody dared. If Mom had taken her talents to a restaurant instead of her own kitchen, her life may have turned out differently. Thankfully for all of us, we were the only customers she wanted, and I couldn't love her more if I tried.

As we waited for Mom, I tried my best to avoid Hope's glare. She made it clear by her loud silence that my coming home to stay was not welcomed news.

I was the gutter ball. The sour milk. The rain on her wedding day. But nonetheless here I was, eating a meatloaf sandwich, Mom's famous potato salad, and fresh beans from the garden boiled in bacon grease. The last time I had tasted anything this good was the last time I had been home.

There are rules in every home and ours was no different. Mom cooked and took care of the home. Dad brought in the money and Hope fixed things. I had forgotten those rules after all these years, but as I sat at the kitchen table finishing off the last bite of boiled beans with bacon, the rules of the house surged back over me like a flash flood.

My mom cleaned the table, kissed me on the head and patted Hope on the shoulder. After that, she disappeared. Her job was over. Her kid was fed and now it was time for her other kid to do *her* job.

Chapter Four

Hope Has a Plan for Your Life, Sinner

From the beginning, Hope did things her way. When she was two, she potty-trained herself. When she was four, she created the toy block committee in her preschool class. When she was six, she founded the jump-rope and monkey-bar assembly. In the third grade, she created a rule that there would be no bologna sandwiches on Wednesday. Why? God only knows.

In high school, she was the only freshman allowed on the senior debate team. When they traveled to Portland for the state finals the five seniors were mysteriously locked in a long-forgotten broom closet in the abandoned basement of their hotel. Hope was allowed to be the lone representative of her school. She finished second...for a day. She later challenged and proved bias by two of the judges and was awarded first prize. To this day, the five seniors still hate her.

"So... Hope..." I tried to be the first one to start the conversation. Break the ice with a hammer and chisel, sort of thing. Not many had succeeded. At least none that I know of and to be perfectly honest, I didn't really care if we talked or not. I missed Seattle. I still couldn't believe I was in Eugene. A second chance would have been nice, but maybe I was on my second chance and nobody told me. But if it was, it would have been nice to have known these things.

"Gibson!"

I jumped in my chair and came close to falling over. I forgot she was there.

"You are in a lot of trouble, Gibson."

Her eyes beamed a death ray through my mid-section. I was afraid to look down.

"You walked away from your problems. Why?"

I tried hard to think. I was never any good at confrontations. Maybe that's why I sucked as a teacher. Try dealing with a teenager whose inches away from your face, outweighs you by a hundred pounds, and is about to toss you through a wall, then come back and convince me.

"I..." The words became lost in my mouth and then tumbled down my throat. "...dunno."

A small smile appeared on her lips. She now had the power.

"You walked away from your job, your responsibilities—people *and* students. They all relied on you."

She paused. Hope liked to do a lot of pausing. I always thought it was annoying.

"You are a weak person," she continued. "I don't know who you get it from. This family is strong. Am I making myself clear?"

"Yes," I lied.

And now it was official. I was a piece of shit from Seattle all the way to Eugene. I made a trail like a slug, slimy and disgusting. I was a thing – an ugly thing, mind you – everyone avoided, and I deserved this. Just ask Hope. Or worse, Lourdes.

"Gibson, you have closed a chapter on a part of your life. The question I have..." the interminable pause again, "is are you prepared to open another?"

I tried to answer but her phone beat me to it. She raised a finger in my direction as though she were pressing the mute button. She listened, ordered a change of plans, and ended the conversation.

"What are you going to do now that you're home?"

Hope's face was growing impatient. She needed an answer yesterday.

"I don't know," I said. I was being honest. I didn't.

"Well, I do." She smiled, obviously pleased that I needed guidance. "You will live here until you figure things out. Mom turned your old room into a greenhouse, so you'll have to sleep in the guestroom."

"The guestroom?" I repeated.

"Yes."

"It's tiny!" I almost followed this with: *What about my Spiderman posters?* But thankfully, I didn't.

"Mom and Dad are very excited you're here," Hope went on, completely ignoring my protest. "Dad's a nervous wreck."

Dad had nerves?

Hope stood and walked around to my side of the table, leaned down and gave me a rare hug. Her face pressed against the side of my head, her mouth inches away from my ear. I suddenly had this feeling I was part of a hit in a mafia movie.

"While you're sponging off Mom and Dad's retirement, you *cannot* lay around," she whispered. "Understand? You need to get a job; a teaching job or a grocery-bagger, I don't care. Oh, and one more thing." She squeezed my shoulders and pressed her lips closer. "Just a sprinkle of advice, Gibson. Try to avoid any kind of romance for a long, long time."

Another call came and she left without saying goodbye.

So there I sat, alone in the kitchen I grew up in. I didn't mind. I liked the feeling of being alone. I could pretend to be anyone and forget where I was. Come to think of it, I was doing that when I was with Lourdes. Is that who I am? Would I rather live a fantasy than a reality, like she said?

Dempsey's Grill

My thoughts traveled to those fantasy games where I would pretend to be a rock star. I can't sing or play anything, so why go there? But I always did. But rock and rollers have problems, too, even if they're rich and have supermodels pounding on their doors...

"Damn," I whispered.

I folded my arms on the table and collapsed my head on top of them. This was bad. Really bad. I even made Dad nervous. I'm twenty-nine, I thought, as the reality of it all came crashing down. Unemployed, broke, and living in my parent's guestroom because being homeless sounded cold.

This was day one. Now what?

Chapter Five

Good Morning, Dempsey

    I woke up in the guest bedroom. It was early in the morning, but I had no idea the actual time.
    The room felt like a prison cell. One bed and four blank walls. No windows, no pictures, no prison guard. But it did have a closet. It also had an odd smell, but I tried not to think about that.
    As I lay amongst my shattered dreams and the strange smell, I heard a knock on the front door.
    "He's still in bed," Mom said, but that didn't stop our guest from running up the stairs. I closed my eyes, placed a pillow over my head and waited. Seconds later, the door flew open.
    "Wakey, wakey, eggs and bacey!"
    A tall, lanky body landed on me, knees burrowing into my legs and hands pushing down on the pillow, as if trying to shove it through my head.
    "You're already awake. Asshole."
    "Good morning, Dempsey," I mumbled through the pillow.

Dempsey's Grill

"Good morning, loser. Now stand up. I want to see what a Seattle lightweight looks like."

I jumped out of bed and smiled. I couldn't help it.

We met when we were fifteen, but it felt like I'd known Dempsey my entire life. Dempsey and his mom moved into the house next to ours on a hot July afternoon. My previous best friend and her mom had moved out a week earlier. I was suffering from withdrawal when he showed up. I had never had a friend move away. We'd been best friends most of our lives and watching her leave was the first heartbreak I had ever experienced. Suddenly and thankfully, the pain eased the day Dempsey moved in.

Dempsey was a tall, skinny kid when we first met. He was still tall, but no longer skinny. About a month into the school year Dempsey had grown tired of being picked on for being the new face on campus. One day he walked into the school weight room and announced: "It's go-time."

Dempsey had a knack for throwing things. He became the first freshman in our high school history to become the starting quarterback.

As time went on and his popularity soared, Dempsey tried his hand at basketball and baseball. By the time we entered our senior year, Dempsey had grown into a 6'5, 200-pound, three-sport legend. He led our football team to its first state title in his junior year and brought home our only basketball state title.

In baseball, where our school always sucked, he helped our sorry team win more games than we lost. But in the end his grades were not enough for college. In fact, he had a bumper sticker—*A Proud C Student*. I have to be honest; I think he was.

Academics wasn't his thing and he was okay with that. There was always a party to go to or girls to meet. On the bright side, he took me everywhere. I tried to tutor him when he was failing algebra, but it didn't work. Too many girls, he said.

When we graduated, he took his trophies home with a smile. He would never play ball again and he was fine with that. He had a plan, he said. He always had a plan. And now you know Dempsey.

"Get in, Bugs, we need to talk."

Chapter Six

A Shit Jam Sandwich

    I could not remember a time when he didn't call me Bugs. Maybe I ate a grasshopper on a dare, or maybe I looked like one, but the name stuck and deep down it was kind of cool.
    "We need to talk, Bugs. I'm in a shit jam."
    "You're in a shit jam? Have you heard my story?"
    "As a matter of fact, I did. Your mom called and told me everything."
    I wasn't surprised.
    "Lourdes was an A1 bitch," he proudly stated. "I predicted this would happen the day you moved to Seattle."
    Dempsey had a way with predictions. He called it a feeling. If the feeling was right, he did it or said it. With Lourdes, he'd said it. Never trust her, he told me. That bitch will lower the boom on your ass. One day she'll wake up and decide your number is up and when that happens, out you go.
    "I'll be damned," I said. "You nailed it."

Dempsey's Grill

"What?"

"Nothing."

I knew where we were going the moment we got into the car. As kids, we had a favorite spot. A giant rock by the river. In high school, we used it to talk about girls or an upcoming game or my struggles in chemistry class. Dempsey said the rock calmed him. It became a tradition to sit together on a Thursday night before Friday's game. Dempsey claimed it carried some sort of magic that allowed him to play at a high level. I always liked the sound it made when the river rushed by. If the rock did have magic, I'd like to think it was the friendship it created for two bumbling kids when both needed something new.

Now, all these years later, if there was magic in that old rock, now was the time to cough it up.

We stood in the middle, surveying the scene. A handful of joggers and parents with strollers passed by, otherwise it was just us. I actually felt calm at that moment. A kind of peace the rock brought slipped passed my sneakers and into my sorry brain. Whatever it was, I accepted it with open arms. Anything to get my mind off the mess that had become my current life.

"Here, hold this."

A shiny beer cap belonging to a brand I had never heard of lay in the center of my palm. I couldn't believe I had forgotten this tradition. Dempsey must have seen the puzzled look in my eyes when I looked up.

He smiled. "You've been gone a while. It's okay. Time to return to old times."

Dempsey jumped off the rock and I followed. We walked to the edge of the river, just enough to get our shoes wet.

"Do the honor, Bugs."

I kneeled and gently laid the beer cap in the water, face up. Dempsey joined me as we silently watched the river carry it away.

"How'd you find that brand?" I asked.

"Buddy of mine lives in Maine. Came from a local brewery."

We followed the cap as it slowly disappeared. Soon a tiny dot and finally nothing.

"I found a new one, Nick," Dempsey whispered to himself. "Miss you, bro."

For a moment we stood on the riverbank, listening to the soft gurgle of the water moving with not a care in the world, just running on and on.

"I need to tell you something, Bugs."

His voice shook me back to reality. To the real world, I was suddenly in. "Did you know I have a birthday coming up?"

"We both do," I said.

"That's right. We're a week apart. I forgot about that. Imagine you and me turning thirty."

He had to bring it up.

I tried fighting off another anxiety attack, but I gave up and let it happen. The number thirty filled my head, drowning out any hope of Seattle and Lourdes.

"I'm still working at the restaurant," he said. His voice sounded dull...bored, even. "Same old job. Dishwasher. Every now and then they let me cook, but only if it's slow."

"Sorry," I said.

Both of our lives had turned out disappointing. Why is that? How do some people find a way to succeed while others don't? Are they born that way? Is it that simple? I worked hard, but I fell into the wrong profession, that's all. I allowed people to tell me what to do and that, my friends, is a weakness we should all learn from. The anxiety attack slowed. Maybe it needed to hear my confession.

"You in there, Bugs?"

"Sorry. I have a lot on my mind."

"No shit there's a lot on your mind. You get dumped and sent packing all in one day. Man, that sucks."

Thanks for wording it so nicely, I thought.

"Oh, come on, Bugs, laugh or cry. It could be worse. You could be staggering around the streets of Seattle, drinking cough syrup. You've got a roof over your head, your mom will feed you right, and you're needed."

Dempsey's Grill

The only person who needed me kicked me out. I did not want to be here. I wasn't the type who could spill their feelings out on the floor. It gets messy, and I don't like mess.

"I said you're needed."

"I heard you."

"You're not even curious why you're needed?"

"I have no energy to be curious."

"Well, find some. That's why we're here."

Chapter Seven

A Man, A Plan, A Restaurant?

I knew the best thing for me was to be alone. I needed to think. I needed to settle down and try to find out what went wrong. I knew Hope would be the first to tell me that and much as I hated to admit it, she might be right. I needed a drill sergeant to emotionally strip me of everything I'd learned and start fresh. Maybe I needed to look at the way Hope lived and follow her ways. That was it. I needed guidance. Or maybe I just needed to learn how to be a pain in the ass.

But then there was Dempsey. He was relentless and he would push and pull until I gave in. Plus, he knew me and that was a big plus for him. I always caved, and now was the perfect time to pounce.

"Why am I needed?" I asked, finally giving in to my curiosity.

"You're kidding, right? You're actually going to make it that easy?"

I didn't have the energy to fight. Dempsey stared at me for a long time. He wasn't the type to overreact or worry about others. He looked away for a moment as if he were catching his breath and then looked at me again. I didn't know what he was thinking, and I didn't want to know.

"So, how is your love life?" I asked. I was hoping for a diversion. I was saying anything to keep his mind occupied. Dempsey's history with women was endless, and I mean that in a good way. With his black hair, blue eyes, and persuasive personality, the odds were always in his favor of being able to score. But one thing never changed; he never seemed to find "The One," or anyone he'd even consider for a serious relationship. *All play and no work, that's my motto when it comes to love,* he'd told me more than once.

"You worry me, Bugs."

Dempsey took a long look at me. It was clear he wasn't falling for my diversion. "Hear me out," he said. "I'm going to make you a business offer. This is something I've been planning for a long time and I want you to be part of it."

"I accept."

Dempsey blinked. "You accept? I haven't even told you what it is!"

I didn't care. I was just killing time until I got back to Seattle. Lourdes was probably changing her mind as we speak.

"I'm all yours," I confirmed.

He didn't say anything at first. He was probably waiting for me to burst out laughing. That's usually how it was between us.

"You still worry me, Bugs. But here it is. I want to open a restaurant slash sports bar. It'll have big screen TVs on every wall. People can come in and have a beer, a burger, or a steak and watch every game across the country."

He paused for a moment and waited. This was the moment I was supposed to say no or laugh. Most people did those things to Dempsey's ideas. That might be the reason he had to try harder than most. A lot of them gave up on him before he could show them anything.

"Go on," I said. "Sounds interesting."

"It does?" he asked, surprised. "I mean...it *is* interesting, and there's more."

He cleared his throat and gave me a nervous grin. He was actually nervous. Can you believe that?

"I'm thinking of calling it 'Dempsey's Grill.' It'll attract the casual sports fan, the clueless sports fan, college kids, and the average Joe who just wants a burger. We'll have tournaments, a baseball team, pep rallies for high schools and during the holidays, we'll dish out to the homeless."

He finished and watched me as I smiled and nodded my head yes. I didn't have the heart to tell him that I would be long gone before his dream failed.

"So... What do you think?" he asked.

"Why your own place?"

He stood up and turned his back to me and walked a few steps away.

"I've got to do something." His voice suddenly shook while his shoulders slumped. "I'm turning thirty. I haven't done shit and if I don't try now, I'll be doing the same damn thing when I'm fifty."

I knew right then that I wasn't alone in the self-pity boat. It was nice to have some company. I admired him for having a dream and I wasn't going to be the one to spill the news that he was going to fall on his ass before he even took a step.

This was a nice little break I was giving myself. It wouldn't be long before Lourdes started missing me. It would start off with a couple of texts and slowly graduate to one call, and then a couple of calls. I saw where this was going; I'd be back in Seattle in a month. Six weeks, tops.

"I need your help," Dempsey continued. "I want to hire the best employees in town who currently hate their jobs and I need someone I can trust to help me."

"I accept."

He still had his back to me. His slumped shoulders and head suddenly moved up. He turned to face me, his expression showing surprise and confusion.

"You would have done the same for me," I said.

"You don't think this is stupid?" he asked. His eyes were bright and full of adventure.

Dempsey's Grill

Well, yes, I do, I thought with some amusement. You will fail. You will panic and then you will get bored and knock up a girlfriend or stalker. One day I'll get a call from you. Your pregnant girlfriend kicked you out and you need a place to stay. You always wanted to visit Seattle, so I'll spend the entire day promising Lourdes you'll only stay the weekend and when you arrive, I'll secretly hope you stay longer. And you will.

"There's no such thing as a stupid idea," I lied. "Look at all the people who laughed at Steve Jobs."

"Exactly."

I'm comparing Steve Jobs to Dempsey. Think about that.

His eyes were focused somewhere far away. His thoughts were either a close second or tied for the lead. I smiled. This was good for him, and for me. It'll get me out of the house, and it'll make him happy. For a little while, anyway.

Chapter Eight

An Invitation with Consequences

The following morning, I received a call. Mom answered and nervously handed me the phone. She stood and watched as if I was about to receive news that would change my life.

"Hello?" I turned away from Mom who was now holding her hands tight to her chest. Even I was starting to get nervous.

"Good morning, Gibson." It was Hope.

"Hi."

I could feel Mom leaning in, trying to capture every word. I thought of my couch in Seattle and was seriously missing it. I never thought I'd miss furniture, but it was just the perfect blend of soft and supportive...something Hope would never be able to understand.

"I want to speak with you today." Hope's voice was menacing and full of doom. "Come over to my house for lunch. If you leave the house at 11:40 to allow for traffic, you should be here no later than noon. Take Mom's car."

"Sure," I promised.

Dempsey's Grill

"Now give Mom the phone."

I handed it to her and sat down to send Lourdes a text, since the previous eight had been ignored before taking a long walk. I was hoping Dempsey and I would start soon. I was getting bored with these walks.

Hope stood proudly by the front door when I arrived. She was, as always, dressed for a party. A Republican thousand dollar-a-plate party, that is. Today she had on a white silk blouse, black slacks, and perfectly combed hair that would have looked swell in 1983. Just once, I wanted to see her in shorts and a baggy shirt.

"Gibson, I asked you to be here at noon." Her voice, as usual, teetered on the edge of a scream. An impatient scream if there is such a thing. "It's eleven after."

"Close enough," I said, and laughed.

"Get in the house," she ordered.

I sat down in her perfect kitchen. The table I sat at was born from a fallen tree I once knew. As I looked around, I noticed not a crumb, coffee-stain, or napkin was out of place. They say every home has a soul. Well, good luck with that. No soul would dare enter Hope's walls.

Hope and I sat in silence in her cold, silent home. In front of me sat a perfectly sliced tuna sandwich complete with low salt chips and a hearty glass of two percent milk. Yes, I'm six-years-old. She sat directly across from me with her adult size lunch consisting of salad, multigrain crackers, and green tea. I forgot to mention our family custom—We do not talk while we eat. Don't even think about it. When I finished eating my first-grade lunch, Hope thankfully broke the silence.

"Mom informed me you spent some time with Dempsey."

"Yes."

"Please tell me it was a social visit and a brief one at that."

I decided to go for broke and tell her Dempsey's plan. She would find out eventually, so I figured I might as well speed it up a bit.

"He wants to open his own restaurant and he wants me to partner with him."

I spoke fast while focusing on the table. Oddly enough, she wasn't all that interested. It usually took me days to explain anything to Hope. When I was a child it took me all summer to ask if she had seen my favorite ball. I reminded myself to talk slow and to sound adult'ish. Yes, I doubt that's a word, but you know what I'm getting at.

"He needs a partner," I continued, and I slowly raised my eyes to hers. "And I'm the perfect fit. We had a long talk and I want to do it."

When I finished, I had an overwhelming desire to ask if I could go outside and play. Thankfully, I stopped talking and allowed the silence to do its job.

"This is important to you," she said after a full sixty seconds of nothing.

"Yes."

I couldn't shake the feeling I was selling her an idea instead of informing her on what I was doing. But let's face it, with Hope, it was always about the selling.

"I agree," she said.

"Thanks?" I tried to hide my surprise.

I glanced at my sister and looked away. Her eyes were fixed on me.

That full second of glancing and catching the stare assured me that for once in my life, she was on my side. She also knew where I was headed. Hope had a way of seeing the future. She knew I was killing time.

"You don't belong here," she added. I wondered if she were talking about me or herself. "But I get it. Why spend the worst moment of your life curled up in a ball? Why wait for happiness to come knocking at your door when you and I both know it'll never arrive."

Hope rose, her lukewarm cup of tea in her hand.

"Frolic at will, Gibson," she announced, as her free hand landed hard on the table. "This is your moment to be free. A tiny moment, but the window is open. Spend a humorous adventure with Dempsey.

His actions will remind you where you may end up. Use him as an example."

She paused, giving her words time to sink in. Her index finger tapped gently against her lips. Her eyes narrowed.

"We will get through this, Gibson," she promised. "Right now, this is the worst moment of your life and I am here to remind you of that."

Chapter Nine

Your Former Bedroom

    I walked out of Hope's house exhausted. Spending any time with her was the equivalent of an emotional treadmill.
    I drove about a mile before I pulled over in an alley. The smell of a rotting something and the sight of a homeless guy taking a nap was all too welcoming. Hope was right. It was painful to admit, but she nailed it. This was a lousy time for me but instead of feeling sorry for myself, I might as well stay busy until I could go home to Lourdes.
    I pictured her laughing and shaking her head at me in that cute way of hers. I could see her hands on her hips, her adorable smile, laughing at my current predicament. Her sweet brown eyes watching and waiting as I trampled off on a crazy adventure.
    "Get it out of your system", I pretended she would say, "and then head north to Seattle where you belong."
    The homeless guy woke and walked to my window. I gave him a dollar and watched him wander off. Lourdes always had a way of making sense of things. *Be a little daring and see what it's like before*

you come back home to responsibility. True, she didn't say any of that, but my mind convinced me she did. What's wrong with a little fantasy exposé?

I drove back to my parent's house with energy. Things were starting to make sense. I left Mom's car in the driveway and rode my bike through town and met Dempsey at work. The rainy days were becoming fewer and fewer, but I wanted rain every day while I was home. The weather was a perfect mood-setter. The rain was a wonderful blanket of misery to remind me with every drop where and who I was. The sun was phony. Nothing more than a false sense of security.

As the clouds parted, giving way to blue skies and a reminder that summer was near, I fought hard at kicking away that happy-go-lucky mood all the way to where Dempsey worked. It was a lie, I told myself. There was no happiness shining down from the sky. Everything was phony.

I parked my bike in front of the restaurant, thinking this was the longest job he'd ever had. It was one of those huge chain restaurants where breakfast, lunch, and dinner had no timetable. He was their main dishwasher.

In some ways, the job was perfect for him. He loved audiobooks and music. He could put on his headphones and enjoy the sounds eight hours a day. Dempsey had tried his hand at other jobs when high school ended. A month after graduation he had moved to Alaska to be a fisherman. He was home by Christmas. The following spring, his uncle got him a job in the logging business. That lasted six weeks. The next summer he sold cars. Actually, the word *sold* is wrong. So is, *tried to sell*. He was fired after two months after being caught driving the fastest cars through town by himself.

Dempsey's mom gave him one of those dreaded 'sit down and let's talk' lectures all restless souls receive from time to time. He was given two options: Find steady employment or find a new home.

After a brief consideration of joining the Marines, an idea that I think lasted all of thirty seconds, Dempsey discovered his current line of work. That was nine years ago and counting.

I never really thought too much of what this job must have done to his mind. Maybe it didn't do anything but make him hungrier for other lines of work. I hadn't really thought about him being anxious or scared. He always seemed to have a plan. Maybe deep down I knew this plan of his would work.

The restaurant was loud, chaotic, and annoying. *Why would anyone want to be a part of this?* I wondered the second I walked in.

Dempsey waved at me from the back room. "My head is popping with ideas." He tossed his apron on a top shelf and walked out. "Let's get outta here, Bugs."

I left my bike at the restaurant and joined him in his beat-up Chevy Vega. I wasn't sure where we were headed, but wherever it was, it was clear he could hardly wait to get there.

"I'm telling you, Bugs, my mind has been going crazy with ideas. I don't know if it was our talk or what, but it's all I can think of."

"What year is this?"

I was far from a car expert, but I was pretty sure what I was sitting in hadn't seen an assembly line in decades.

"It's an '83. An old girlfriend's brother works in a junk yard. He rescued it from getting crunched. Beauty, huh?"

It took a few minutes to start and we had to rock it back and forth, but slowly the Vega coughed and came to life.

"Don't worry. Takes her about a mile to get going. I've got a buddy in town who's going to turn her into a class princess."

"Where exactly are we going?"

The Vega rocked and momentarily stalled but as promised, got going about a mile down the road.

"Research, Bugs. There's a bar next to the college. We might be able to find some talented beer-pourer or server who hates their job as much as I hate mine."

"You haven't put a lot of planning into this have you, Dempsey."

"Come on, Bugs. How hard can it be?"

"A little planning doesn't hurt," I suggested, as the Vega coughed and sputtered.

"Planning? Shit Bugs, you're way too organized. Listen, you walk in, find someone with that pissed off look in their eye and promise them some sunshine and rainbows, and bingo! They're all yours."

He gave me a disappointed look as if I should have had this simple task of employee savior laminated and stapled to my wall.

"There are times when I wonder where your head is, Bugs."

I happened to look down and notice the Vega had an 8-track. Adding to my further surprise was Dempsey's impressive 8-track collection.

"Nice, huh?" he said.

"Does it still work?"

"Bet your ass. I found a bunch of 8-tracks at a hock shop. This baby will be rocking when I'm through with her."

"A real chick magnet," I said, wondering what type of woman would find herself drawn to something like this.

"Huh?"

"Nothing."

We pulled up to the bar and waited for the Vega to stop shaking and coughing. The lines in the parking lot were faded, two lights were broken in the sign and the front door looked as if it could fall off any minute.

I lied and told Dempsey I would meet him at the bar, saying I was going to the bathroom when in reality I was looking for a payphone. I wanted to keep my dirty little secret from him.

I had been trying to call Lourdes every day since I came back, but every call went to voicemail and every text unanswered. All I wanted was a five-minute conversation; it didn't matter what was said, I just needed to hear her voice. I had heard her voice every day for two years and now, nothing. The withdrawal was killing me.

I found a payphone at the end of the hall. Luckily it was out of sight of the bar. I had a backup plan if Dempsey suddenly appeared around the corner. I'd tell him my phone died and I was calling Mom to get her grocery list. I surprised myself at how quickly I was able to create more lies. The lying tree was popping out branches everywhere.

"Hello?"

Her soft voice danced sweetly on the other end. I could tell I woke her up. She only took naps when she had a headache. Sometimes we would cuddle during the day. That was the best time. It was not planned. Not our normal schedule. Outside, everyone was busy with their lives. Late for appointments, rushing to pick their kids up at school, worried about meetings but inside, it was just the two of us. Time didn't exist.

"Hello?"

"Lourdes. Hi...it's me. Gibson."

I was nervous. I had no idea what to say. In fact, I was surprised she answered. In my haste to call I forgot that the payphone would not tell her who was calling. My hands were suddenly wet. Sweat appeared on my face. I froze.

"Gibson," I was now certain that I woke her. "I can't talk right now."

"Why?"

I sounded panicky, desperate, but I didn't care. I felt out of control and I hated it. I wasn't supposed to be living like this. Talking on a payphone in a campus bar, hanging out with a high school friend and not to mention my two other favorites: Broke and living with my parents.

"Gibson, please. I thought we had an understanding."

"What understanding?"

I knew she could hear the frustration in my voice. The loss of control. I just wanted a conversation. I wanted a clear understanding of what I did that was so wrong. Yes, I lost my job and for that, I'm sorry, but people lose their jobs every day. I'll get another one. I thought we had something...I thought you and were a team, weren't we?

"It's just..."

"I wouldn't do this to you," I blurted out.

"Gibson, please."

I hated how her voice remained so calm. I felt as if I were a child being told 'No' but in a gentle way.

"Fuck your please. I want a fucking answer," I whispered.

Dempsey's Grill

The click on the other end was my answer. I knew when I calmed down I would regret this. I hated feeling desperate. It's the loneliest feeling in the world, isn't it? Not to mention she hates the F-word. Well, kind of late for that, I realized.

I made my way back to the bar and Dempsey was sitting at the counter. He ordered us beers and onion rings. If there was ever a bad time to drink, this was probably it, but I knew it wouldn't take much to get me started.

"Damn, man. I thought you fell in. What's wrong?"

He placed the beer in my hand and gave me a long look. If I had told him I called Lourdes he wouldn't be surprised. If I had told him what I said, he probably would laugh and say, 'Good for you'. Old friends understood those things. They knew when to push and when to pull back. He was better at this than I was.

I shrugged my shoulders and smiled. "Nothing." It was all I felt like saying.

"Sit down, Bugs. Let's talk business. I'm not really sure where to start but I figure places like this are a beginning."

"This sounds like a huge place you have in mind."

I was still shaking from the phone call but thankfully the beer was calming my nerves. I wondered if this was how it was going to be. Would Dempsey and I spend our days drinking in a bar, hashing over plans to open a business that would never be? I finished off my beer and hoped so. There's something to say about drunks—they forget about the past, at least for a little while and right now, a little while was better than nothing.

"I'm not sure what the place is going to look like, but I do know if I can fill it with employees who give a damn, I've got a chance."

"True."

Truth be told I wasn't listening all that much. I just wanted another beer. Doubling the buzz that was on its way sounded like a nice idea.

"I'll need a building that can support a restaurant and bar. I want it located near the college but finding something like that might be a bitch."

"Money might be a bitch, too," I said. I was staring at the floor, studying all the crushed peanuts and lottery tickets. Is it so hard to throw things in a trashcan?

"You mean a loan," he added. "I got it covered. I've been saving for years, plus Mom said she'd help me."

"You must have saved a hell of a lot."

"As much as I could. Most of my money came from some land my mom gave me when I turned eighteen."

I looked at him, surprised. "You never told me about that."

"Because I didn't give a shit. I sold it about a year ago to a farmer. He offered me $75,000 and I took it."

I sputtered in my beer. "No shit!"

"I damn near spent it all on earrings for this girl until I came to my senses."

"What happened?"

Now, you may think blowing all your inheritance on earrings would be a dumb mistake, especially if it's for some girl you just met, but keep in mind we're talking about a guy who once traded his car for a watch. And the watch wasn't all that great.

"The place she wanted me to buy them from had a no return policy. Can you believe that?"

I grinned. "Shit happens for a reason."

"So it does, Bugs, so it does."

"You boys want another beer?"

I turned to say no. It seemed I wasn't in the mood to pour my sorrows over an afternoon drunk after all. Not yet, anyway. Plus, I had this crazy idea of borrowing Hope's minivan and sneaking it up to Seattle. I doubt Hope would mind. But instead of saying no, I looked up and smiled into a familiar face.

The woman smiled wide. "Well, well, if it isn't the boy with the funny name." Her name was Gail. We met in the first grade. Lunch time, to be exact.

"Gail? You're all grown up!"

The beer buzz washed away. Adrenalin had now replaced it and began rushing through my veins at a feverish pace. The boredom and dreariness that had overcome me vanished.

Dempsey's Grill

She smiled again. "I hope so."

She had grown nearly a foot. Her strawberry blonde curls had straightened but her green eyes were just as bright as the last day I saw her.

"When did you get back?" I asked.

"I was going to ask you the same question." When she smiled, her dimples reminded me of all those summers lost.

"I moved away, and it didn't work out," I said. "So now I'm back."

I kept it short and sweet. No sense spilling my guts this soon into our reunion.

"Same here," she said.

Our smiles told each other that both our answers were lies. Both of us had pages and pages of details, but for now at least, why bother reading it?

"Where are you living?" I asked.

"My mom's old house. A couple of blocks from here." Her mom was a basket case alcoholic. I was amazed she was still alive.

"Let's plan a date," I said. "We have a lot of catching up to do."

"I'll give you my number before you leave."

Gail walked away, taking orders from other afternoon beer drinkers. I had a forgotten how she made me feel. You forget a lot from when you're fifteen. I had serious doubts I would call her. This was not the best time and I was not the best company. I had no doubt she was busy in her own life.

I had forgotten about Dempsey until I caught a glimpse of his stare. He had been sitting there the entire time watching us. I'm glad he stayed silent.

"Who the fuck is that?" he whispered.

His eyes moved to the space where she was and back to me. I couldn't tell if he was angry with me or surprised. I remember in our younger days he was always pissed off if a girl talked to me first.

"Gail," I answered.

"I got that. I mean who is she?"

I glanced up for a moment to make sure she wasn't close enough to hear. "We grew up together. In fact, your old house used to be hers."

"Really?"

"They moved out the summer you moved in. Your bedroom used to be hers."

Dempsey stared in her direction. We watched her deliver a pitcher of beer to two guys who could not take their eyes off her.

"I masturbated in the same room she was naked in? Dude, introduce me."

"No. We're leaving."

"Not until I say something."

"Dempsey, I seriously doubt your masturbating line is going to score with her."

"Excuse me, Gail," he called out. "I have a question for you?"

"We have to go," I said in a voice way too high, panicked.

I walked to the door. It was a mistake. By then Gail had made her way over to Dempsey who leaned forward with a smile. I could see the words floating in the air...

I-Masturbated-In-Your-Bedroom.

Oh shit!

My hands moved back and forth over one another as I ran to them. My hopes of swatting the words into a jumbled mess failed. My fear of Gail kicking us out and never speaking to me again heightened. Or worse, her getting turned on by his line followed by me laying Dempsey out right there on the bar counter.

It all comes down to sex, doesn't it?

By the time I had reached them, Gail and Dempsey were laughing like two old chums at a reunion party. Gail had her hip leaning on the table while Dempsey was making an obvious effort not to peer down her shirt. For once, he seemed to be trying to behave himself. Normally by this stage in his seduction routine, the object of his desire practically had her shirt off. Maybe Gail was just better at fending off horny guys since she worked in a bar.

"Gibson, I never knew you had such interesting friends."

"Those are the best friends to have," Dempsey said, and winked.

I forced a smile and quickly sat down. My knees were buckling and my lower lip was quivering. I held my knees together and bit the inside of my mouth. I'm pretty sure I drew blood.

Gail smiled sweetly at me. "I think you have some explaining to do."

I leaned forward and attempted my best to utter words that might make sense. I had no idea what those words would be, but I was willing to throw out anything, hoping it would stick. This was bad. This was really bad. And to make matters worse, she looked as if she was excited.

"Gibson, come closer," Dempsey ordered. He placed one hand on my shoulder and the other on hers. He's touching her. *I* haven't even touched her. Bastard!

"Meet our first employee."

"Partner," she corrected, "But yeah, I'll do anything to get the fuck out of here," she added in a whisper.

I smiled and started to sweat. This was bad. This was really, really bad.

Chapter Ten

The Hand I Held

Gail and I met at a restaurant on the other side of town, away from our relatives and away from Dempsey. We said we wanted to talk business, but who were we kidding? Both of us wanted to eavesdrop into each other's lives.

"So how bad is it?"

Gail shrugged. "The worst job I've ever had in my life," she said. "I come home smelling like beer, which is really weird when you're sober. And my boss is a sexist pig."

"Sounds like you picked a winning profession."

"Don't start, mister Unemployed Teacher."

"Temporary unemployed," I reminded her. "There's plenty of teaching jobs. I'll land another one."

I took a bite of my burger and a few fries drowning in ketchup. When I looked up, she was giving me the same smile she gave as a kid when she caught me in a lie.

"You're full of shit."

I tried to argue but the burger stuck in my mouth had other ideas.

"I haven't seen you in fourteen years, but some things never change. You are a terrible liar."

"I will land another teaching job," I repeated.

Gail just sat there and smiled. As kids we'd learned that different looks had different meanings. It was our silent way of talking in case we were in mixed company, even if it was just the two of us and the occasional waitress asking if we wanted a refill. Still, I was glad Gail didn't just come right out and remind me of my failures. She knew my life was a mess, no matter how many pounds of sugar I tried to sprinkle on it.

"I still remember the day you left," I said softly. "I'm standing in the road watching you and your mom put the last box in her car. I kept thinking you were going to stop and come to your senses."

Her eyes looked misty. "I was hoping you'd grab my hand and start running."

"Two fifteen-year-olds thinking they were in love," I said, laughing.

"Running off into the sunset," she added.

"Where would we go?"

"That's the worst thing about reality, it's not like the movies. Those looming issues of having no money, being underage, plus Mom had the car and would've run us down."

"Your mom hated me."

"She only hated you because she caught us...well, you know." She stopped and cleared her throat.

And there you have it. All in a nutshell, all rolled up into one tiny ball of yarn, Gail was the first girl I ever loved, and also the first girl I ever had sex with.

That's fine if you're an adult. Let's say you waited until you were twenty-something on your wedding night, or a horny nineteen-year-old, for that matter. But when you're fifteen, it's right up there with the atomic bomb. Your mind is still growing, you're just a dumb kid and you have convinced yourself that you are in love. How many stories like this have a happy ending? I know! Zero.

"But everything worked out," Gail reassured me. "We both moved on and had lives."

I nodded but didn't say anything. I was still thinking of her mom shouting as I tried to get dressed. I never did find my socks.

"Hey, I'm sorry about the unemployed teacher comment. That was a little too much."

She reached across and held my hand and in a nanosecond, every memory of her I ever had from the age of six to fifteen came back. The scar on her thumb that she sliced with the can opener when she was seven, the single black hair that always grew back on her right index finger no matter how often she plucked it with a disgusted look on her face, the way she always bit the little fingernail on her right hand.

It was the first hand I'd ever held that didn't belong to a relative. It was the hand that pulled me out of a mud puddle in the first grade, and the same hand that pushed me back in during the fourth grade. This hand had held me when I laughed, or cried, or when I was just bored.

Oh shit.

I released her hand and pushed the half-eaten burger away. I had to get out of here. I would get on a bus, sit in front of my old house and beg Lourdes to let me sleep on the couch, the front lawn, anything to get back into her life. Eugene wasn't my town anymore. It was a joke. I fought back the urge to run. Plus, where would I go? Yes, the bus stop was an open option but all the buses leaving for Seattle weren't scheduled to depart until 7am. Trust me, I checked.

Instead of running, I said, "So, tell me about your boyfriend."

"Fiancé, but I don't have a ring."

"Congratulations."

"Thank you."

I sat and waited for details but when I saw the conversation had ended, I gave it a little push.

"What's his name?"

"Bruce."

Bruce. I was unaware that name was still being used. "How did you two meet?"

"I was down in Fresno working at a truck stop. He was one of the regulars."

"A truck-driver, I take it."

"Yes. A truck-driver." She caught my sarcasm and lifted an eyebrow at me.

I got the impression Bruce wasn't her favorite topic. Being her fiancé, you would have thought this would have been a happy occasion. I wasn't going to press too hard, but I did want to find out who this guy was.

"Have you decided on a date?"

She paused longer than I would have if it was me. Finally, she looked up and smiled. "Bruce is on the road a lot. We need to work around his schedule. But we talk almost every day."

"Where is he now?"

"Somewhere out east."

"Doesn't sound like a lot of fun," I said, then added, "How often do you get to see him?"

"He shows up out of the blue. Sometimes I'll come home and there he is, or he'll call and tell me he's a mile down the road."

I didn't say anything. It wasn't what she said, but the tone. The sound of her voice gave off warnings that this was a topic that needed to go away.

"We need to work a lot of things out," she continued. "I wish things were different. I think being on the road as much as he is changes a person." I watched her play with her napkin. She looked so alone, scared. It was all I could do not to hold her. I do believe if I had I might be describing a different scene. Gail looked up and smiled. The thoughts that had gripped her and held tight had now released her and left her in the present again.

"So...we're running away with Dempsey?" She gave me a pleading grin, begging me to smile with her. Anything, her eyes screamed, to get away from this topic.

I obliged and at that moment, we realized we were a team. We didn't have to fight our battles alone. "I can't believe I offered to help him, and what about you, Miss Easy? How did you let some strange guy pull you into his fantasy world?"

"I've got a weakness for tall men with black, shaggy hair and big blue eyes."

"Damn," I mumbled. "I can't compete with him."

"Relax, old lover. I don't think I'm his type."

"And if you were?" A touch of jealousy seasoned my voice.

"Trust me, he's not my type either. Too much of a train wreck for me."

Our evening ended with a hug in the parking lot. Thankfully we split the bill as my wallet was running on fumes and I had a feeling hers was not far behind. We were meeting Dempsey at his house the following morning. She would come over, say hi to my parents and then we'd leave. Both of us knew it was crazy, following Dempsey's dream, but I think we were at a point in our lives where a crazy dream was perfect and in some crazy way, it made sense.

Chapter Eleven

Clothes Make the Man

I was upstairs getting dressed when Gail arrived. I was running late. What else is new? After our lunch I had driven straight to the mall. The rags I had been wearing were showing their age and now this is where a psychologist might come in handy, I didn't want to cheat on Lourdes.

Yes, this is where it gets weird.

If I wore the same clothes with Gail that I wore with Lourdes, I would be cheating on Lourdes. I'm pretty sure the anxiety caused by that thought drove me to the store and forced me to fork over $200 I didn't have for a new wardrobe. I could have used that money on bills, but what the hell, I looked nice and let's face it, we're all weird about something.

"Why hello, darling! My, you have grown into a beautiful young lady." My mother greeted Gail with confetti and a parade. I began to sweat buckets. It got so bad I had to jump back into the shower. When I got out, I heard Hope's voice too. Oh no.

Unlike Lourdes, who was a mystery to the family, Gail's history with my family ran deep. From the day she presented my mom with a homemade birthday card when she was six, to the day we lost our virginity, my family was a part of Gail's everyday life.

There were times when I was jealous. I wished Mom had as much to say to me as she did to Gail, but I always passed those thoughts off to typical teenage drama.

"Why, there you are!" Mom smiled as I made my appearance. "We thought you might have drowned. It is so nice you two are having a visit," she demurred. "Such little adults you two are. It is so cute."

"Mom, they're almost thirty," Hope said from her position near the kitchen, doing a dynamic prison guard imitation. Her posture perfect. Her right hand clutching a coffee cup, the other neatly behind her. If her free hand had been holding a nightstick, I wouldn't have batted an eye.

Hope examined my new wardrobe with raised eyebrows. Her casual glance at Gail confirmed she understood my new look. With a slight curve to her lips, followed by a silent sip from her mug she signaled that my motive was understood.

"And what are you two crazy kids up to today?" Hope calmly asked.

"I'm going to drag your brother into his room, listen to some records, smoke some weed and make out." Gail gave Mom a wink and a hug goodbye. Hope glared at me as I followed close behind. Hope's nightstick was now clearly visible. I was hoping mine wasn't.

Chapter Twelve

Dangerous Furniture

Dempsey sat on a stool. It actually looked new. He stared at the few shards of glass Gail had missed. He twisted his hands, coughed, tried to put his hands in his pockets and then seemed to realize he had no pockets in his sweats. Even though we were sitting in his house, I got the feeling he was out of his comfort zone. I started to feel guilty. Here I was complaining about where I lived and I'm pretty sure if my parents knew what kind of condition Dempsey was living in, they would have had him move in at once.

"I don't have anything in the fridge," he apologized. "Otherwise I'd offer you something. I'll buy lunch when we finish. Let's get down to business." Dempsey reached into the darkness and balanced a laptop on his knees. He listed off his ideas. "The biggest problem we have is finding the right location. Before that happens, we can't do shit."

"I wouldn't go that far," Gail said.

Dempsey gave Gail a quick glance before returning to his laptop. I was curious and a little concerned how well they would work together. Gail wasn't exactly the groupie type Dempsey was used to.

"The University district is a prime sport," she agreed, "but they're rare, and expensive."

"I know, and that sucks, but we have to get a spot near campus."

"Not really." I watched Gail wait until she knew she had his full attention. "All you need is a plan B."

"I don't have a plan B, Gail. I swing for the fence or I don't swing at all. Tell her, Bugs."

Gail shook her head. "So, you're going to pack it in if you don't get a primo spot? Every business wants a great spot but there are only so many available."

All this talk was nice and I'm sure I would have been knee-deep in it, or at least ankle deep, had it not been for a spring in Dempsey's couch and its fascination with my right testicle.

"I want college kids," Dempsey continued, as the spring jolted body-numbing pain through my groin. "We bring them in, we'll get their parents, their teachers, and their neighbors. Everything has to center around the college kids."

"I agree," Gail countered, "but the restaurant doesn't have to be outside their dorm window. We can't control the location, but we can control the menu. Let's focus on that."

Gail glanced my way with a satisfied grin. I did my best to return one of my own but let's face it, anything hitting the balls pretty much shuts off the mind. Looking back, it's still a mystery why I didn't stand up or at least scoot over for relief.

"We need a burger," he said. "Something that's unique, one of a kind. Maybe a special patty or bun or some damn thing."

Gail sighed. "A burger is a burger. You can't reinvent the wheel. Let's focus on the items we can put on the burger."

Pain shot down my leg and raced to the bottom of my foot. I had no idea a jammed testicle could create such havoc. On the bright side, Dempsey was being challenged. Not all his ideas were gold.

Dempsey's Grill

"I know a burger's a burger, but we need a gimmick." Dempsey's pitch was so high my toes went numb. "We can't be some everyday burger joint. We need something that's different from the others."

The spring had a brother and it seemed hell bent to dance with my non-spring damaged testicle. Turns out they were a perfect match.

"Ahhh!" I sprang to my feet, unable to feel my lower body. My right hand cupped my groin while my free hand searched for answers. Gail later said I reminded her of a mannequin in a sex shop. I never asked if she'd ever seen one up close or was only guessing.

It was a moment ripe for explanation. I should have described how the spring in Dempsey's cheap-ass, dime-store couch had jammed into my future children's home like a laser beam. Gail's and Dempsey's odd stares would have evaporated.

Instead, I shouted, "Steak fries!" My face was sweaty, my smile uneven. I must have looked a little odd.

"Steak fries?" Dempsey repeated, his voice concerned.

"Every place has average size fries. We need thick ones." I sounded surprisingly clear and confident. If my testicle could speak, not even close.

Dempsey sat silent as he studied my groin-clinching hand. Thankfully, Gail did not. Her eyes moved from my groin to the couch. An understanding look spread across her face. Rather than ask the obvious question, she took my idea and added another layer. My numbing mid-section would have to wait. "Give every table a basket of steak fries after they order. Sort of an all-you-can-eat kind of thing."

If there was such a thing as a living hell, I'm pretty sure I was at ground zero. Oddly enough, my mind was ripe with ideas. "Potatoes fill people up," I added. My free hand rose in the air like an injured dictator. "We could save on food cost."

"Small, thick burgers!" Dempsey's voice grew louder with excitement. "Holy shit, Bugs. You're a genius!"

My numb toes woke up as pain gave way to relief. Not the kind of relief one would expect after a long sought-after pee, but close enough.

"Remember the beer," Gail added. "Thick fries. Lots of salt equals lots of beer."

"Micro-beer!" Dempsey was at an all-time high. "That fancy overpriced shit the college kids love!"

"Remember Mom," I groaned as a tiny ache worked its way to the top. "The Fourth of July."

Gail grabbed my arm and gently navigated me to a safe non-spring stool. Dempsey, on the other hand, had no clue or care. He was too busy taking notes.

"Your mom! Holy shit, Bugs. She would have different kinds of cheese and toppings and shit. We'll get her recipe and play around with it. Holy shit!"

Dempsey returned to his laptop. His eyes wide, his grin wider. He never did see us leave.

"Let's get your sore balls out of here," Gail whispered.

Chapter Thirteen

A Needed Embrace

Ever since my move back, the first half hour of my day was always the worst. If there was ever a moment of suicidal tendency, that was it.

On Tuesday morning I woke in what was, at the time, a strange and rare good mood. I felt adventurous and full of energy. I wanted to do something, to make something. I had the sudden urge to build a birdhouse. In an instant, I was in my dad's workshop. I could count on one hand the number of times I had been in there but regardless of the reasons, there I was. I was surrounded by gardening tools, screwdrivers, wood glue, duct tape, and table saws.

I found pieces of wood, nails, glue, and a hammer. It dawned on me in that instant I had never built anything in my entire life. In school, I avoided shop classes. 'Why build when you can buy?' was my motto.

Dad walked in as I stood in front of his work bench. He stopped and stared at the mess scattered before me. I'm sure he was surprised as much as I was that I was not only in his shop but was building something. Immediately, he inspected my work.

"Building something?" he asked.

"Good morning, Dad."

I was impressed with my effort. Big enough, but not too big. An opening wide enough for a small bird to enter but not big enough for starlings or blue jays. I nodded my head with approval. Not bad. Not bad at all.

"What is it?"

Obviously, I was the only one who approved.

"Um, a birdhouse."

"Nails or glue?"

"Nails."

We stood in silence, staring at the only thing I had ever built. I wasn't sure what to do next. What do shop guys say at a time like this? There must be a code of conduct.

Without warning, my dad walked out. It was the longest conversation we'd ever had. I wasn't sure how to handle it.

Dad's shop had three doors. There was the one leading to the driveway and one to the backyard. The third door was hardly ever used and was squeezed behind the boat. It led to the narrow walkway. As I stood in front of the workbench, wondering if the birdhouse was finished the seldom used door behind the boat opened. Was Dad coming back for another look? I could feel the familiar anxiety rise in my belly.

Instead, I heard my sister's voice. It sounded like she was crying and talking on her phone.

I don't know why I stood still. In fact, it took some time to realize I had stopped breathing. Whatever my reason I froze where I stood. Just me, my birdhouse, and Hope's private conversation.

"What kind of a marriage counselor are you?" she whispered. "Of course I tried talking to him. Is it my fault he won't answer? I have exhausted every means—don't tell me to calm down! Todd is sneaking around."

I carefully laid the birdhouse down. As I did, I could feel the angel on my right shoulder telling me to leave but it was the devil on the left doing the serious talking and to be honest, he was far more convincing. I stood and listened.

"We've been drifting apart for months," Hope continued. "We disagree on child rearing and he hates my home decorations. Can you believe that? Home decoration is who I am!"

Todd, my brother-in-law, was a nice enough guy. At least I thought he was. The perfect starter husband for any young woman. Tall, nicely tanned, thick, blond hair does not discuss politics, a closet Oregon State Beaver fan, and has the single most annoying laugh I have ever known.

We have nothing in common. Once the hellos are out of the way we're usually stuck on what to do next. I discovered if I brought a book along, it seemed to ease the tension after our initial greeting had ended. I would sit and read while Todd took a nap.

Hope and Todd have two kids, both named after the Reagan and Bush dynasties. The oldest is Laura, age six, followed by her younger brother, Ronnie, age four. I had no clue what they even looked like. They probably had no idea who I was, either. If, by the rarest of chances, they ever saw me in their home, I am sure they would scream and run, yelling, "Burglar!" or "Kidnapper!" They were usually away at school, summer camp, or some sort of educational activity. You get the idea.

"And the bedroom," she whispered.

Oh no. This was my punishment for listening to the devil.

"I can't remember the last time we had sex," she sadly continued. "Three months, ten months, a year? And I don't even miss it."

I slowly turned to the door leading to the backyard. My plan was to make a clean getaway. As I took the longest steps my legs could, Hope began to calculate as only Hope could. Counting last night, she and Todd had spent eight months, two weeks and three days without sex. I had no doubt this was an accurate number. According to Hope, Todd tried to cuddle, but it made her itch. He attempted foreplay, more itching. Kissing the back of her neck, arms, the back...painful itching. I began to wonder if she had a skin condition. Maybe she was just allergic to Todd.

Hope stopped talking and silently cried into the phone. I knew it was only a matter of time before she caught her breath and began another round. Lucky for me, my legs had carried me to the back door where my hand lay inches from my getaway.

My hand froze as it hovered over the door handle. One of the door handles had a very loud squeak to it. Was it this one or one of the other two? I forced my brain to think. *Come on, work it*, I begged. Was there a squeak when I walked in? How about Hope? Anybody? Hurry, before she delves into the really weird stuff.

But a strange thing happened as my thoughts raced; I began to relate. Hope's world was falling apart. The life she had grown accustomed to, the face she saw every day and the voice she heard every night, all the little things she took as routine were now being ripped away and she had no control over any of it. This ugly moment had a mind of its own and no amount of complaining, pleading, or tears would prevent it from having its way.

As I sat on the curb in front of a home I thought was mine, I realized all she wanted was what I wanted. I pulled my hand away from my escape and followed her muffled sobs. I waited until she saw me and when she did, I pulled her into my arms and held her tight.

All I wanted on that lonely day in Seattle was a hug and a reminder it would all be okay. When it didn't happen, I knew then I would always be alone. My sister didn't have to suffer the same fate.

"It's going to be okay," I whispered as I hugged her a final time and walked outside. As the door slowly closed, I saw a softness in her eyes I had never seen before. In that moment I wondered if we had found a connection.

The door squeaked, in case you're curious.

Chapter Fourteen

A Stand-Up Guy

Again, I woke up in a good mood. It was Wednesday and I was meeting Gail in a few hours. Maybe I was upbeat because of Gail. The adventure and spending the day with ideas and her were a perfect combination.

As I settled in and examined my thoughts, my good mood might have come from Hope. Spending time and hearing her problems made me realize I wasn't the only one walking around messed up. But still...this was Hope. She was born with her shit together. How is it possible she could be so screwed up? How can a person who can organize a committee with nothing more than a sticky note and a latte, not have it together under her own roof? Are we all that way? Is it possible everyone we meet on an average day is completely fucked up?

I stopped thinking about Hope, Gail, and Dempsey. As I lay in bed staring at the ceiling, I realized things could be worse. I, too, could be trapped in a dead-end marriage. I could have kids I didn't like, or a job that was slowly killing me...that road was well-traveled, but how many of those people do we know?

My mind drifted back to Gail. I started to smile and as I did my phone rang. I glanced over and saw the name. Lourdes. Gail's voice, her smile, and the way she made me feel — safe and confident — suddenly vanished.

As I stared at Lourdes's name a heavy blanket of loss and loneliness covered me. Its warmth was ice cold; a reminder of who I really was. I should be with her, I thought in a panic. This is all wrong. This room, this house, the people I saw every day. Seattle is where I belong.

Right?

I'm on a break, I promised. A little get away. I'm just killing time. I'm just waiting it out until I get back to how things should be. Now it made sense. We're taking a break. That's it. I picked up the phone and said hello. Her voice sang to me.

"Hi," she said. She sounded excited. "What are you doing?"

I didn't answer right away. I wanted to, but I seemed to have forgotten how. Was she lost, like me? I convinced myself, yes. Yes, she was.

"Hello? Gibson?"

"Hi."

My voice sounded funny. I felt like a sixteen-year-old talking to a girl for the first time.

"Did I wake you?"

"Yes," I said, stumbling. "No, no... umm...I was getting dressed. I just stepped out of the shower." I don't know why I lied.

Guilt stung my throat, my hands and my back. I could not believe I was thinking of Gail when Lourdes called.

"You sound busy," she said. "I'll call some other time."

"No!" I shouted. "I mean...no, now is fine. How are you, Lourdes?"

She paused a long time before answering. I wondered if she, too, had been distracted. Was there someone else in the room with her? I could hear noises in the background. Could be the TV. That's it. It was just the TV.

Dempsey's Grill

"I'm fine, I guess." Her response sounded more like a question than an answer. What could it mean? Did she miss me? Should I leave today? I could be in Seattle by tonight. I had to remain calm. We're just talking, I reminded myself. That was all.

"I don't know," she continued. "Life is so confusing, isn't it?"

"Yes," I agreed.

I said nothing else. She did the same. Our silence grew louder by the second.

"Gibson, what's wrong?"

"Nothing," I lied.

"Tell me the truth. I know you too well."

"You do." I smiled. Why is she doing this? I realized she must have something to say. I could feel it.

"Sorry," I continued. "You caught me in a sleepy mood."

"I'll call you later when you're awake."

I felt she was slipping away. Which, come to think of it, was the reason I was in Eugene.

"Wait," I begged, jumping out of bed hoping my head would clear. "Why did you call?"

I heard more noise in the background. Footsteps, a voice and something else I couldn't make out. Too loud for the TV. No, the TV must be really loud.

"I..." She stumbled over her words and paused. I wondered if she was waiting for someone to leave the room. "I just wanted to hear your voice and I wanted to make sure you haven't forgotten me."

"That's impossible."

"Good."

I imagined her smiling. Looking off to a faraway dream, pretending I was there, her eyes full of tears. I closed my eyes and saw our place. It was all so clear. The colors. The smell.

Someone called, "Lourdes." Was she in a store? On a street? I couldn't tell. I didn't want to know.

"I have to go," she said, hurried. "Take care of yourself."

"Lourdes, listen, we—"

She was gone.

I stood in my underwear, alone and in my parent's guest room, staring at my phone. I waited patiently like most of us do when a secret is about to be told. But phones are good at keeping secrets, aren't they? I took a long shower and left in time to meet Gail. It felt wrong. I wondered if I should stop seeing her. I know what you're thinking; I'm not seeing her, so what's the problem? If that is what you're thinking, you're right. But things were getting messed up in this crazy head of mine and guilt was having its way. It felt good talking to a friend, but I felt like I was cheating on Lourdes simply because of who Gail was, because of our shared history...because we'd once promised to love each other forever and ever.

As soon as I got into my parent's car my phone rang. I jumped, causing double pain to my legs as they collided with the steering wheel. I looked at my phone and saw this time it was Gail. The usual emotions of joy and nervous anticipation arrived as it does with any call involving a girl. I wondered if these emotions wave goodbye when one turns thirty.

"Hi," I said. I knew my voice sounded weird.

"What's wrong?" Gail asked without hesitating.

"Nothing."

"Your voice sounds weird."

See, what did I tell you?

I could hear her leaving the house. A door closing, keys jangling, the sounds of traffic and people.

"Change of plans," she said. "Dempsey didn't show."

"Huh?"

"No text. No call. Not a damn thing." Gail was mad and this was bad. "It's like he walked into the woods and disappeared."

"Are you sure you've got the right address?"

I knew that was the wrong question the moment it left my mouth. I'm pretty sure I reached up and tried to shove the words back in.

"Of course I've got the right address. I don't have time for this, Gibson. I thought he was serious."

Dempsey's Grill

I closed my eyes and gave them a long rub. I couldn't blame her for getting mad. She was in a dead-end job and Dempsey showed her the promise of something better. Hell, he even looked professional at his house.

"Look, I'm sure it's just a misunderstanding," I said. "The moment he realizes he messed up he'll feel terrible. Give the cook who's coming in for an interview a call and reschedule."

"That's not necessary. He's standing right in front of me."

Now I was getting mad. "Okay, um...reschedule." Yes, this was my brilliant idea. "Tell him Dempsey doubled-booked."

"Fine," she said through gritted teeth. "No worries."

I searched back as far as I could, trying to remember what Dempsey would do when good things came his way. It didn't take that long to figure that one out. What's that old saying? "Old habits die hard."

Which leads us to our current situation.

If there was one thing that Dempsey was consistent at, it was the art of celebrating. It could have been something as simple as cleaning his room when he was a kid to something major like hooking up with a hot girl, or the one time he got a B on an algebra test. Whatever the case, Dempsey always found a reason to celebrate and I had a feeling that between Gail, myself, and his new idea, this was a time to celebrate.

I stood in front of Dempsey's door with my hand raised to knock. I knew I'd find his car at his house, what I didn't know was what I would find on the other side of the door. Before I could knock, two young women opened the door and walked out. They were the same type he always hooked up with, only this time they were a little older, still in their early twenties, but at least not jailbait.

The women walked past me without a word. They looked exhausted and bemused. I almost offered them a ride but before I could, they headed to the bus stop. I turned my head to the front door, which hung ajar. I slowly took a step and another. Soon I was surrounded by the dusky darkness where sunlight was not on the guest list.

I ignored the vampire rule where invitations are a must and slowly pulled back the curtains. Visions of vampires and sleepovers in coffins warned me to pull away as the room grew bright. To satisfy my worrying thoughts I turned to find an empty room. My final action ended by opening the window. To this day, I'm positive I heard the house say, "Thanks!" Unfortunately, it could not be said that the occupant was equally grateful.

"What the fuck!"

Dempsey staggered from his hiding hole using one hand to protect his eyes and the other to hold up a towel. Sadly, the towel left little to the imagination.

"Oh. Hi, Bugs." He didn't seem surprised by my company. In fact, he acted as though I belonged where I stood.

"You didn't see anybody walk out of here, did you?"

I barely heard a word. My eyes were locked on his forehead. Well, not exactly his forehead. If I must be technical about my observation, I was staring at the duct tape wrapped around it.

"Dempsey, what the hell happened?"

He ignored my question and wandered to the kitchen. "You want some coffee? I know I do."

I took a step into his so-called kitchen, which wasn't all that far from his so-called bedroom and equally so-called front room. To be honest, I was curious why they even bothered putting up walls here since he basically lived in a box.

"Dempsey, your head."

He slowly raised his hand to his head and lowered it without thought. It wasn't until he started the coffee that he answered my question. "Oh that. I was out celebrating, and I met these two classy ladies. I think one of them is married."

"You think?"

"I'm pretty sure her husband showed up.'

"Dempsey..." I took a breath and forced myself to look past this. "There was an interview with a cook this morning. You were supposed to be there."

"Today?" He paused and scratched his head, which did little to no good given the current situation. He even ignored the piece of duct tape stuck to his finger.

"Oh, shit," he said, remembering. "That was today. Did Gail take care of it?"

"No, Gail did not 'take care of it.'"

We slowly turned our heads to the voice. The open door framed a lone figure with her hands on her hips. Wonder Woman came to mind. Thankfully, I kept that thought to myself.

"Oh, shit," Dempsey whispered.

Chapter Fifteen

Duct Tape is Not Enough

"This is bad," Gail said, as she slowly removed a piece of duct tape. "Dempsey, hold still."

"Wow, this is bad," I agreed taking a closer look. "Now what?"

"Put another strip on," he ordered. "I've got plenty."

We talked Dempsey into sitting on the couch. Gail had me fetch some wet towels while she took over the duct tape removal duties. At first, she wanted to cut off his hair, but Dempsey would have none of it. Even if he had, the chances of finding scissors in this place of clutter were next to none.

"Why did you make me put my pants on? They itch."

Gail glanced at me and rolled her eyes. "You're kidding, right?"

"Why would I kid?"

Getting a full view of Dempsey and his loincloth disguised as a towel was all she needed to order a quick change. "I would like to be the only girl in town who has not seen your penis. I was surprised

Dempsey's Grill

when Dempsey disappeared into his room and reappeared in his famous rainbow polyester sweats.

"Good," she said. "Now sit down and hold still."

Gail grabbed a wet towel from my hands and pressed it against his head. She glanced at me with concern as she slowly pulled away another strip. "Tell me, just what the hell happened here?"

"Well, I got to thinking," he explained. "The idea of us three working together was the best plan I have had in a long time. It was so good I figured I earned a mini-celebration."

"Mini?" Gail asked.

"That was the plan. One drink and go home."

"And where was this place?" I asked. I already knew the answer. Five dollars on 'Caesar's.

"Caesar's." He said with a wink.

"Caesar's," I repeated. "I don't even know why I asked."

"You know me well, Bugs."

In case you missed it, Eugene, Oregon is the home to the University of Oregon where like all Universities, there is a large population of young, intelligent, curious, and sexually adventurous people. Conveniently located only a few hundred yards from campus, Caesar's is one of the main places they meet.

"So, I'm sitting at the bar, minding my own business when these two amazing ladies said hello. Now, I take one look and I see they don't have a drink in their hands, so I buy. Next thing I know, I'm buying more drinks and then they're taking me out on the dance floor. I swear, Bugs, I don't know how these things happen."

"Weird, isn't it?" Gail added, her voice dripping in sarcasm.

"I know!" he agreed, his voice growing with excitement. "All of a sudden some guy turns me around and smashes a beer bottle over my head. I get up and toss him over a pool table. Now I'm not only horny, but angry. That's a great combination, by the way."

Gail gave me a long look as I did my best not to smile. Stories like this were common in Dempsey's world, but new to her. I knew I should say something, but nothing came to mind.

"Turns out one of them was married. She said they were separated but he got mad anyway. I would have felt bad if I had time to think but I was pretty drunk, so thinking wasn't at the top of my plans. Anyway, I guess we ended up here. I must have found some duct tape to take care of my head."

Dempsey took a final gulp of coffee and held out the mug for me to refill. It was obvious he was pleased with his story. To be honest, if this were a different time I would have been disappointed for missing out, but this wasn't one of those times. I think a lot of it had to do with Gail. Her mom was an alcoholic and drinking turned her off.

Was this only the beginning of Dempsey's mini-celebrations? And if it was, how long before he left us behind? I looked over at Gail and wondered how long it would be before Dempsey and his partying ways turned her off. Would she see me as a follower, waiting on him hand and foot the way she waited on her mom?

"Gibson?"

Would she pack her bags the way she did when we were kids this time in disgust?

"Gibson."

Would she tell us to get lost or worse, would it just be me?

"Gibson!"

I turned to her direction as she tossed the final bloody duct tape into the trash.

"We're taking him to the hospital."

Chapter Sixteen

Friends Like This

It took five stitches to put Dempsey back together. The doctor told us not to let him drive or operate heavy machinery for a while. Even though he didn't show signs of a concussion, he shouldn't be alone.

Gail and I said nothing as we walked him out. We were both trying to figure out what to say about all this, but how do you tell someone with a stitched-up head that you only agreed to this wild scheme because it was important to them? But wild schemes require dedication and hard work, and if Gail and I are the only ones doing all this while he parties with married women then, maybe it's time to ask ourselves just what the hell are we doing? Somehow, it felt wrong to tell him all that as he staggered out of the emergency room.

I opened the passenger door and stood there to help him in, but Dempsey ignored me and kept going. We watched as he walked to the road and for a moment I feared he would step out into oncoming traffic. Instead, he sat down on the curb next to the traffic light pole, under the Walk/Don't Walk sign.

"Did they give him drugs?" Gail whispered.

"I don't think so."

"Is he always this weird?"

Slowly we walked to him, both of us unsure what to expect.

His head hung between his knees, his knuckles interlocked in front of him. He could have easily been mistaken for a beggar. All he needed was a sign asking for help or beer money. I took a step toward him and Gail followed. I was worried about the traffic and where he was sitting. He could have aimed for the picnic tables instead of flopping down six inches from traffic.

I placed my hand on his shoulder, hoping he would say something. He didn't.

"Dempsey," I hesitated. "What's going on?"

He lifted his head and looked me in the eye. It was a look I hadn't seen in years. He stood and walked to the trees near the hospital. Gail started to say something but stopped when I placed my finger to my mouth.

We stood under the shade, waiting for the tall skinny guy with a head full of stitches and eyes full of defeat to say something. His face was full of desperation and loss along with a mixture of panic that all of us could understand. I think that's why Gail and I said nothing. We were all a part of this particular loser club.

"You think I'm crazy," he said, staring at the ground. It wasn't a question. "I don't blame you. I think I'm nuts too."

We didn't argue.

Dempsey focused his attention on Gail. He looked tired and used up and for the first time since I knew him, frail. I never thought I'd say that about him, but it was true.

"Gibson told me about your mom," he said. I watched as he ran his fingers across his head. "I have a feeling what I did last night is giving you second thoughts. I know if I were in your shoes, I'd be thinking that."

"Dempsey..." Gail tried to speak but he would have none of it.

"Gail, please, hear me out."

He stood and walked towards her until they were a few feet apart. I was afraid she'd walk away, but she didn't. Her mom's drinking problem was a topic she didn't like to share, and I shared it with Dempsey without asking if I could. But she didn't move.

"From here on out, what I did last night will never happen again. I promise you—I promise both of you. All I'm asking for is a chance," he said. There were now tears in his eyes. "I've got an idea and I think it'll work but if it doesn't, at least I'll know I tried. I'm twenty-nine years old, and all I've got to show for it is sore hands from scrubbing dishes. Every day a piece of me gets chipped away. It won't be long until there's nothing left to chip anymore. If I don't do something now, I'll never have the drive to do this again and that's the scariest thing I've ever said in my life."

I knew where he was coming from. Hell, who doesn't? It was at that moment I realized Dempsey wasn't talking about himself, he was also talking about us. I looked over at Gail. I could read her eyes; she saw it too. Three adults hanging on to their twenties by a thread and completely fucked. Wow.

Gail walked over and hugged him. I stood in the middle with my arms wrapped around their shoulders. Sure, Dempsey got carried away at times, but this time he had an idea, something that gave his life meaning...a purpose. And Gail? I could tell there was more to her story and I knew in time I would find out, but until then, I would just hold her.

"I'm not going anywhere," she said.

Gail glanced at me waiting for an answer.

"Me either," I said.

We looked at each other and smiled. Why not, our eyes agreed.

"You guys are just feeling sorry for me."

"Not really, buddy," I said. "We're all fucked up. Might as well do something together."

"I love you guys," he said with a huge grin. "I knew something good would happen today."

I started to feel good. Really good. I actually made someone happy.

"Okay then," Dempsey said, grinned and stepped back. "We meet tomorrow. I'll draw up a plan."

" What about the interview?" I asked.

"Later. Let's get organized first."

Gail stood by my side, looking at me as Dempsey walked away then disappearing into the city streets. A tiny smile on her face appeared through her messed up hair.

"You ready for this?" she asked.

"No."

We started to laugh.

Chapter Seventeen

William's Grill

Running a restaurant is a lot like running a factory. There's a building that makes stuff, there are people who put it together, and there's some people who wants the stuff. The idea is to get enough of these people to want it all the time. If that happens, the owners get rich, the workers make a good living, and the people who want the stuff are happy. Maybe it's not always as easy as that, but you get the idea.

Now, before the idea can spring into action, the creator must decide what to make. Will it be high-end fine dining?

Your coat, sir? Compliments to your tailor.

Casual?

Sit anywhere you like. Your waitress will be with you in a minute.

Or is there something specific in mind? Italian. French. Greek.

Or maybe—

"Burgers and fries. Like we first talked about."

"You're kidding," I said. "I thought you wanted to change that to steaks and fancy chicken and stuff?"

"Screw that, Bugs. I can only do what I know, and I know a good burger when I see one."

That's true. Growing up there was only one place to go. All three of us remembered riding our bikes to the old part of town to a broken down building with a hand-painted sign out front. Inside was the home of the most amazing burgers on the planet.

"Like at Willie's? Or was it William's?" I asked.

"I remember that place," Gail said. "It always smelled good when you walked in."

We sat around my mom's kitchen table, trying to remember details of that place. It was early evening, just after dinner, when Dempsey and Gail stopped by. We had tossed ideas off the wall and for once we finally found something that stuck. Were we trying to copy it? I don't think we thought that far down the road, but I do remember it was the first time all of us were on the same page.

We stopped my mom as she walked past us to do some gardening. My parents weren't the eating out type, but maybe they remembered this place.

"Blue building," Mom said after thinking about it for a moment. "The owner sold the property back in the '90's. Your dad knew the owner's cousin. I think he was a fisherman because he always smelled."

"Wasn't the owner's name on the sign?" Gail asked.

"And wasn't the owner some tall skinny guy with white hair?" Dempsey wondered.

Now we were picking up speed.

"Crew cut," I added. "He always wore a tie."

He had an uncanny way of remembering names. I was always addressed as Mr. Baker. I thought it was cool.

Gail said, "If we hadn't moved, I probably would have worked there. He wanted his restaurant to be a kid's first job so they could learn responsibility."

"And the place was called William's Roadside Dinner," Mom remembered proudly. "This is fun. It's like a game."

Dempsey's Grill

I smiled. I knew she'd remember.

"Guy Williams," my father's voice announced.

Dad had been in the hallway the entire time listening but unlike his natural state of listening and walking away, he surprisingly joined in.

Dad continued. "He bought the place in 1970, window orders only. It was opened for dining in 1975. I helped him with the windows that spring. We had to even them out because he had them crooked. He was going to open another one, but he didn't want the extra work. He made a fortune when he sold it."

I stared at Dad for a long after he finished speaking. It wasn't the history of the place that grabbed me, but the fact that my father spoke several sentences in a row.

"Is he still alive, sir?" Dempsey asked.

"Don't know," Dad said with a shrug.

"He moved to Springfield when he retired. He might still be there," Mom added.

She made her way outside to her gardening. She must have figured her work was done. The three of us sat in silence, slowly sipping our ice teas.

"I wonder if he remembers what he cooked those burgers on," Dempsey wondered.

Gail and I didn't answer, but I think we knew where this was heading.

Chapter Eighteen

Scouting for an Outhouse

The following morning the three of us drove to Springfield in search of Guy Williams, former owner of William's Roadside Dinner.

"Let's assume those burgers weren't anything special," Dempsey announced. "They're just plain old hamburgers any of us could buy. What did Guy do to make them so damn good?"

"We're just assuming everybody liked them," Gail corrected. "You two remember it better than I do. Can you remember it being busy?"

"It kicked ass," Dempsey said, remembering. He was right. There always seemed to be a line to the door and sometimes out the door. The smell was so good I'm surprised there weren't puddles of drool where customers waited.

"What if he's dead or he can't remember?" Gail asked. "Old people go senile."

Dempsey shook his head. "Hush, I'm thinking."

It turned out the gentleman in question wasn't senile, but Gail's first omen was correct. Guy Williams died in 1995. It took two hours

Dempsey's Grill

and five wrong Williams before we finally hit the jackpot. We found his cousin in an old farmhouse on the far end of town.

"Let me get this straight," the cousin asked. "You're lookin' for that ol' grill Guy use to cook on?" The cousin went by the name of Harvey. Harvey was a short man who appeared to enjoy chain-smoking and fast food. I say this not out of opinion, but as a fact proven by the numerous cigarette butts and fast-food wrappers that littered his property. He had the worst comb over and largest beer belly I'd ever seen.

"Yes sir," Dempsey said, taking command of the situation. "We would like to take it off your hands, if that's fine with you."

We do?

"Hell, take it all," Harvey happily replied. "He gave me this fuckin' junk in his will. No use to me. We can haggle a price."

The grill, along with other kitchen goodies courtesy of Williams Roadside, rested in a large, open shed surrounded by evergreens and oak trees. They had survived the elements thanks to a large thick blue tarp that was tightly wrapped and held together by elastic rope. I had a feeling the cousin had little to do with the work of keeping them so secure. They were also located behind several cords of wood.

"What can you tell us about the grill?" Dempsey asked.

"Whaddya mean?" Harvey asked. The ten-minute walk from the house to the shed had clearly exhausted him. He had taken the load off by relaxing on an old stump.

"Well, what kind of history can you tell me about it?"

"History?"

"Yes. History," Dempsey pressed.

"You eat off the fuckin' thing." Harvey followed this with a high-pitched hyena style laugh. I smiled just to be polite. Gail, on the other hand, joined in. I'm pretty sure she was laughing at him and not with him.

"Does it still work?" I asked.

"Fuck if I know."

Another round of hyena laughs followed.

We located the grill courtesy of a felt tip marker in which someone – probably not Harvey – had meticulously wrote in detail the description of each item that had been wrapped. As we sorted through the clutter, a woman I assumed was Harvey's wife, joined us. Her name was Lou, and she watched over us with a suspicious glare. Harvey wasn't the only one who seemed to enjoy fast-food and chain smoking. His, shall I say, 'charming' wife, had also put on a few pounds. My guess was that their days of dancing the night away were long gone. Gail turned and said hello, her warm greeting returned with an icy stare.

Gail turned away from Lou and caught my eye. We immediately joined Dempsey as he attempted to work a deal. On a normal day, I would have been knee-deep in the conversation. Who doesn't like an afternoon talk of old restaurant grills?

"We cleaned her up good," Harvey said with pride. "No grease or anything. All shiny."

"Why did you keep it?" Dempsey asked.

"Fuck if I know."

I was afraid another hyena laugh was in the works. Luckily it died as a puzzled look crossed his face. "Too expensive to haul to the dump, probably."

To be honest, I didn't care. I really had to pee. I had to fifteen minutes before we even got here. Looking around at the fields and farmhouse, I recalled the phrase, coined by a genius some time ago: *The world is my urinal.* I had every reason to believe that genius was talking to me.

Reaching the emergency stage, I knew I had to act soon. With the house not being an option, I noticed two thick trees on the far end of the lot. They gave me the impression they didn't mind a little urine around their trunk and if they did, I was in no mood to listen. Isn't it nature's law for bodily functions and tree roots to come together?

Gail made her way back to the grill. Dempsey was reconsidering the asking price and was now deep in negotiations. Thankfully, Gail joined in giving me a straight path to cosmic relief. She knew I'd always had a bladder with absolutely zero patience. Thinking back, my only mistake was telling Gail my bathroom issues. Had I kept my misery a secret, all the stuff that came after never would have happened. On the other hand, I wouldn't have found out about her mom the way I did.

I was inches from a clean getaway. A nice wide trunk of a hundred-year-old evergreen disguised beautifully as the world's most welcoming urinal. My kidneys applauded; relief was inches away but on that interesting day, an inch was not enough.

Gail grabbed me by the elbow and pulled me to a dead stop, causing my kidneys to groan.

"Just thought you'd like to know I think that building over there is an outhouse." She smiled innocently, pleased with how thoughtful she was as my bladder tried not to explode.

I was about to thank her while making a run for it but unfortunately I was delayed.

"What the hell?" Gail took a step back, taking me with her.

I was certain I would never pee again.

"Let me guess...you work for Danilson's?"

Lou, and more importantly, Lou's rifle, blocked my path to the outhouse. My bladder misery took a back seat to another priority.

"Goddamn scout," Lou growled. "I knew it. Thick as fleas, all of you."

Lou and her rifle took a step toward us, causing Gail and I to take a step back. It was an interesting dance, one I hoped would end soon.

"What the hell? The only scouting we were doing was for an outhouse," Gail said. Rifle or no rifle, Gail was angry.

"Shut up, missy," Lou snarled as she waved the rifle between us. "And you, I saw the way you were looking around. I know what you're up to and I know what you're looking for."

"Lady, you don't understand I was just—"

"Don't you 'lady' me. I understand just fine!"

I could hear Dempsey's voice as we backed into the clearing. Gail told me later that she did that on purpose in hopes that Dempsey would see us. In theory, it was a great idea. Note that I said theory.

"All the way out here to buy a goddamn grill." Lou took another step aiming her rifle at Gail and then at me. "Who the hell does that? I'll tell you who, a goddamn—"

"He was trying to find a place to pee!"

Gail took a step forward, her face red with anger. I started to pull back but stopped halfway. Something was happening.

"Pee?" Lou asked.

A curious look spread across her brow. She lowered the rifle. Not a lot, but enough to tell us we had her attention.

"Pee." Gail repeated, slamming her elbow into my ribs.

"Yes." I added. "I really have to go, and we are really here to buy the grill. That's it."

"Oh."

We stared at her as her curious glare transformed into understanding and then embarrassment. The three of us shared a guilty smile, thus allowing my bladder to remind me of its current issues.

Lou lowered the rifle until it was aimed to the ground. Trust and understanding floated like a bubble on a birthday wish but like all bubbles, its lifespan was on short supply and as what should come as no surprise on this really weird day, it popped into oblivion.

"Hey, lady! Put that fucking gun down or I'll turn your fat ass to shit!

Lou's rifle had a mind of its own, at least that's how it seemed. It spun around, aiming at Dempsey, the owner of the voice who had promised to turn its master to shit. Within seconds, all three of us were lined in a nice little row, our hands pointed high, our faces full of dread.

"We had it under control," I whispered.

"How the hell was I supposed to know?" Dempsey whispered back. "You got to admit this is kind of funny."

Dempsey turned to Gail, assuming, I can only guess, that his final comment would be agreed upon with a snicker or two. Instead, Gail replied in silence with a death-stare matched only in a Charles Manson documentary.

Harvey calmly walked past us while slowly pushing his hat back to scratch an itch. He had the look of a child questioning who ate the last cookie, knowing full well it wasn't him.

"Problem, Lou?" he asked.

Lou explained in what I could guess the only way she knew how.

Dempsey's Grill

"These thieving pricks were scouting around, and I caught 'em. This joker tries to pretend he needs to piss and next thing you know, this other joker comes running over calling me a fat ass."

"Is that so?" Harvey paused and gave the grass a long look. He didn't come across as the kind of guy who did a lot of thinking. I wondered if he was contemplating a new hobby.

"What the fuck is a scout?" Dempsey asked.

I opened my mouth to answer, but Dempsey wasn't finished.

"Hey mister, all we want to do is buy your grill. I swear."

Lou whispered something into Harvey's ear, causing another round of head scratching. In the meantime, Dempsey and I had inched forward, acting as human shields for Gail. She later admitted she thought it was cute, if not stupid.

As we stood with our hands in the air, I still had my bladder to contend with. I wasn't sure if I had to pee or not

"Will you shut up?" Gail whispered.

Check that. I said it out loud.

"That's what this is all about?" Dempsey turned toward me with a rare glare.

I opened my mouth to answer but Harvey beat me to it.

"I think you three should leave." He wore an apologetic smile. It was a nice look.

We slowly lowered our hands and backed away. For a moment, things seemed to have returned normal. For a moment, that is.

For reasons I'll never understand, Dempsey grabbed my arm and Gail's and ran.

"Dempsey, what the hell are you doing?" Gail shouted.

He had no time for her question. It was clear he had a plan and to be honest, I was curious to see how it played out. We ran back the way we came, veering off slightly.

"Wood!"

I understood. A cord of wood is four feet by four feet by eight feet and in that moment, Dempsey had a plan.

"Over!"

* * *

Hours later while sitting in the emergency room, Gail and I questioned why we jumped over the four-foot-high pile of wood when we could have put on the brakes. We concluded there are times when the mind shuts off the voice of reason and opens the floodgate of stupidity.

I cleared the pile with ease and performed a tuck and roll. Proud of my achievement, I turned to witness my friends' vaulting skills who sadly, were not as lucky.

"Son of a bitch!"

Gail landed hard on her ankle while Dempsey landed flat on his face. He later admitted the experience was a sad reminder that his athletic days were over. He raised his head as a stream of blood gushed over his eyes and off his chin. He also complained of a sore shoulder. We never got a clear number how many stitches he popped, but Gail guessed most if not all of them.

"Hurry!" Dempsey scrambled up and ran alone to the car while Gail used me as a crutch. Dempsey stumbled, fell, got up and fell again. We paused as the voice of reason settled in. Lou and Harvey were nowhere to be seen. Maybe retreated inside the house, possibly to go find more guns.

By the time we reached the car Dempsey was a bloody mess. Gail wasn't all that great either. "It's swelling like a balloon," she said as I helped her in the back seat.

"Do you think it's broken?" I asked.

I didn't wait for an answer. Dempsey was still freaked out by Harvey and Lou and I just wanted to get out of there.

Gail glared at Dempsey as she attempted to rub life back into her ankle. "Why the hell did you drag us over the wood pile?"

"I didn't drag anybody!" Dempsey had taken his shirt off and was using it as a rag. I was relieved since this was my parent's car.

"The hell you didn't," Gail argued. "If I hadn't jumped, I would have looked worse than you."

For the next five minutes they argued, stopped only by Dempsey's phone. It was Harvey asking if we were still interested in the grill.

Dempsey's Grill

"We're back in business!" Dempsey shouted as blood dripped off his chin.

"Oh goodie," Gail grumbled, shaking her head.

Chapter Nineteen

En Morpheno Veritas

    We drove to the emergency room in silence. I was curious where Dempsey was going to store the grill, how it was going to be set up, does it work, that sort of thing. But most of all I was curious what we were going to do next. I had to admit, the adventure was fun. It reminded me of a treasure hunt Gail and I had played as kids. Of course back then, nobody messed up their shoulder, popped their stitches, or hurt their ankle.

    I looked in the car mirror and attempted to give Gail an encouraging smile. She glanced at me and looked away. I then focused on Dempsey. He reclined in the passenger seat as much as he could. He looked uncomfortable as he cradled his odd shaped shoulder with his shirt wrapped around his head. I decided to stay silent since he looked like he was in a lot of pain.

    When we arrived at the emergency room I put Gail in a wheelchair. A staff member pushed her inside while I held onto Dempsey. We looked like survivors in a biker fight. I felt like laughing

Dempsey's Grill

when I thought of that, but I figured the timing was way off. The same assistant who stitched Dempsey together the first time was there to help.

"They had an accident," I said, as Gail and Dempsey were wheeled away.

"What exactly were you guys doing?"

She was a young, energetic, possible college intern. Plastered on her head was a giant question mark.

"We're opening a restaurant." I couldn't think of anything else to say.

I sat in the waiting room for about an hour as Gail and Dempsey got patched up. I knew this was all temporary. The world that I belonged to was on hold and waiting on the sidelines, ready to take over. It had the power, my world in Seattle, that is. My struggling profession as a teacher, my relationship with Lourdes, both on life support, yes, but it was still alive...barely...and that counted for something, I supposed.

Dempsey had a slightly dislocated shoulder. Gail had a badly sprained ankle. Both were advised to rest for a week. No heavy lifting, no running, and by no means try not to repeat whatever it was we were doing that caused all this mess. I made up that last part, but I have a feeling the doctor either told them that or should have.

I drove Dempsey home first. The doctor gave him something for his pain. Whatever it was made him pretty useless by the time we got there. Slowly and gently, I eased him out of the car. He held on to me with his good arm while we took baby steps to his house.

"I'm a fuck-up, Bugs," he mumbled.

"I know," I agreed.

He wasn't going to remember any of this, so I figured a little honesty didn't hurt.

"I don't even have a girlfriend."

"I know."

"Seriously man, I use to lay everyone."

"You still do."

"Ya, but they leave before I sober up."

We stood at his front door as I wrestled with his keys.

"You're lucky, Bugs," he whispered. "You got a mom and dad to go home to. I don't have shit."

We stepped inside his dark, cold house. I reached for the lights, but he told me no.

"I don't want to see anything." His voice sounded weak and empty.

I dropped him on the couch and left. It felt lonely and weird and wrong, but I left anyway. I still had to take Gail home. As I walked to the car I wondered if I should have taken him to my parent's house instead. Knowing Mom, she would have treated him like a king. Then I thought of Lourdes and her dislike of people who cared for strays. I could hear her in my head clear as a bell: "They're just taking advantage of you. Now you'll end up feeding them and taking care of them and cleaning up all their messes and have nothing to show for it. Don't be a pathetic loser and fall for their sob stories. They need to learn to take care of themselves."

Well, I'd done my part and more. I'd gotten Dempsey patched up and brought him home. No reason to let him burrow more deeply into my life like a handout-seeking tick who would couch surf until we were both old and gray.

The ride home with Gail was almost the same as it was with Dempsey. She, too, had been given something to ease the pain. She wanted to sit up front and talk to me. I figured she'd fall asleep. I was wrong.

"I loved my mommy," she giggled.

I smiled but said nothing.

"Did you know my mommy?" She leaned over and slowly played with my ear.

"Yes," I said, and smiled.

"She used to drink a lot and that made me sad. Then one day everything stopped."

"Good."

I figured it would be best to answer with one-word sentences. The last thing I wanted was a long drawn out conversation with someone who was knee-deep in pain pills.

"I wish we never moved away." She sighed and closed her eyes, relaxed, but I could tell she had more to say.

"It was really hard making new friends." She looked at me with sad eyes, her arm laying on my shoulder. "I kept looking for a best friend like you. I wanted someone to talk to just like we did, but I couldn't do that with just anyone. Come to think of it, I don't think I ever did meet anyone like you."

I looked over and smiled again. I wanted to tell her the same. Sure, Dempsey was a great friend, but he's a guy. If you want someone to laugh with and make fun of you, you talk to a guy, but if you want someone to listen and to understand and most of all to be honest and say things you may not want to hear but should, well...you make sure that person is a she.

"Sex was cool," Gail continued. "It was sort of weird, but I knew it would happen."

She turned away and looked at the sky. It was swimming with stars and the moon was full.

"We were curious," she added. "But that's not why I missed you."

Her breathing had changed and her hand relaxed. I was pretty sure she was asleep.

"Do you know why I missed you? " She suddenly raised her head and looked around, her eyes big and lost, as if she had awoken from a nightmare.

"Why did you miss me?" I asked. I kept my voice low and soft.

She didn't answer right away. She lowered her head and closed her eyes. I could tell she wanted to curl up with a favorite blanket but there was none around, and her swollen ankle would have none of it even if she tried.

"We used to cuddle." Her voice was tired and full of wishes. "Remember those days? Two kids pretending they were adults. We talked or took a nap or watched TV and that was fine with us. It was being together. That's all that mattered. And you know what?"

This time she opened her eyes and looked at me. I wondered if it was the drugs talking or something deeper.

"I never met anyone like you no matter how hard I tried."

She reached over and held my arm. In the darkness, I could tell she was looking at me. I saw her smile. I smiled too.

"Do you know how many guys just want to cuddle?" she asked.

She didn't have to answer I already knew. She answered anyway.

"Zilch. That's something else I found out when I moved away."

Upon arriving, I helped her out of the car and up the porch steps into her living room. Unlike Dempsey's place, her mom had the lights on and the place looked warm and friendly. I didn't see her mother and didn't ask where she was. I figured Gail would tell me if she wanted to. She sat in the recliner and elevated her feet. I placed a blanket over her and started to leave.

"Please stay. I don't want to be alone."

"You're not alone. Your mom's here."

"Mom died."

Her voice trailed off. Sleep was near, but not near enough. She looked at me with understanding eyes as shock spread across my face. This time her eyes were awake. What if they hadn't given her drugs or maybe they'd worn off? A sad smile appeared. The kind of smile that says, I know, I can't believe she's dead, either. We looked at each other wishing things were less complicated. A place where you know you belong, and you don't have to say special words or pretend you're someone else. But that place doesn't exist, does it?

I lay on the couch and listened to Gail's steady breathing. She fell asleep after I assured her I would stay. I don't know how long we slept but when I awoke the sun was already up. I laid the crutches the hospital had loaned her nearby and quietly left. It was the most peaceful and restful sleep I'd had in months.

Driving home that morning, I kept thinking of Gail's mom. How did she die, and from what? Yes, it had been a lot of years since I saw her, but sometimes we foolishly believe certain people will live forever, especially parents. Gail's mom was strong and brave and safe. You just knew nothing bad would ever happen when she was around. But death? She lost a battle. What battle and how long did she fight? Was she in pain? Was she scared? Was Gail with her when she died? So many questions. I was afraid to ask, but I had to know. What if Gail had no intentions of telling me. Do I press for answers when I see her again, or do I wait? This is her mom we're talking about. Her mom is dead, and I want to know what happened.

And then there's us, I thought. Is this friendship real or are we just passing through? Some things were meant to be. But are we talking long term or just a short stay? You always hear about it. Two people bouncing around in life suddenly ending up with each other, like a gravitational pull where no matter how hard you try running in another direction it's going to win the battle. So why do I fight it? Last night I slept in the same house with someone who gave me the most peaceful night I can remember, and this includes being with Lourdes. She also gave me some terrible news. If that isn't fate, what is?

I pulled into my parent's driveway, enjoying a quiet confidence. For once I saw a tiny hint of direction. The fog was still there, and I had no doubt it was going to be there for a while, maybe forever, but I could see something else and it felt good. For a moment, that is.

Chapter Twenty

I Hate Lemonade

I didn't get out of the car by myself, Hope did that part for me.

With a clinching grip I was dragged from the driver's seat onto the driveway where we once played as children. I believe her favorite game was follow the leader. Guess what role she played?

Hope stood over me as I lay on the ground, a phone in her hand and a wild, worried look on her face. Something happened while I was gone, I realized. Something terrible had happened. I could feel it. Dad cut his hand off in his workshop or Mom had a nervous breakdown. Or maybe the house caught on fire!

I had a hard time believing Dad would panic even if his hand had been separated from his arm and Mom, let's face it, she could have a series of strokes and still manage to fix dinner at 5 p.m. on the dot. But these truths, these major pinpointed facts of life, for now reigned useless. I was way too worried about Hope's next move.

"Get up," she ordered.

I didn't.

Dempsey's Grill

"Now!"

I did.

"Where were you?" she demanded. "I've been calling you all morning."

As I got to my feet I gave a short wave to our neighbor Mrs. Tennyson, a nice lady who always seemed uncomfortable around Hope, even when Hope was a child.

Hope snapped an angry glare in Mrs. Tennyson's direction and waited until she ran back into her house.

"It's called a cell phone, Gibson," she said, waving hers in my face. "You turn it on and answer it when someone calls!"

"Are Mom and Dad okay?" I asked.

I'm not sure if the question was too abrupt or if it was the sound of my voice. Either way, I was given an angry glare before she answered.

"Gibson," her voice low and growly, "always answer you cell phone.

I tried to sound reasonable. "Hope..."

"Do not 'Hope' me!"

"I didn't have it on me. What do you want me to do?"

She turned her back with her arms folded, her mind shut down to any unwanted visitors. That would be me, by the way. I raised my arms in the air in a sign of desperation and walked away. That was when she dropped the bomb.

"I talked to Lourdes."

I stopped in my tracks.

"I don't know what you were doing last night, and I don't want to know, just keep your phone on so we can reach you."

Hope walked past me as I stood frozen in place. "Lourdes?" I asked.

I realized she wasn't going to stop. I followed. "Lourdes?" I repeated. I continued to follow. Hope continued to walk. Did I mention Hope likes to be chased?

"You should be nicer to her, Gibson."

I was getting mad and scared. Let's face it, I was more scared than mad. Hope talked to Lourdes. How much worse can it get?

Hope walked into the kitchen. I followed. She was a leader who demanded attention. I should never have given in. I should have acted uninterested. Bored even, but I didn't. I stood and watched as she slowly poured us glasses of lemonade. With the ease of a class A barmaid, she carefully placed a glass in front of me. A coaster lay perfect underneath with a lemon slice wedged neatly on the rim of the glass.

She sat across from me, the tick-tock of my parent's grandfather clock growing louder with each passing second. She waited until enough silence had passed. I have no doubt her mental clock was ticking, waiting for the right time to speak. A third of her lemonade had disappeared while mine was still full. The napkin she laid out so delicately in front of her lay untouched while mine huddled in a crumbled mess. Hope was in control; this was her environment where every detail was perfectly planned.

"You need to understand her point of view." I jumped at the sound of my sister's voice. Not a lot but enough for her to notice. She smiled.

"You're lucky to know her. Lourdes is an intelligent woman. She has direction and if you are smart and if you listen to her she will take you places."

I took a long drink.

"That little fun you had last night is excusable. You're a grown man, and..." she paused uncomfortably. "Indiscretions happen."

Now it was my turn to be uncomfortable.

"Hope, nothing happened last night. What did Lourdes want?" I tossed what little was left of my shredded napkin on the table. I finished off my lemonade and pushed it away. I had to get out of there. "Why did she call you? I didn't know she even had your number."

"I called her."

Hope calmly took a sip and dotted the sides of her mouth with her spotless napkin. Her entire action was theatrical to the core. Damn it, I admired her.

"I wanted to know why you were here." She waited for this to sink in, her eyes watching me as the words stumbled around in my head.

Dempsey's Grill

I suddenly felt cold. "I told you why I'm here."

Hope had a small smile on her lips. "I had to hear her side of it."

"Really." I wanted more lemonade but refused to ask. Hope had enough control as it was.

"She's happy you're away," Hope explained. "She can breathe. You were smothering her."

Hope reached across the table and grabbed my hand. I suddenly felt like a child being told Santa was killed on his way to my house.

"Gibson, she needs space. With you, that didn't exist. She may want you back someday and if she does, don't mess it up. People like her are rare.

This happens when you're in love with someone smarter than you," she said in a sorry way. "Envy is as bad as jealousy. It hurts."

I stared at my empty glass. It suddenly occurred to me that I hated lemonade.

"Gibson, you hurt her but now that you're away you're giving her a chance to heal and for that, I'm proud of you. At first, I didn't understand but now I see what you're doing, and it's brilliant. You're allowing her to breathe and grow and all the while you're nurturing her."

She released my hand and took a proud sip. She slowly leaned back and produced a satisfied smile. I got up to leave, figuring her speech was over. Unfortunately, I had just witnessed the introduction.

"I didn't know you had it in you," she said.

Act Two had begun.

"All this time I thought you were just stumbling around with that man-child of a friend of yours and what's-her-name, that trailer park bartender, but I see now you have a plan. A brilliant plan."

She leaned close, gripping both of my hands. I swear I saw tears in her eyes. "I am so proud of you," she whispered. "Intelligent leaders are misunderstood and rarely respected. I have been misunderstood and disrespected my entire life. Lourdes and I face challenges every day, but we always have hope. Pun intended."

She paused and giggled.

"Our goal is to find someone who understands our qualities, takes a step back and allows us to fly, to grow, to teach others what we know. Most men would never think of such a thing. They are too busy with sex and power. It consumes them. They can't tell one from the other. Their busy penises take over their lives. But not you, Gibson."

Of course not. Why should I have sex on my mind or a busy penis?

"You decided to take a step back," she continued. "You admire her. You respect her and you had the courage to walk away."

Hope shook her head with admiration. Her pride bursting with all kinds of bubbles.

You may be wondering why I didn't set the record straight. Why I didn't remind her that Lourdes kicked *me* out. If she hadn't, I would have still been there. The local fruit cannery was hiring; I could have worked on the loading dock. We lived near the lake and her dad had a boat. It slept three. You get the idea. When you hate your job it's easy to get fired. There was no respect, no courage, no anything. I got fired from a job I wasn't good at and my girlfriend kicked me out. Being homeless in Seattle wasn't my thing and my parents, still had a welcome sign in front of their house. I could have told Hope all of that. My record would have been clean, but then what? Lectures over admirations? I was left with the only logical choice.

"Thank you, Hope. It feels good to do something right."

I was happy our talked ended on a positive note. This was rare.

"Is there anything I can do for you while you're home?" she asked.

And there it was—Opportunity.

Chapter Twenty-One

So-Called Friends

    I waited until the stars came out. That was when I knew it was going to happen. When I was a boy, I use to pretend the stars were alive only for my entertainment. They would blink twice to say hello and once to say goodbye. They never spoke, instead they listened, and when they listened, they smiled. As a boy, it felt good to have a sky full of friends.

    And so, I sat on the front porch on a warm summer night, looking to the stars for a sign of approval. My phone rested deep in the palm of my hand. My thumb on Lourdes's number. My heart racing, my mouth dry, I pushed the number, the stars gasped, and my arm slowly carried the phone to my ear. I waited.

    My mind traveled back to my high school years. Sure, it was a pain in the ass. All that worry and trying to be cool, hoping no one figured out the real you. But it was easy when you had a friend like Dempsey. He was the type of guy who did all the work. All I had to do was follow along. He would smile at the cute girl and her friends. If they said hi, he took it to the next level. The conversations were creative: Music, clothes, hair, and during all of this, he would pull me in and ask them my favorite question...have you met my friend, Gibson?

It was easy when you didn't have to try.

Lourdes answered on the first ring. She always did but it still caught me off-guard. I wanted to run, and she knew it. She had control. I wish I saw that, but I doubt it would have done any good. Maybe it was just good ol' fashioned habit.

"Yes, Gibson?" Lourdes answered with the speed and cutting edge of a razor. In all our years together, it was never, "Hello," or a friendly, "Hi." It was always, "Yes Gibson?"

A shiver raced down my spine as her voice shot through my right ear and exited my left. If I heard her voice today it would probably sound the same. As always, I didn't know what to do. I froze. The silence lay as dead as November leaves.

"Yes, Gibson?" she repeated. Her voice impatient. The razor sharpening.

"Lourdes." My voice shook. Now what? I should have used cue cards. "My sister called you." I tried to say it as a statement instead I sounded like a child. "Is that right?"

Lourdes responded with silence. It was a habit I should have been used to but wasn't. "Hope and I had a long talk," she finally said. "Are you doing well?"

"Yes, I'm fine," I quickly replied. My own attempt with silence an obvious failure. I guess she was doing fine.

"She is worried about you and so am I."

"Oh," I said.

"You're regressing. Old habits turning into bad habits. Hope is frustrated."

Now I was silent.

"And that dishwashing friend." Lourdes sighed. "Not to mention that bartender girl. Why? These people will drag you down into their gutter. What is happening to you, Gibson?"

I wanted to tell her those gutter people were my friends...my real friends. *Go to hell!* I wanted to scream. *Fuck you!* I tried to yell. *I'm having a great time down here. What do you think of that, Lourdes?*

At least I'm surrounded by real people and not the phony plastic version of your reality! Speaking of phony, how's life in the Emerald City, bitch!

"I don't know," I whispered.

I sunk lower on the concrete step and listened to the long pause.

"I don't know," she repeated my words. "I feel like a mother hen talking to one of her runaway chicks."

"I didn't run away."

Finally, a true statement.

"You might as well have." Her voice started out low, calm and controlled, but with one sentence, it turned into an angry vicious snarl.

Lourdes sighed loudly and said in a tightly controlled voice, "You worry me, Gibson. You really worry me."

I heard a voice in the background. I thought the voice asked if everything was all right. "Hang up the phone, honey. Come back to bed."

"Don't worry," I whispered.

In fact, don't do anything. Go away. Stay away.

"I will always worry about you, Gibson. You could have been so much more." She paused for a moment. Her way of letting the words soak through the fabric.

"Think about what I just said. Look at those so-called friends of yours. You think you can trust them but you're wrong. They're dragging you into their world. Hope is terrified. She can't sleep. Thankfully, your parents don't see it. You are confused, sad, and lonely. I understand why, but this is your time to grow. Move forward instead of backward."

I tried pulling the phone away, but it wouldn't move.

"I'm afraid they already have a firm grip on you, Gibson. I can see their claws tightening around you and it makes me cry."

I wasn't given a chance to respond. A cold silence followed by a click said goodbye. Slowly I dropped the phone to my side. The stars above heaved a sigh of disappointment.

A part of me was angry. These were my friends, not hers. I met them long before I knew Lourdes existed. We had a history full of childhood and teenage years. On the other hand, I saw it. It was the last thing I wanted to see, but it was there. The idea of growing up was to move forward, but what direction was I headed? Was I moving at all?

Maybe this was my fault.

There does come a time when you must face the music. Could the music I was listening to be the reason why I was sitting in front of my parent's house, and not in my living room in Seattle? Did Lourdes show me a picture of who I really was and if so, was it too late to erase it?

"I blew it," I whispered.

I sat alone on the steps for the longest time. How many times had I played out here? Running around with my cap pistol or Nerf football. A time when my mind was innocent of grown-up thoughts. A time when I could spend my day full of wonder and adventure. I remember a time when twenty-nine sounded old and crippling. Who wanted that? My youth was a time where problems were easy to control, and tasks were handled with grace and composure. Confidence and risk taking were all in a day's work, and most of all, now listen closely kids, this is the biggest lesson of them all, you were not afraid of anything.

I was so lost in my thoughts I didn't hear him drive up. I knew by the time I saw him he had already figured it out.

"Hey man," Dempsey smiled. "Everything good?"

I put on a fake smile and said hello. He joined me on the step without a word. We sat for a while in silence. I didn't know what to say.

"Deep in thought," he allowed. It didn't come out as a question.

It wasn't that hard to figure it out. A phone in my hand, still steaming from a lopsided conversation, my eyes lost, frustrated, sad, and angry. Dempsey only knew one person who could turn me into this. He understood Lourdes. He didn't know her all that well, but he knew her type. He knew what they were capable of and how they could turn a normal guy into mush. But he never got in the way. Not once did he try to push me away, but I wish he did.

"Lourdes," he said with a defeated smile.

My defeated head nodded yes.

"What's the next move?" he asked.

I shook my head left to right. Why say anything if I didn't know?

"Does she want you back?"

"She didn't say," I said with a shrug, but I knew the answer.

"I want you to know I'm really glad you're home. It means a lot to me that you're here. I missed you, Bugs." I knew from the moment I got home he felt this way, but I was still surprised to hear it. "And if you repeat what I just said to anyone I will beat the shit out of you."

Guys have a hard time expressing their feelings, don't they?

Dempsey and I sat in an uncomfortable silence for a long time. Did I mention guys aren't good at expressing their feelings?

"How's your shoulder?" I asked. It was one of those panic questions.

"Still sore. Doc told me it'll take time. I can't lift anything heavy for a while."

I shook my head and grunted. My immediate reaction was to hit him in the arm. It's a common exchange with guys who wish to show their admiration for one another. Since hugging is out of the question, beating each other senseless is the obvious choice, but with his shoulder still in the tank, I passed. I never told him his words made me feel better. It's nice to be needed. I thought about Lourdes's comments. My dishwashing friend, as she put it. How I'm being dragged down to *his* level, according to her.

"Still plan on getting that grill?" I asked.

"I don't have a truck," he said with a surprised look. I'm pretty sure he thought I was leaving.

I smiled. "I know where I can get one."

"No shit?"

To this day I can still see the comical look of disbelief on his face.

Chapter Twenty-Two

Enjoyable Wrecks

I started to knock on her door, but she opened it before I had the chance. She lowered her eyes and smiled. In my hands were two coffees. Large and strong.

"You look great," I said, as she grabbed the coffee from my hand.

That was a lie. She looked like roadkill warmed over, but sometimes lying is a good thing.

Gail walked to the kitchen with a slight limp. Her leg was wrapped halfway to her knee, her strawberry blonde hair lay tangled in a mess, and an extra-large Oregon Ducks football shirt covered most of her. I did, however, sneak a peek at her long, naked legs as she walked ahead of me.

"Thank you," she said. "Body likes coffee."

"It sure does," I agreed.

We said our cheers and took a long sip.

"Your mom."

I didn't know what else to say. I looked down at the floor and up into Gail's eyes. My face told her I knew. I hoped she remembered. She looked away for a moment, hesitant of what she might have said the night before but when her eyes returned to mine, they were calm and confident. She remembered.

"How did she die?" I asked cautiously.

"Liver cancer, lung cancer, heart failure. You name it. Pick a card. Pick a poison."

I waited. If she wanted to tell me more, she would.

"Mom hated California," said. She seemed to gather her thoughts, then pushed on. "One day she gives me a call and tells me she wants to die in Oregon. About a year ago, we found this place. She sold her house and we moved in. I moved her bed into the front room so she could look out the window because she loved watching people walk by. 'Life keeps rolling on,' she used to say."

Gail looked away and took a long drink. "She died five months later. We were holding hands."

"When...?" I tried to finish but couldn't.

"The first Sunday in January. It was still dark out and it was starting to snow. She loved the snow. She'd take us up to the mountains and we'd sled all day."

I smiled. "I remember."

"It wasn't supposed to snow that day, but we had an inch by the time the day was over."

I reached across the table and held her hands. We finished our coffees and ate raisin bread fresh out of the toaster.

"Tell me I didn't say anything stupid when you brought me home."

"Silent as a clam," I lied.

She looked up at me in mid-bite and smiled. She knew I was holding back.

"How's the ankle?"

"Doctor said it'll be stiff for a while. I think it's feeling better."

I wanted to tell her the same thing Dempsey told me. I was happy to see her again and to be with her again, and how much it meant to me. She was one of the few people in this world I listened to and took advice from. His words had really hit home. Never take a friend for granted, however, this is me we're talking about, and my twenty-nine-year-old-self had one thing on his mind. I didn't want to know but I asked anyway. "Where's Dale?"

"Bruce," she corrected. "Oklahoma, Or Kansas, or Missouri. Far away." She fetched a sigh. Her voice sounded flat, defeated. Then again, maybe she was just tired.

"When will you see him again?" "He keeps saying soon and I keep believing him."

I made a mental note to stop asking about Dale or Bruce.

"Dempsey called," she said, remembering.

"He did?"

She took another long sip and before continuing. "He said he caught you in a bad mood. He said you looked sad."

Her eyes watched me over the top of her cup. She slowly took another sip without looking away.

"I was."

"Women can drive a nice guy crazy, am I right?" She smiled.

"Why is that?" I really wanted to know.

"Hobby."

If there is one thing that gives friends an advantage over lovers, it's the ability to read emotions. They are the ones who know when something is wrong. They see it in our eyes, our walk, and our talk. I saw it when I asked about Dale or Bruce. A tiny flicker in Gail's eyes. A deadly mixture of loss, fear and the inability to control the future. Of all the things we face, the easy things to handle are fear and loss. It's a part of who we are, but it's also the part of being out of control that drives all of us batshit crazy.

"Speaking from experience, huh?" I asked.

"What?" It was easy to see her mind was elsewhere. Somewhere in Kansas, Oklahoma, or Missouri. So many poisons. So many gift shops.

"I said, is driving a guy crazy one of your hobbies?"

Dempsey's Grill

She sat back in her chair and smiled. Her eyes looked far away.

"He's been away so long I don't think I can call it a hobby. I doubt there's a word for it."

"You're still in better shape than me," I added. I winced. I needed to change the subject in a hurry. "So, how's work?"

"I'm taking a few days off. Ankle." She pointed.

"So...you have some spare time?"

"To heal, yes. To fight another round with the woodpile? Probably not."

"I'll take that as a yes."

Gail gave me a questioning look as I smiled and finished off my coffee. "Gibson, why do I get the feeling you came here for other reasons?"

I smiled and explained. "Simple. We go back and sneak the grill out of the shed."

Gail stared at me. "Why?"

"Because," I said, then hesitated. Yes, maybe this was a bad idea, "You see, Dempsey wants the grill."

"No," she said, while rubbing her hands through her hair. "Try again. Why are we sneaking it? I thought Dempsey was buying it?"

"Well..." now I was the one rubbing my hands through my hair. "Dempsey is buying it but we can't drive up and take it."

I bit my lip and waited for her to ask why. Gail took a sip of her coffee, silently watching me instead.

I tried to explain. "Harvey is having second thoughts about us on his property. Dempsey talked to him and the guy was a little worried." I wasn't going to force her to do anything, especially on an ankle that was just starting to heal. "In fact, Lou," I pointed out, "thought all of us were troublemakers. Or maybe that we were there for other reasons. Harvey said she's really paranoid."

I waited a few seconds before delivering the last line.

"Those burgers were good though, remember? And if it was the grill that made them so good, maybe Dempsey's plan has a chance at this. Right?"

Gail sat on the couch playing with her hair for what seemed like the longest time. I didn't want to stare, and if the sunlight hadn't found its way in I would have left, but I stayed and watched as the sunlight displayed the lovely lines of red and gold intertwining as though they were a couple dancing away on a summer day.

"Yes," she said. "I'll go on your crazy grill hunting chase."

She limped into the kitchen and tossed another raisin bread into the toaster. I noticed her limp wasn't as visible as when I first came in. A little spring to her step had taken over.

"You do realize I know what you're up to," she said from the kitchen. I smiled and said nothing. "This is the same kind of stuff we did as kids, and you know I can't resist."

Gail returned from the kitchen taking a bite of her buttery toast. She sat next to me and held the bread up to my mouth to share.

"So, what's the plan?" she asked.

For the first time since the day I saw her in the bar, I saw the familiar flicker in her eye. The same flicker I saw when we were kids chasing raccoons and squirrels. But most of all, I saw a flicker convincing me to sneak away to that special place we were told not to go.

"We have to show up really late." I took a small bite.

"How late?"

"Around midnight."

"Won't that wake up Lou?"

"According to Harvey, she watches a lot of late-night movies. We'll sneak in, pay the guy, and leave."

Gail finished off the remainder of the toast and gave me a long stare. This would be the processing part where questions were sure to follow.

I knew this could be the deal breaker. She was thinking again. I didn't wait for an answer. Instead, I added another twist.

"I'll probably go back to Seattle after this is over. You'll probably leave too. I'd like to help Dempsey before I leave and I think it would mean a lot if you did too. He doesn't have a lot going for him right now."

Dempsey's Grill

The bullshit wagon wasn't that heavy. A lot of what I said was true. "Plus," I added, "I like his idea. It might work."

She moved closer to me. Silence exploded against the walls. Her mind processed the pros and cons of my offer. I had said enough...maybe too much. Maybe it was time to go. In fact, it was definitely time to go.

"You really think you'll go back to Seattle?" Her voice sounded sad, or maybe it was my imagination.

"Yes...and you?"

"Absolutely. Missouri, Oklahoma, here I come."

The drawback of knowing someone so well is they can read your mind. So there we were, two liars convincing no one that we were just killing time. In truth, we were train wrecks enjoying the ride. I knew there was a reason I loved being around her.

Chapter Twenty-Three

Ice Cream from Former East Germany

    I pulled a cuticle off my thumb, played with it and did the same to the other thumb. So, there I sat, in my car with two sore thumbs. As a child, this was the normal standby whenever I was nervous. I never did it around Lourdes. She never made me nervous. She just made me sad. I started to reach for the pinkie when a thought popped into my head.
    "Let's go over the rules one more time," I said.
    "Again?" Dempsey groaned. "This is the third time, Bugs. Come on."
    Gail turned sideways and leaned her back against the car door. She nodded to Dempsey, and then turned to me and smiled.
    "Humor me," I begged. "I get a little tense when I'm in Hope's house."
    "We take off our shoes," Gail sighed, "and smile before entering."
    "We compliment her interior decorations," Dempsey added, "and we love whatever the hell it is that we eat or drink."

They paused, looking at me for approval. I approved.

"Wait Bugs, we forgot something!"

"No, we didn't," Gail argued.

"We did. We're supposed to stand outside until she invites us in or some shit like that."

"The vampire rule," Gail remembered, giggling.

We were ready but I still didn't want to go in. Asking Hope for anything took a lot of energy and most of the time I didn't have it. From my teenage years until today it was an endless loop of emotions stabbing me in the gut. Most of the time the buildup was so intense I gave up and canceled all plans of whatever help or favor I needed. School projects, broken toys, an extra piece of gum, you name it. All undone because of my never-ending fear of confronting my sister.

But today was different. I had a team and hopefully they would give me the courage to ask Hope for a favor. We were ready. We were parked in front of her house and on time. The rules were in order. The plan was solid. Small talk and trust were a possibility. Find a common ground, I hoped, and slowly prepare her for the request.

Gail calmly watched as I nervously played with my fingers again. It was an act she'd seen before, but never seemed to bother her. Until today, that is.

"Gibson, stop it!"

I did.

"Why are you so nervous?"

She leaned back against the passenger door, her feet resting on the edge of my seat, her ankle elevated.

"Hope is territorial," I confessed. "She's also controlling and has issues. We need to earn her trust and if that happens, then we can move on to other topics."

I was given thirty seconds of silence and then...

"Grow some balls, Bugs!" Dempsey opened the back door and got out. "We're here to borrow her truck. Big deal. I'm going in."

Gail smiled. "I think we're ready. All is well, trust me."

Trust her, I thought. They had no idea what they were doing. They were innocent children walking into a mine field. Playing jump rope with a python while juggling hand grenades disguised as plates. Nobody listens to me. Why is that? I asked myself. How is it every time I have an answer to something, I am the last one to be listened to? Not once in my memory has anyone ever come to me first with a question. I'm always the last resort.

As these thoughts rolled inside my head it suddenly occurred to me I was sitting alone. As I looked up I realized to my horror Gail and Dempsey had already knocked on the door.

They knocked on the door!

And now they were being greeted by Hope.

Without me!

I did the only sensible thing. I panicked.

In a moment of decision making that still puzzles me to this day, I tried to leap out of the car by way of the passenger door, hands first. My legs and feet tangled between the steering wheel and front seat, causing pain and numbness to my knees and ankles but that was minor league compared to my pride that just so happened to be severely bruised.

I can only think of one reason why this course of action made sense at that time. Her name was Hope. As you know by now, my sister had a way of shutting off all form of reason in my head and this current spectacle was a prime example of such a thing.

So, there I was, feet tangled and stuck inside the car while the rest of my body closely examined the marvel of Hope's beautiful concrete driveway. It was nice, in case you might be wondering. A few cracks, but overall solid, very solid. To be honest, my plan was to channel the inner child inside of me – age seven to be exact – and do my best to pretend I was invisible. Sadly, I went so far as to close my eyes and make a wish.

"Gibson? What, exactly, are you doing?"

I opened my eyes and looked up.

Hope stood inches away from my face, her hands on her hips, her head shaking back and forth in typical big sister disappointment as she leaned over me.

Dempsey's Grill

Gail and Dempsey stood behind her, puzzled looks on their faces. Dempsey simply stood where he was while Gail, on the other hand, quickly slapped her hand over her mouth and doing her best to hold back a laugh and failed miserably at it.

I managed to untangle my legs, pulling my lower body out of the car and stand. As I walked to the house with a slight limp, Hope turned to Gail and Dempsey.

"Please come in." It sounded less like a request and more like an order.

For me, she had other plans. She held her hand straight out in typical Nazi conduct, stopping me on the front porch.

"You, stay put."

Hope turned around and followed Gail and Dempsey inside while I stood alone in her driveway. Confused and afraid to move, I was about to call her name but stopped short. That type of action might arouse attention from her neighbors and in Hope's world, no attention is a good thing from the dreaded liberals on her block.

"Here," Hope said, walking out to me. "You fell on a grease spot. Put these on."

Hope turned and walked inside leaving me alone with my grease-stained pants and her husband's green and hot pink pajama bottoms. As ordered, I put them on.

"Adorable," Gail smiled.

"Are those baby farm animals?" Dempsey asked.

Once the photo op was complete courtesy of Dempsey and Gail, I entered the kitchen.

There are rules in every home. Some are strict, some are relaxed. Some run a tight ship while others run no ship at all. It should come as no surprise that Hope's ship was tight. Really, really, tight.

Shoes were removed immediately upon entering the home. They were placed on the concrete area of the entryway far from the wooden floor. The guests were escorted to the kitchen, unaware that their clothing, socks, and hairstyles were under close inspection. If they passed the test, Hope would allow them to sit at the kitchen table, but if they failed, they would sit outside. Only two people know this: Hope's husband and Mom. I only found out about this after Todd had one too many pre-dinner drinks and proceeded to tell me all her house rules and how much of a "heifer bitch" she was.

Yes. Heifer bitch. I have no idea what that means either. Even though Hope and I had never really gotten along, I still couldn't approve of Todd talking about my sister like that. I'd taken away what was left of his microbrew and dumped it out. Petty, I know, but you gotta stand up for family, even when you can't stand them.

Ice green tea was the customary refreshment for all new guests. It was slow brewed with the perfect number of tea bags measured precisely with the correct amount of water. Hope even added an expiration date. A tablespoon of honey was added to the hot water. She said it helped to release the natural sugars. I must admit it was pretty damn good. I never met anyone who turned down seconds.

Unless you were her children, her husband, her painter, or her electrician, odds are you only saw a choice of the entryway, the kitchen, the patio, or the guest bathroom located next to the garage. I was once told by a friend whose mother once showed the house during her real estate days that the house covered 3600 square feet. There were at least five bedrooms, two full baths, and a miscellaneous room which measured close to 1100 square feet.

During Todd's drunken rampage, not only was she a heifer bitch, but she collected hundreds of life-like dolls. The kind where the eyes follow your every move.

"It's her favorite room," he told me while pouring himself another round. "It's a fucking nightmare."

I could only imagine. Despite his drunken ranting, I felt sorry for the guy.

"Nice patio," Gail said as Hope ushered us outside. The table was big enough for six people.

"Yes, Hope," Dempsey agreed. "It's really nice out here."

I smiled and joined my friends. I was surprised we were not seated at the tiny table for four complete with plastic stools and sippy cups.

Dempsey's Grill

Hope and I exchanged quick glances but nothing more. The animals belonged outside. Respect the rules, her quick glance said. Aside from the tasty green tea we were served homemade glazed doughnuts and ice cream.

"I apologize for the ice cream," Hope said as she laid the half gallon container in the middle of the table. "I hope you like it. Normally, my ice cream is homemade, but I was pressed for time and this is the best I could do."

Hope gave me a hard stare as Dempsey and Gail eagerly scooped large portions on to their plate. I failed to give her the standard 72-hour notice. Our arrival was a mystery and, as I would find out during this visit, there was a hefty price to pay for such a mistake.

"The ice cream is from a small town in what used to be East Germany," Hope explained. "It arrived a few hours ago."

"You mean you special ordered ice cream just for us?" Dempsey asked. He looked at Gail and me and shook his head in amazement.

Dempsey held up his glass to Hope. Gail and I followed.

"Thank you, Hope." He smiled. "For going above and beyond. Homemade everything and ice cream from East Germany."

"Former East Germany," Gail corrected.

"Whatever. You are too kind."

For a second I saw a rare glimpse of humility in Hope's eyes. I also saw something else, but I'll get to that later.

Hope said, not unkindly, "It was nothing. Part of being a good hostess."

Hope and Dempsey held a look with one another a little longer than normal. I glanced at Gail to see if she saw what I was thinking. Gail looked over at me with raised eyebrows.

For a few precious moments we sat in silence enjoying our treats. Hope carefully nibbled her glazed doughnut and tiny scoop of ice cream while the rest of us savored our second and third helpings of both. Dempsey was the first to speak and I'm glad he did. Asking Hope for a favor is right up there with asking the President for the missile launch codes. Dempsey turned to face my sister.

"Normally I would use some cheesy pick-up line to ask for what I want," he joked. "But you're an intelligent woman, Hope, so I'm just going to give it to you straight."

I watched Hope as Dempsey talked. Her eyes were narrowed, and she was biting the inside of her cheek. This wasn't going to go well.

"There's an object that needs to be moved," Dempsey continued, "and, how do I put this?"

"You want to borrow my truck," Hope stated, looking at Dempsey.

"See? I knew it! I knew you were smart."

"You flatter me," she said, blushing.

Dempsey looked her from head to toe. "And gorgeous, too," he mumbled.

Alright, that's enough! I'm drawing the line here. This was my sister he was hitting on.

"Yes, we want to borrow your truck," I said, butting in. "Can we?"

"I think I remember you," Hope continued while ignoring my question. She gently laid her elbows inches away from Dempsey, her hands cupped, her chin resting on top of them and the worse part, her eyes looked...horny. Fixed and glazed, to be bluntly honest. "I rarely meet Gibson's friends, I don't want to, if truth be told, but I remember you."

"You two've met a couple of times," I said. "We stopped by at that apartment you use to live in. Mom paid us to move your new couch and—"

"You're taller," she continued, cutting me off completely. "Big." She smiled and glanced at his arm.

"And smarter," he added.

"Are you wearing contacts? Your eyes are very blue."

Oh, good God, they're leaning in!

"Blue," he said. "And you have a nice smile."

Hope blushed to Dempsey's flattery with a smile and a hint of desire, her eyes glued to his. Her lips parted, her hand touching the back of her neck, their eyes locked like missiles ready to launch.

Chamber opening. All systems go!

Dempsey's Grill

I suddenly had this weird sensation I was ankle deep in a romance novel. One of the badly written, cheesy ones.

I believe it's my duty to step in if I see my sister having eye sex with my best friend. As I opened my mouth to say something, hell anything, Gail spoke up.

"Um..." Gail grabbed my hand and squeezed. Her eyes gave me the familiar shut-up look as she quickly asked a question. Clearly, she saw what I was seeing. "Any chance we can borrow your truck?"

"Yes," Hope snapped, momentarily taking her eyes off Dempsey's dreamy blues.

A tiny bird panicked and flew far away. A chipmunk ran for its life, a garden worm dove deep into the dirt, and old lady Hamilton from across the street asked her dog if he, too, heard that hideous noise.

"Excuse me," Hope apologized, collecting herself momentarily. "Of course you and your friends may ride in my truck. It will need to be washed first. The road dust dulls the color."

"I'll wash it before I bring it back," Dempsey promised.

Hope admired him while taking a long, relaxing sip of her iced tea. She gently laid the glass down and slowly dabbed the edges of her mouth, all the while keeping a commanding stare on her willing prey. "Sorry for being nosy, but what exactly are all of you up to?"

I opened my mouth to answer but Dempsey beat me to it.

"I'm starting a business," he proudly smiled.

"I know." Hope leaned forward, elbows back on the table with chin resting comfortably – again – and her face much, much closer to his.

Dempsey took the green light with ease and told his story. He explained each adventure with colorful detail and humor. Gail and I actually caught ourselves laughing. Hope exchanged casual glances in our direction but continued her focus on the storyteller.

"I'll drive," Hope said.

"Bad idea," Gail answered. "Really, really bad."

Hope turned toward Gail. "Honey, I understand your concern, but it is my vehicle and I always I drive."

"Hope, Lou is scary," I advised.

"Lou?"

Dempsey went on to describe Lou in a very creative and colorful way. Hope didn't flinch. To this day, I envision them both in a series of world-tour steel cage matches.

"She's mean," Gail cautioned. "She'll put you in the hospital."

Hope slowly leaned back in her chair with her arms folded across her chest. We paused and waited as deep thoughts spread across her face.

"Well, if I recall correctly, there's good reason to think those folks are involved in... let's say, illegal activities. So we'll need to be careful and just—"

"How can you just get up and go?" I interrupted. "What about the kids?"

"Kids?" Gail asked. I forgot to tell her.

"I have a boy and a girl," Hope said to Gail.

"You're a mom," Dempsey announced.

The words did not come out as a question. If anything, they came out...aroused.

"So, what do we do with them?" I asked after a long uncomfortable silence. "We can't take them with us."

"Who?"

Dempsey's arousing statement had now taken all thought and normalcy away from Hope's highly sophisticated mind.

"Your kids," I said, glaring at Dempsey.

"Oh, the kids."

Hope snapped out of it and turned her focus on me.

"That's easy. They're at a leadership camp for the next two weeks."

"Ah, leadership," Dempsey said and smiled winningly. "That's impressive. How old are they?"

"Six and four," she said proudly. "They're attending a young republican leadership camp in Southern Oregon. The camp creates a vision of how to follow the proper ideas of our Grand Old Party. Also, they learn about nature, or something like that."

"Wow!" Dempsey's eyes grew with amazement.

Dempsey's Grill

"Yes!" my sister said, animated now. "They follow the ideas and history of the Republican Party from its earliest days to now. The group leaders give examples and workshops and teach our children how to apply them in their everyday life."

"That is so neat," Dempsey said. His eyes full of wonder, lust, and fascination.

Hope smiled. "I only regret the YRC wasn't around when I was a child."

"The YRC?" Dempsey asked.

"The Young Republicans' Club," Gail answered before Hope could.

I flinched.

Hope pursed her lips and ignored the interruption. Hope hated to be interrupted. "Yes, it's a good way to introduce leaders our children can relate to like Reagan and the Bush dynasty. We also discuss Congressional leaders and the wives who were home supporting their husbands' beliefs and careers. But most of all, it is the foundation of belief and goals from our great Republican leaders that we teach and build in our children's minds."

I slowly pushed away from the table after a long moment of awkward silence.

"Cool," Dempsey said with admiration.

"Yes, indeed it is 'cool.'" Hope washed herself in his baby blues. "Very cool." She nodded to Gail. "I'm surprised someone such as yourself would be involved with an organization like the YRC. I hadn't realized you were so conservatively minded."

Gail laughed. "Not really."

I never asked Gail's political views. Didn't care, to be honest, but this was Eugene, the liberal capitol of the world, and in that moment of our world, we lived in a time where a Democrat ruled the highest office. Republican housewives and past presidents were easy pickings on every street corner in the Land of Liberals.

"I must be confused then. You know about the YRC and you're not a conservative." Hope smiled like a coyote about to pounce on its prey. "Please tell me I didn't invite some sort of liberal activist into my home."

I tore another cuticle as I nervously waited for an answer.

"Who me?" Gail laughed lightly. "No, I'm pretty moderate. I swing both ways."

"Huh?" Dempsey perked up.

"Dempsey," I muttered. "So how did you come to know about the YRC?" Hope turned her full attention on Gail. Poor Gail.

"It's a funny story, kind of. I just turned twenty. Mom and I were living in Fresno and I needed a job. Mom pulled some strings and got me a job in a campaign office."

"You got into politics? No shit." Dempsey was pleased but I didn't know why.

"Hardly," Gail corrected. "I was assisting the campaign manager. In other words, I did lots of coffee and muffin runs and stuck signs into people's lawns."

"Who was the candidate?" Hope asked.

Yay, politics at Hope's house. This is nice and safe, I thought. I love calm waters. Anyone need more ice cream? Tea? A gun?

"Jack Niles. He was a Republican running for the 5th district," Gail explained. "He wasn't around much, but I did see a lot of Ron."

"Ron?" I was curious.

"My boss. The campaign manager and oh, was I smitten." Gail paused, reliving her time with Ron. "Energetic, intelligent, charming. He lit up a room wherever he went. I often wondered why he wasn't running. His pet project was finding grants to fund things like the YRC. 'Hook em young,' he used to say."

"Sounds like you found the ideal man." Hope smiled.

A jealous fever replaced the icy shiver. Suddenly I was hot and uncomfortable. To make matters worse, we were out of ice cream.

"For a little while, until..." Gail trailed off.

"Until?" Hope prompted.

Gail had our full attention. "I can't believe I'm telling you this." She paused and shared an embarrassing giggle. I smiled too as her dimples took center stage. She finished the remainder of her iced tea and continued.

Dempsey's Grill

"About a month before the election we were running even. Some polls had us ahead. We were all excited. One late night, Ron was going over speeches and asked if I could edit." I was thrilled. I was actually doing something creative. It was after midnight and I was exhausted and somehow, I spilled an entire cup of grape juice on my white shirt. So there I am, trying to rub it out with hot, soapy water while Ron is insisting on baking soda. Well, that led to my shirt on the floor with Ron's pants joining them and us on the break room table."

"I love grape juice," Dempsey chipped in, smiling in the only way Dempsey could. I didn't make the connection, but I smiled anyway.

Gail blushed. "It wasn't my proudest moment."

"Nothing to feel bad about." Hope smiled and patted her hand. I was seeing Hope's softer side. It was nice. "Both of you were young and free. It happens."

"I wish," Gail muttered.

"You wish?" Hope repeated.

"Turns out Ron was a young-looking thirty-six. Married, three kids, house in the burbs. You name it. They contracted him out of L.A., but that wasn't a big secret, however, he didn't have a wedding ring and he never talked about his home life."

Gail stared off into space and shook her head.

"That sucks." Dempsey shook his head and was about to say more. He never got the chance.

"So... you were the 'other' woman," Hope said.

I had joined in with Dempsey as he laughed but now, I turned my attention to Hope, puzzled by the way she was glaring at Gail and then it hit me.

"You bet I was, and I didn't even know it." An ice-cold, lava-killing shiver rolled down my body as Gail laughed at her own mistake. "I was so caught up in this beautiful, sexy man who only had eyes for me it never dawned on me that he might be full of shit."

"Of course, honey. Why would it?"

"Hope's arms were now crossed. Her eyes a mystery, her fangs bared.

"I know, so anyway this goes on for a couple of weeks until one night, I'm in his hotel room when someone knocks on the door. We ordered pizza and jumped in the shower so figured we had time. I answer it with a towel draped around me and my hair dripping wet, my stomach growling and when I open the door, there stands a pregnant woman with three little kids."

My eyes shot to Hope pleading, begging, if you want the truth, to just stop.

Gail did not ruin your life. Do not...

"What happened next?" Hope asked, her voice dripping in icicles.

"I'm looking past her wondering and where's the pizza and she's looking past me wondering why her husband is as wet as I am. Let's just say it got really ugly after that."

For the longest time none of us said a word. It might have only been a few seconds but believe me, it felt like an hour.

"So, who won?" Dempsey said eagerly, as if he was asking about last night's Big Game score.

"Dempsey," I mumbled. I figured now was not the best time for a guy to speak.

"We all lost," Gail said. "Ron was fired and of course, I had to skip town. But get this, while—"

"So, he kept her pregnant while he ran around with his fly unzipped?" Hope interrupted. Gail tried to open her mouth and comment, but Hope wasn't finished. "So many hussies and he chose you. Wow...good job. You win the prize."

Oh no, we're going down that road. In my moment of panic, I tried changing the subject. "How's Todd?" Have I failed to mention how my mind shuts down in moments like these?

Hope leaned forward with the weirdest smile I'd ever seen. Slowly, she moved her glass out of the way and did the same to Gail's.

"I had a friend who drove a hundred miles on a hot day with no air conditioning because her cheap husband forgot to fix it while she was eight months pregnant."

"That's...awful." Gail's voice was soft and innocent, like a freshman at a senior toga party.

Dempsey's Grill

"And when she reached the end of those hundred miles, do you know what she found?" I could tell by the dawning light in Gail's eyes she realized Hope was not pleased with Gail's tale of her youthful indiscretion. "She found her beloved husband, who promised to love and honor her until death, getting blown by a cheap fucking hussy in a goddamn hotel room!"

The world that we lived in had suddenly changed. Birds stopped singing, kittens stopped playing, and the all-you-can-eat waffle bar on Hines street ran out of waffles. For the first time in its long history, the world lay silent.

"Listen Hope, I'm sorry about what happened to your friend. I never wanted to be 'the other woman' and I broke up with Ron as soon as I found out."

"You think no one gets hurt. That's the problem with all you free love, liberal hippy types. Well, people do get hurt, Gail. Families get destroyed. Driving a wedge and ripping out our hearts! Goddamn clueless whores! That's exactly what you are!"

"Hope, it wasn't like—"

My sister cut her off like a lawnmower blade. "Just trying to sleep your way to the top! Have you ever thought for one second about the lives you are ruining, or the trust you are shattering?"

Gail stood up. "I'm sorry, Gibson, but I'm not going to just sit here and listen to this judgmental..." she glared at Hope, who was now also on her feet, fists balled at her sides.

"Get out of my house." Hope pointed toward the door. "Women like you shouldn't be allowed around decent families."

I glanced at Dempsey, hoping he'd take his cue to leave. No such luck. Dempsey only had eyes on Hope.

Gail stormed into the house, out the front and slammed the door. I opened my mouth to say...I don't know, *something*, when the door flew open.

"For the record," Gail announced loudly as she marched back into the ring, "I didn't know he was married! It's not my fault his wife was so busy breeding she didn't even notice his wandering gaze. He lied to me just as much as he lied to her, so I don't see why you're so pissed at me, Hope. I didn't do anything to you."

"Ladies," I pleaded with a panicked grin. "Let's go back to our pleasant non-male hating conversation. Please? Hope? Your truck?"

"Shut up!" they shouted in unison.

Hope strode across her patio to stand face to face with Gail. Picture a steel cage match minus the screaming drunks and you'll come close to what I witnessed. I was hoping for a handshake and goodwill. Not today.

"So, tell me, homewrecker. Did you have to pay for your abortion, or did it come out of his wife's purse?"

Gail shook her head, a savage grin on her face. "You're pathetic. No wonder your husband cheats on you."

"*Get! Out!*" Hope screamed and snatched Dempsey's iced tea glass. I didn't know if she really would have thrown it at Gail's head, but fortunately, Gail didn't wait around to find out. She ducked back into the house and a moment later we heard the front door slam again as she exited out to the front yard.

"So, when do we leave to get my grill?" Dempsey asked. Both Hope and I turned and stared at him.

Chapter Twenty-Four

The Trouble of Love

Dempsey was in love. Don't ask me how or why but trust me, he was.

Maybe it was the way he followed Hope as she chased Gail to the front door. Or maybe it was the simple, to the point, statement he made as we sped away.

"I fucking love your sister, Bugs. Any chance we can come back?"

Getting Gail into the car was the easy part. Calming her down? Not so easy.

"God! No wonder her husband's out messing around. Gibson, your sister is one uptight Republican nut job." As we pulled out of the drive, Hope stood on the porch, glaring. Gail rolled down the window and yelled, "And she's got a fat ass, too!"

The look on Hope's face nearly made me burst out laughing, but I managed to stifle the urge.

"She doesn't have a fat ass," Dempsey defended as he waved to Hope from the backseat.

"Shut up, Dempsey!" Gail looked so upset I almost suggested another trip to the emergency room.

"I'm sorry," I said. I really was. "She's having some marriage issues and I think your story triggered something."

"Maybe you should have kept your thoughts to yourself," Dempsey suggested. His voice was cool and confident. He really had the voice of someone in love.

"The hell I will," Gail snapped. "I don't see how it's my fault her husband cheats on her."

"I'm sorry," I repeated.

I took Dempsey home first. As the three of us sat in silence thinking of what just happened, it suddenly occurred to me. "We still don't have the grill."

"You've got to talk to her, Bugs. We need her truck."

"Bullshit Dempsey," Gail interrupted. "I'll have two abortions and fuck every married guy in town before I say another word to that crazy bitch."

"You're going to stop calling her names," Dempsey ordered.

"You're backing her up?" Gail stared at Dempsey, her expression going from shocked to hurt to angry in about four seconds. "Smooth, Dempsey. About what I expected. Way to put the team first."

"What the hell is that supposed to mean," he demanded.

"Well, let's see," Gail held up her fingers and began to count off. "Dominating, intimidating, name-calling, possibly violent. I have one more digit remaining. Any suggestions from the cheap seats?"

Her voice rose with each word. It didn't take long before she was shouting.

Dempsey shook his head. "Are you telling me that's the kind of women I like?"

"No, I'm giving you the weather report. What the hell do you think?"

"I'll tell you what I think..."

And so, they continued. Ten minutes, fifteen, maybe twenty. After a while, time doesn't seem all that important.

I did my best to drown out Dempsey and Gail's shouting match. My mind took me back to a pleasant time of music, dance, and love.

Dempsey's Grill

None of the three involved me, of course. As their shouting continued, I wondered what my former neighbors in Seattle were doing. The little lady from across the street who always waved when she saw me. Hank the plumber who, to the surprise of all of us, painted his house hot pink with mauve trim. And last but not least, there was little Mary, who had just graduated from training wheels to the big time.

Are all memories like this? Is it all about picking and choosing? In other words, is a memory no different than searching for apples in a giant bin? The big, pretty red ones always win out while the dimpled faded ones get left behind.

"...so, you're telling me this is all my fault?"

The shouting match had lessened to a somewhat reasonable tone with actual, identifiable words as we pulled up to Dempsey's home.

"It's really simple, Gail, apologize to her or don't," Dempsey said. His voice had now calmed to a reasonable tone. "Whatever you do, stop being a pain in the ass. So, Hope lost her temper. Big deal. She's under a lot of stress and you weren't helping with your cutesy story about banging a married man. If her husband cheated on her, he's a dick. This isn't even about you. Get over yourself."

Gail stared at Dempsey for a few seconds. I could practically see the gears whizzing in her head as she considered different ways to kill him and hide the body, but instead, she shook her head and turned to me. Her eyes gleamed with tears.

"Sorry, Gibson," she said. "I'm out."

Dempsey slammed the car door and stormed inside. He even slammed the door of his house. I wondered if that'd ever happened before.

Gail and I said nothing. I didn't feel like talking; what I felt was disappointment. I remembered the feeling I had when Dad drove me home from the bus depot. It all came back like a nasty stomach virus settling deep in my gut.

There would be no grill. No restaurant. No dream. Dempsey and Gail would never speak to each other again. And Hope? Forget it. She was too busy sticking pins into her liberal voodoo doll.

"I'm leaving," Gail said. Her voice exhausted.

"Let me drive you home."

"No." Her face looked defeated, lost, and afraid. We were both in the same place, weren't we? "There's a bus stop down the road. I need to be alone."

I didn't watch her leave. Who wants to see an ending to a bad play when it had so much promise? I sat behind the steering wheel in front of Dempsey's house for a long time. I didn't want to go home.

Chapter Twenty-Five

Running Away

When I woke the next morning, I lay in bed staring at the ceiling. We had planned to do some work on the menu. I had coaxed Mom's recipe for her bacon green beans out of her and we were going to try pairing those with garlic mashed Yukon potatoes and a bleu cheeseburger. After Dempsey and Gail's fight not only were our lunch plans ruined, all my plans were ruined. I was back to square one. Alone in the guest room, I knew if I didn't do something more than likely wouldn't want to get up again. I dragged myself out of bed and donned my running shoes. Running always made me feel better, gave me energy, and helped me clear my head.

So, I ran.

For the next two days all I did was run, sleep, and eat. It was great. Well, maybe not great, but it took my mind off everything. When I wasn't running, I was staring at my phone. A part of me wanted Lourdes to call. Me calling her was out of the question; who wants to sound needy? Okay, maybe I am needy. There, happy? My fear was that I was one of those who enjoyed it. Could I be one of those people who found no reason to help themselves because it was too much fun being knee-deep in misery?

I may have to self-medicate, I thought.

Twice during my runs, I ran past Dempsey's and Gail's houses. Confrontations were not my strong suit, so naturally I skipped the part where I would knock on their doors and demand resolution. Each time I ran past, I would slow down a little bit, hoping they would see me and happily invite me in for pie. *Gibson!* they would cheerfully call out. *Come on in! Have a slice or two. Hell of a night, wasn't it*? After pie, the scene would cut to our favorite music, and typical of every fantasy, it would fade to black.

Didn't happen. Shocker.

Hope came over twice. She did her best to avoid me and would only speak to Mom.

What I missed most of all in my friend's absences was the adventure and the idea that something positive may come out of it. When you're busy chasing a dream, it doesn't allow you to stop and look around. The three of us were in the last months of our twenty's. The adventure became a nice, colorful band-aid hiding the ugly sore that had already started to turn green.

I had to get a job, any job, and it had to be done now. Dad would probably give me one of his rare talks; Now's the time for responsibility, you're not a kid anymore. You need to pick up the pieces, accept the fact that life doesn't always turn out the way you had planned and oh, by the way, the lumberyard is hiring.

At least in my mind that's what he would say. Truth is he might ask if I was working and that's as far as it would go. I liked my version better.

Eleven Days Later—I got a job!

With the help of the self-proclaimed number one job-finding agency in the valley, along with their connections to the University of Oregon, I was given the opportunity to apply and accept a position on campus.

Thirty-five hours a week, assistant janitorial worker, University of Oregon.

Dempsey's Grill

I laughed and cried most of the day. Funny, I always thought that was just a saying.

"It's a job," Dad said.

"That's great, honey." Mom said. I smiled, doing my best to match her enthusiasm.

I was surprised how much I enjoyed the work. The name gets a bad rap. When you think about it, somebody has to do it, but nobody wants to. The University had an image to keep. A clean image that is, and I was part of the team that got it done. Dad nailed it when he said it's a job. It got me out of the house, it kept me busy, and gave me a sense of worth. Not to mention a paycheck.

We worked all over campus. We fixed, we cleaned and replaced as needed. Most of the time I was in large buildings by myself. My hours were extended after a week to forty hours. One day I was given two hours of overtime, a pat on the back, and a promise that I may have a future.

Once when Mr. Wallace, my boss, and I were scraping mold off the ceiling in the boy's locker room, I asked what his ambitions were as a kid.

"P.E. teacher," he said. He stopped and looked around at the empty lockers and shower stalls and laughed. "I got close."

I wasn't sure if it was my imagination, but I swore I detected a small amount of disappointment in his voice. "Do you ever wonder where you'd be if you were a teacher?" I immediately concentrated on the mold, pretending it was the most fascinating thing I ever saw. I was afraid I pried to deep.

"Oh sure," he replied to my relief. "Sometimes when the wife is snoring too loud, I'll lie in bed and wonder how things would have been if I'd worn a condom instead of playing Russian roulette."

I remember he paused and laughed for the longest time. Clearly the Russian roulette line was a keeper.

"I'll tell you this much," I listened for him to finish but when I turned his direction, I saw the laughter in his face had disappeared. He had something important he wanted to say, and I was going to hear it. "There's nothing like choosing your own path. When it's chosen for you, it's like a bitter taste that lasts longer than it should. There's your life's lesson kid. Wear a goddamn condom."

I saw Gail and told her about my new job. I had a beer and left a five-dollar tip. A down payment I said, to a night out. Her truck-driving boyfriend called, filling her head with promises, but his promises were broken when a load in Texas took priority. I saw the disappointment and desperation in her eyes and had to wonder if she saw the same in mine.

We promised we would get together. Maybe next week. Maybe next month. Or another lifetime. Our defeated smiles said goodbye as I walked out the door.

I turned my attention to Dempsey and wished Gail could have come along. Life changes in a second, doesn't it?

Dempsey had gotten a promotion. He would be the head cook for breakfast and lunch. He saw me when I walked in and waved me to his workstation. He was backed up with dishes half a mile. A new boss, younger and a foot shorter, glared from his post in the wings. The boss gave me an uncomfortable smile followed by a long stare at Dempsey that said we'll talk later. I waited for the boss to leave and asked if I could help. He smiled and passed. His mess, he said.

We tried to cover up the silence with meaningless words, but it was no use...something was missing. I left him alone with his mile-high stack of dishes along with the angry boss. I wished him luck on his promotion along with a promise of another crazy night, but we both knew they were just words. I glanced back one final time. His dead eyes programmed to neutral while his red-faced boss shook his finger at the dishes and at him.

Dempsey looked up and smiled and in that moment, I could almost believe he was back with his crazy dream of owning our own restaurant; being our own boss. It was all so simple. We'd kidnap Gail and go chase that dream before it all became a distant memory. It seemed so real.

And then he turned back to his dishes.

Life is what you make it. Sometimes old friends become strangers overnight. Some say that's a good thing, but why does it have to be a reality?

Dempsey's Grill

I had gotten into teaching for the summers off. What other job can give you three months leave? That was an easy choice, but it never occurred to me to ask myself if I was good at it. Guess I should have thought that part through. My decision to dive into a profession I was neither good at nor motivated led me to where I stood. I took a deep breath, turned, and left my friend behind.

Chapter Twenty-Six

We're Getting the Band Back Together

Mom and Dad were gone that night. Their anniversary was in a few weeks and Hope had found a photo of them when they were dating. She thought it would be a great idea for a gift, so I offered to help by increasing the size and adding a frame. I had just finished printing out the picture when I decided to go outside.

My parent's home had an old fashion wraparound porch. As a child, I played under that porch during our many spring rains. I was relaxing on the porch when I heard a car pull up and my first guess was my parents had come home. We'd make small talk, what restaurant did they celebrate at, that sort of thing. I wanted to thank them for allowing me to come home and to show that I put in a productive day of job-hunting. Mom would give me a puzzled look, perhaps saying, "Our home is your home," or she might ask if something was wrong. She would feed me her famous meatloaf, which was her cure for most ills in life.

My parents always entered the house through the back door so I waited for sounds of their arrival and would greet them after they settled in, but I heard nothing.

A car had parked in our driveway. I could see the reflection of headlights from where I sat but still, nothing. As I stood to investigate, a sharp voice cut through the night.

"Sit down, boy!"

The voice was menacing, fearsome, military, and would have sent a shiver down my spine had it not been followed by a familiar giggle.

"Damn it, Gail, I had him."

Dempsey and Gail walked out of the shadows. They looked different than the last time I saw them. Dempsey wore a clean, button-down summer shirt, dark blue jeans that for a change looked new and sparkling white tennis shoes. He even had a haircut and was combed. Shocking.

Gail smiled as they walked to the steps. She wore a beautiful green linen shirt that flared around her shoulders and white shorts cut at the perfect length, allowing all to see her long and amazing summer legs.

"Permission to come aboard," Dempsey asked, as they waited on the bottom step.

I smiled and waved them in. I wasn't sure what to expect. Their friendliness, especially Gail's smile and Dempsey's discovery of wardrobe coupled with the hairstyling was a little unnerving. Was I being cornered as vampire bait? Strangely, the idea was exciting.

They sat down on either side of me in silence. I could smell Dempsey's cologne and Gail's perfume. A mixture of cinnamon, lavender, and musk. Her lips were glossy and sparkly, and it was all I could do not to stare. A stranger would have guessed they were the perfect couple. A bit of jealousy rose within me as I wondered if they were.

"We're sorry," they both said. They stopped and laughed.

"Dempsey and I had a long talk and—"

"We're idiots," Dempsey said, closing the sentence for her. "We're a team, Bugs. But we're only a team if you're with us."

Gail turned and laid her hand on mine. There was a certain calmness about them that put me at ease. It was as if they saw something I didn't.

"We're all in the same boat," she said. "You, the unemployed ex-teacher, me, the sorry ass bartender, and Dempsey, the dishwasher geek."

"We've got nothing to lose," Dempsey added with a shrug.

He was right.

"Hopefully, we didn't lose you," Gail said. Her green eyes smiled as her hands squeezed mine. "Dempsey and I had a long talk today and we realized we were both afraid of the same thing."

"We don't want to lose you, Bugs. One more screaming match and you'd probably move away for good."

I shook my head. "I can't exactly leave town, but maybe lock myself in my parent's house."

"What's in your hand?" Gail asked, looking at my stack of job applications.

I showed them and explained how I had spent my day.

"Do us a favor and put them on hold," Dempsey said. "We have a better idea."

Gail was nodding with enthusiasm "We want you back on the team, Gibson. This plan will only work if you're on board. If not..." She trailed off.

"If not, the dream's dead," Dempsey finished and leaned forward, his normal goofy grin missing in action. "No pressure."

I sighed. What could I say? I had resigned myself to finding a "real" job and suddenly, here they were.

"Look, Bugs. You're my good friend and you're Gail's good friend, but Gail and I just met. There's no bond, no team between us." Dempsey gave me a long look. I had to be honest and not say yes just for their sake. Even if I had a week to think about it, I doubt that would be long enough to make the correct decision. On one hand, I needed money and getting a job would answer that. Still, the idea of chasing a dream was exciting. I had no wife, no kids, so the only responsibility I had was me. But what would I get out of it? The weight of how much was riding on this hit me hard.

Dempsey's Grill

"We split ownership three ways," Dempsey added.

I made up my mind.

"I'm in," I said. "Now what?" So much for taking my time.

Dempsey and Gail looked at each other, and then at me.

"No sense wasting these new rags," he said. "Let's go, Bugs. Tonight, we dance...tomorrow, we fetch that damn grill."

Chapter Twenty-Seven

The Biggest Boy on the Block

We drove to Harvey's house the following night. I would have liked to go in the morning or afternoon when it was nice and light – and the police wide awake and in heavy force – but since Harvey was afraid of Lou, we went at night; midnight, that is. Most of the area was asleep with all kinds of creepy images dancing under the moonlight.

Hope's truck was out of the question, which meant Dempsey, Gail and I would pay for the grill and find some other means of transportation later. I had a bad feeling about this, especially since I was now invested in one third of the operation, but I trusted Dempsey and went along.

Hope was coming over to pick up the picture of our parents. I sent her a text explaining it was under my bed. Knowing full well she'd want to know where I was going, I beat her to the punch, explaining I was headed over to her client's property to pick up the grill.

Dempsey's Grill

When all of us look back at our lives and examine the decisions that we made, and most importantly, where those decisions take us, they can all be credited to a small handful of actions. It can be an action that appeared meaningless at the moment, but in the big picture it was the giant boulder that shifted the landscape to another direction. For our little team, it was that note. That little piece of white paper sitting on my parent's kitchen table. To this day, I wonder how much it changed our lives.

We drove to Harvey's house and found our way down the middle of the long dark driveway. The lone streetlight had burned out, adding to the horror-movie trope. We were nervous but too proud to admit it. We took Dempsey's car, the '83 Vega and somehow all managed to fit in the front seat. Gail sat on my lap with her feet stretched across Dempsey's legs, while Dempsey struggled to drive a car only meant for people under six feet tall. Have you ever wondered why tall people own small cars? Yeah...me, too.

"This is creepy," Gail said as her arms tightened around my neck.

"Not that creepy," Dempsey argued. He was lying. I could see his knuckles turning white on the steering wheel.

"I don't remember it being so dark," Gail said. I knew she didn't want to be here. Hell, none of us did.

"Dempsey, how come we had to come with you if all you're going to do is pay for it?" I asked.

"I don't know."

"You're scared, aren't you?"

"No!"

"Dempsey?"

"Okay, a little."

We drove in silence until we saw the house. Immediately, I thought of Lou and her shotgun.

"Lou's in the house, right?" I asked.

Gail gripped my neck tighter.

"Yes," Dempsey answered. His voice was sharp and nervous. "Harvey said her favorite show is on now."

We all had the same uneasy feeling and we were in no mood to laugh. We drove past a giant open gate where the road came to an end. Dirt and grass became the norm. There was a light near the shed where the grill sat. A motion detection light had spied us and was now showing off the property's newest visitor.

The plan was simple: Pay, leave, and come back later to collect, preferably during the day.

"Can you trust this guy?" Gail whispered.

"He gave me his word, Gail. I don't see a problem."

Famous last words.

Dempsey stopped about a hundred yards from the shed. We could see the tarp that covered the grill. The three of us sat alone under a cool country breeze, enjoying a summer night and I opened my mouth, about to mention the calm of country life when I was interrupted by the door to the country house opening.

Harvey stood on the steps, surveying the scene. Slowly, he reached into his shirt pocket, retrieved a lighter, and lit a cigarette. He smiled and walked toward us.

"How do?" he greeted amicably.

Gail and I watched while Dempsey got out to meet him. Harvey smiled, made a quick gesture to the house and back to Dempsey. They shook hands and walked to the shed. Later that night, Gail and I agreed Harvey didn't see us. If he had, that might have changed the way things worked out.

As Dempsey and Harvey took their walk I looked back to the house and saw the glow of the TV through the curtains. I was caught off guard as Gail grabbed my arm. I turned in her direction and saw a puzzled look on her face. Her finger pressed tight against her lips, a warning to silence any words about to escape.

Listen, her eyes said. I did. I heard it too and nodded. A low hum. We looked at the house and then to the field, then back to the shed. Dempsey was gone.

Gail moved to the driver's seat. I watched as she carefully positioned herself between the seat and the steering wheel while carefully avoiding the horn. She sunk low into the seat, attempting to hide herself as much as possible. Without thinking, I did the same.

"What's that low humming sound?" I whispered.

She didn't answer.

Dempsey's Grill

"It's too dark." Her face was worried and scared. Suddenly, so was I. "Too quiet."

Both of us looked around, jumping at noises that weren't there. It was too dark to see, too quiet to hear. Everything is fine, I kept telling myself. Weird noises happen all the time out in the country. A little humming noise never hurt anyone. We're here to buy a grill, that's it, unless it's a haunted humming grill. How exactly is this scary? Why don't we just leave if it's so damn scary? That's a great idea. We'll come back during the day and pick it up under a bright blue sky. It seemed like a simple plan and you know why? It is a simple plan, ladies and gents. Not a hip whole lot of imagination on that one. No siree, Bob. It's just a big chunk of metal, that's all this grill is. You heat it up, slap a piece of meat on it, and in a few minutes, dinner time. If you can find something scary in that description, tell me.

The worst part of it all is our memory, which is nothing more than a vivid imagination. We have convinced ourselves that this grill, this piece of scrap metal makes everything taste better when in fact, now this is a terrible thing to say, but let's face it because we're all thinking it, the real reason we're sitting in this cramped little car while our friend plays nice with the country hick is clearly an act of desperation. Our lives suck, and this damn grill just might make it better.

"Shhh..."

Gail grabbed my shoulder and turned to me, her big eyes spilling over with fear, curiosity and excitement.

"Where's Dempsey?" she whispered.

I sat up and looked around. No voices or anyone were near the shed. Where else could they have gone?

I wanted to get out of the car and take a look, but Gail grabbed my arm and held me in place. "Don't move," she ordered.

I had no problem obeying.

"What the hell is going on?" she whispered. "He should have been back by now."

She was right.

"I know."

Where is he?

"Is he smoking pot, drinking? We're out in the sticks, I'm sure it's all around us."

"He never smoked pot," I corrected. "Neither of us did. He said it messed up his thinking."

"His thinking." She giggled.

"I know." Now I was giggling.

We stopped and took a moment to look at the house. All this worrying about Dempsey was ridiculous. In fact, later, when things settled we both agreed it wasn't worry that concerned us, it was the idea of putting Dempsey in charge. Little did we know it would come back to haunt us.

Gail shivered. "It's chilly out tonight. He didn't take a jacket."

"He's tough."

"Well, I'm cold."

It was too dark to see anything but for the record, I didn't look at her chest. I know, I'm the king of self-restraint. Give me my brownie points, damn it!

"Maybe we should huddle together," Gail suggested. Was her voice a bit lower? It sounded lower, sexier. "For you know, warmth."

She scooted closer.

"Yeah, for warmth." I cleared my throat. I was beginning to have this feeling we were on a date. Gail and I were never on an official date where handholding, movie, popcorn, and a possible smooch on the doorstep were possible. We had been too young for all of that. At least that's what I like to say. To be honest, we probably thought it was ridiculous to spend our valuable cash on one another when it could be spent on better things like pizza. Plus, if we had the urge to smooch on each other's doorstep, all we had to do was walk across the street. Still, the idea that this was beginning to feel like a date was making me—

"The damn gear shift is in the way."

"Huh?"

Gail rolled her eyes at me. "Focus, Gibson. I said I would cuddle with you, but the damn gear shift is in the way."

I glanced down at the damn gearshift. She was right; it was in the way. At that moment, I hated it and was grateful at the same time.

"I have an idea." Gail took her right leg and gently moved it over the gearshift. The rest of her body followed with the grace of a midnight dancer. She settled her body on my lap with her head resting on my shoulder. I closed my eyes, enjoying her closeness. The silence, the stars, her warmth. It was all good.

"Do you think we would have dated?" she asked. Her warm breath tickled my neck.

"I was wondering the same thing."

"You were?"

She raised her head, her eyes inches from mine. We smiled. I could smell her hair. Lavender and wildflowers. Perfect choice.

"Why not?" I said. "We were friends and we had a lot in common."

"Like both being horny teenagers? At least, I didn't get preggo."

"We were safe," I sputtered.

To be honest, at the time I didn't remember putting the condom on. I was the same as any kid experiencing sex for the first time. The shock of having sex eliminated any worry about consequences or other forms of rational thought.

"The only reason we were safe was because I showed you how to put it on," Gail sadly noted.

"How did you know what to do?"

"Please." I could tell she was rolling her eyes again.

I was curious. "Seriously. You seemed like you knew what you were doing but that was your first time, too...right?"

"Mom taught me all that stuff," Gail confessed.

"You're kidding?"

"Did you know Mom and I were only sixteen years apart? She didn't want me to make the same mistake."

"I think I remembered her thirty-first birthday just before you moved away."

"She showed me how using veggies, carrots, and cucumbers. Had me practice a couple times." I was getting a picture of what that must have looked like.

"Did you eat them afterwards?"

"Now that would have been a weird custom," she giggled. "We ate the cucumber, but not the carrot."

"Thin skin?" I guessed.

"That, and we were afraid it would have that condom after taste."

I wrinkled my nose.

Gail snuggled tighter in my lap. Her right arm nestled comfortably around my waist. We continued to listen to the silence, watching the stars and following our memories.

"So," I asked. "The cucumber. Was it...big?"

Gail snickered. "Always a comparison, huh?"

"I'm just curious."

"It was a big boy. Largest on the block." Her voice sounded relaxed, restful. I wondered how long before both of us fell asleep.

"Mom had to downsize," she continued. "The condoms kept tearing."

"Really?"

"She bought smaller ones and they worked a lot better."

"So it wouldn't slip or tear," I said, amused.

"Exactly."

I thought I heard a noise from the shed and held up a hand. We listened in silence, but I didn't hear anything else. I shrugged.

"Were you disappointed when I didn't live up to the cucumber?" I asked.

"Of course not. Mom told me all about that. She said as long as it worked, size was nothing more than bragging rights."

Bumper Sticker.

"And you were okay with that?" I reminded myself I had been only fifteen. I was a growing boy, but who the hell am I kidding? How can anyone compete with a cucumber? Especially the 'biggest boy on the block.'

"Yours seemed to work. Of course, I had no one to compare it to. Besides..." she ran a hand down my chest, stopping just above my jeans, which seemed to be getting tighter. "As I recall, I was pretty pleased, even if you were just a boy."

"But I'm not anymore." Was I getting defensive?

Dempsey's Grill

Gail repositioned herself, sat up and looked me in the eye. Her hair had loosened and was now lying close to my face, some of it touching my nose and chin. Her mouth and mine were separated by mere inches and through the darkness, I could see a small grin on her face.

"Lucky for me, I'm not interested in boys anymore. I'm a grown woman and I like grown men." She leaned closer to my ear, her teeth gently biting my ear lobe, whispering softly, "I'm betting you're more experienced than the last time we were this close."

"I've learned a few tricks," I admitted in a shaky voice. My hands had found their way inside her blouse. Her skin was soft and warm despite the chill of the evening.

"I like tricks," she confessed.

The thought of Gail being engaged, or soon to be, or whatever the hell it is you want to call it, never even entered my mind. We had a history. We saw each other grow, change, and move away. I never knew what it was like to miss someone until she left and to be honest, I had never stopped missing her. But none of that mattered on that cool, summer night. It was a confusing time, a different place, which is why I didn't object to her fingers as they unzipped my pants.

Her breath was warm and minty. Her lips soft and full of memories. My hands moved around her waist as she moved her eager hips and rested them on top of mine. Reaching below the seat, she pressed the lever that guided us all the way back. She could feel I was enjoying this. Her smile told me so. As my hands slowly reached the front of her pants, with my one and only goal being to lose them, a muffled noise caught our attention. In our moment of fun and play and soon to be sex in the passenger seat of Dempsey's cramped car, a ruffle of bushes and a muffled cry caused our plans to come screeching to a disappointing halt.

"What the hell is that?" She pushed away, rising to look around. Her unbuttoned shirt fell open, her green bra peeking through. I suddenly realized where we were and was reminded with a cold slap of reality that Dempsey was still missing.

Another muffled sound followed. Gail climbed back to the driver's seat, both of us looking at one another and then back to the mysterious sounds.

I was officially confused and afraid. "Is that Dempsey?"

"I don't know." Her eyes looked back and forth in the darkness.

I zipped my pants and got out of the car. Everything was silent...again. I took a few steps away from the car and looked back as Gail also stepped out.

"What?" she asked.

It suddenly made sense. Why didn't I see this coming?

"Of course," I said, then started to laugh. I wasn't laughing because it was funny. No, just the opposite.

"What are you laughing at?" She sounded scared and shaken.

"You not going to believe this," I said as I walked back to the car. "We're in the middle of a—"

And then it happened. I wasn't surprised.

Chapter Twenty-Eight

Arms Waving, Running About

A long time ago, marijuana became legal in Oregon. This wasn't one of those times.

Dempsey ran through the bushes far away from where we stood, his shirt torn, his hands waving high in the air. I stood frozen in place, not understanding what I was seeing but at the same time not all that surprised. Chaos seemed to follow Dempsey wherever he went.

He stopped and stood at the far corner of the property. For a confusing moment I thought of asking Gail why he was standing so far away, and then I realized he was lost. I waved in his direction and was about to yell to him when his head turned, as if he'd caught sight of me. From the bright property lights, I could see the confusion drain out of his face. He looked relieved but that quickly changed into something else. I opened my mouth to ask what his problem was, but I was too late.

"*Run!*" he screamed.

He ran to, then past us with no signs of slowing down. Not even a pause to say hello, how are ya? Gail and I watched him run past before turning to look at one another. Gail's head swiveled in the direction Dempsey had come from, her eyes growing wide. I didn't want to look.

"*Run!*" she screamed.

She grabbed my arm and pulled, giving me little choice but to follow. I tried to see what we were running from. Lou and Harvey stood in the middle of the property, each holding a rifle aimed in our direction.

I froze. I met the eyes of the two people holding their guns aimed at what I was sure my head. I started to say something, but Dempsey yanked me away before I had the chance. He pinned me against the side of the house, his hand pressed against my mouth, a look of panic on his face. It was the type of look I'd seen in movies but not in real life.

"They're growers," he whispered. "They think we're here to take their weed."

I motioned for his hand to uncover my mouth. He did.

"What the hell does that mean?"

"It means they're going to kill us."

"Why? We just want the grill."

"They don't know that."

"Will you two shut up?" Gail whispered.

Gail moved her way to the front of the line to get a better view. She turned away and looked back at us and neither of us liked the look in her eyes. I was afraid they were moving in for the kill.

"Bugs, they've got a ton of pot and we stepped right in the middle of it. They think we're some rival grower or some damn thing. Whatever it is, they're paranoid as hell."

I gave Dempsey a long look. I wasn't sure what to do. Confronting them or running were our only two options.

"I'm going to talk to them." I pushed myself away from the tree.

"No!" Dempsey and Gail whisper-shouted. Dempsey pulled me back. "Those assholes don't fuck around, Bugs. They are convinced we're here to take their shit."

"Why?" Gail demanded.

"I don't know." Dempsey looked sheepishly at the ground.

If any of you have friends you have known for a while, there are certain words, phrases, or looks that can set off alarms. To anyone else, the phrase, *I don't know*, would just be a simple sentence explaining a lack of information. But I knew Dempsey. According to him, we were in trouble, probably going to die, as in doomed, and he had done something to cause whatever shitstorm was about to ruin our night.

I grabbed Dempsey's shirt and pinned him hard against the house. Dempsey is the strongest person I had ever met but he wasn't putting up a fight.

"You don't know?" I repeated. "What the hell did you say to them?"

"Nothing," he lied.

Whenever Dempsey uttered the phrase, "I don't know," I knew it really meant, "I poured on the bullshit really thick and everybody believed it"

...for a while, anyway.

"I might have said a few things," he uttered. "I kind of told them we were somebody else."

"Get your skinny asses out here," Harvey shouted.

"You might have said a few things?" My fear was giving way to exasperation.

"Dempsey, what the hell did you do?" Gail took a step toward, him demanding an answer.

"I...um...might have told them we wanted a discount on the grill."

"A discount," Gail repeated. Her eyes were wide, confused.

I dropped my head and waited. He wasn't finished.

"Continue," I said.

"Well," Dempsey stammered, "when they told me they had all that pot I sort of came up with an idea."

Gail took a giant step forward and shoved Dempsey against the wall. I think she might have hurt him.

"An idea?" she seethed.

Her fist curled into a ball on his shirt while the other fist held tight under his chin. Her face was inches from his.

"What kind of an 'idea'?" she demanded.

He laughed. "Wow, you're pissed."

"Dempsey," I pleaded.

"Well, you're going to laugh when you hear this," he promised. "I told them we were pot dealers too, and we'd undercut them if they didn't give us a discount on the grill. I might have added that we have guns and weren't afraid to use them."

Dempsey let out a laugh and acted surprised when we didn't follow. He stopped when he saw the look on our faces.

"Forget you guys," he said as he turned and walked away. "Damn good idea, I think."

He made it about two steps before Gail kicked him from behind and knocked him to the ground. I was now more afraid of her than the gunslingers.

"We're drug dealers!" she shouted.

Her words came out more as a statement than a question, which was probably a bad idea at the time.

"Sorry," he mumbled.

I had a simple goal that would not only clear everything up but create a nice memory afterwards: I would grab Gail and gently push her to the side; from there, I would help Dempsey up and brush him off. I would call out to the actual drug dealers and let them know as I was coming out that I had no gun. We would clear up this mess, share a few laughs, along with a beer or two, maybe a late-night movie with Lou, and finally pick up the grill in the morning as originally planned.

"I'm going to shoot your sorry ass!" yelled Harvey. A warning shot rang out.

My plan didn't happen.

The first shot exploded about two feet above our heads. The second shot went wide right, obliterating a poor tree. There was a third shot, but I was too busy running for my life to see where it went.

We jumped behind a woodshed. I think all three of us were in shock. Dempsey muttered something that sounded like a prayer.

Dempsey's Grill

The memories of that evening carry a variety of emotions: Anger, fear, curiosity, denial, just to name a few, but if one memory stood out above the rest, it was the experience of being shot at and how little it resembled what we see in the movies. Did you know that being shot at can take an average man and turn him into a screaming three-year-old? Trust me, I know.

"I just pissed myself! Holy shit, it ran down my leg!"

Dempsey tried shaking his leg while keeping his head low. I never asked what exactly his goal was. Not to mention he could have kept this experience to himself and none of us would have been the wiser. But when it came to imitating a child, sadly I was in Dempsey's league at the moment.

I panicked. "We've got to get out of here...out of here...out of here! Who has the car keys? The keys, the keys, it's just a question...just a fucking question...the keys...the keys...Oh fuck!"

"Dempsey has the keys," Gail answered. Her voice sounded surprisingly calm.

"I'd give them to you, Bugs, but I think I pissed on them, too."

A bullet flew over our heads as we discussed the piss-coated car keys.

"Why don't you wash them off?" Gail calmly advised. "I heard drug dealers have wells all over the place."

"They do?" This from me.

Gail flashed a sarcastic smile. How could she be so calm?

In my moment of panic, I had an idea. "Where's the car? If we can get to the car, we have a chance!" That was the only thing I could think of. Beyond that, it was nothing but haze.

"Do you still want me to wash the piss off the keys?"

"Shut up, Dempsey." My anger had boiled over. "I don't want to hear any more about your piss!"

Another bullet flew by causing a beam to shake. Harvey and Lou were closing in. The sounds of their footsteps were closer.

Without warning Gail suddenly leaped into the open and faced them. I watched as her long legs stretched high above me, her arms relaxed to her side, her face determined and fearless and her hair, those long strands of strawberry-blonde waves were dancing against her shoulders in perfect rhythm to the warm summer breeze. I love dangerous women.

"Find cover, assholes! We're packing some serious shit and unlike you sorry fucks, we don't miss!"

See what I mean?

Gail's arms stretched out in front of her, her hands shaped into a make-believe gun. Dempsey and I lay frozen with our mouths hanging open and eyes big and bright. Without warning Gail reached down, dragged me to my feet and ran like hell. I had no time to think.

Chapter Twenty-Nine

Trigger-Happy Hicks

    Gail ran ahead while Dempsey and I did our best to catch up. We didn't say a word. I wanted to turn around and look but I was too afraid of what I might see. I didn't hear anyone behind us.
    We didn't make it to the car, but we found the road we came in on and followed it. My sides hurt from running so fast, but I didn't care. I think Dempsey wanted to stop and catch his breath or throw up but every time he tried, Gail and I grabbed his arms and pulled.
    Everything was a blur. The ground we ran on, the sky above, the air in our lungs, all of it a dream. I guess that's what happens when gun-packing marijuana dealers are chasing you. I can't remember how far we ran: A mile? More? Less? I don't know. But I do know it was the scariest run of my life. We found a ditch along the trail and jumped in when we couldn't run anymore. As we caught our breaths, we looked around for any signs of imminent danger.
    "It worked!" Dempsey smiled. His face was full of exhaustion and fear.

"They could have shot you," I said, turning to Gail. My heart wanted to explode.

Her eyes were wild with excitement. "I know!"

"They really could have shot you," I repeated. This time the reality was settling in. "You could be dead! One shot would have ended everything."

One shot. Everything gone. What the hell was she thinking?

I grabbed her and held on tight. My mind began playing tricks. I was holding her dead body. A bullet through her head. Her blood covering my shirt, my skin. Her arms no longer holding me. I fought back hysterical tears. I babbled as I held her. At that moment I didn't really care. All I could think of were all the things I wanted to say but didn't. I thought we had time. We always think we do, don't we? There is always tomorrow, next week, next year. I had to smell her lavender wildflower hair, feel her touch, and see her smile one more time. I had to convince myself she wasn't dead. A bullet didn't take her away. She was holding onto me in a ditch in Springfield, Oregon, hiding out until the pot-growers quit hunting us.

"It didn't happen," she whispered.

Gail brushed away a tear from her face and mine. I had cried. She smiled and kissed the spot where the tear once lay.

"Will you two find a room or crawl to another ditch?" Dempsey asked. He was now smiling. Amazing.

"I have an idea," Gail said. "How about we feed you to those trigger-happy hicks."

"Watch it, Gail!" Dempsey sounded mad but he knew he deserved worse.

"Why couldn't you pay for your grill and leave?" she asked. "Like a sane person."

"Our grill," he corrected. "Remember, we all agreed we were in on this together."

"You're right, Dempsey," she countered. "Our grill. So, tell me, Mister Deal-Maker, why were Gibson and I sitting in your car waiting? This should have been 'our' deal, too."

Dempsey pointed his finger with his mouth open to argue, but his finger pointing was as far as he got.

Dempsey's Grill

A car was coming.

Chapter Thirty

Speak to the Trees

Two giant searchlights on the passenger and driver's side lit up the night. The car drove slowly, gravel crackling under its weight, the searchlights scanning back and forth between the brush and trees.

They were coming for us.

"They're closing in," Dempsey said, panicked.

Dempsey jumped out of the ditch to run. Instead, as soon as he hopped out he froze, resembling the most perfect make-believe mannequin I ever saw.

"Dumb shit!" Gail shouted. "Get down!"

She tried to grab his legs, but he was too far away. I started to crawl out but it was too late. They'd seen us. We didn't move. The car didn't move. It was a high-midnight standoff. Our luck wouldn't strike twice in one night so I did what any normal person would do in a situation like this.

"*Run!*"

Dempsey's Grill

Dempsey was the first to go, followed by Gail, then me. Gail pulled ahead of Dempsey and pulled him to the side of the road. I followed the sounds of breaking branches, along with the help of an occasional beam of moonlight. I had no idea where she was leading us, but neither of us argued. The car raced by, the headlight beams passing through the trees. They seemed to know where we were going and were planning on heading us off at the end.

Gail stopped behind an evergreen with Dempsey and I right behind her, waiting for her next move.

"I can hear the river," she whispered. "We'll go down there and run to the bridge."

"Hell of a plan," Dempsey approved. Right now, being rescued by sharks might've seemed like a good plan to him.

"How do we get there?" I whispered.

I saw a beam of light moving through the tress. Good. They were still in the car.

"Follow the trail," Gail said.

Dempsey started to say something but turned toward the sound of the car backing up. He grabbed Gail, Gail grabbed me, and we did our best to hide deeper into the trees.

The car backed up into our view, the searchlight pointing in our direction. The large evergreen did its job; the car pulled away. Dempsey gave a thumbs up and Gail smiled. So did I.

And then something really bad happened.

I had no idea my phone had such a loud ring. You would have thought that over time, someone, somewhere, would have made a comment about it. It would have rung in a quiet house, a movie theater, an elevator or a library...you get the idea. At some point somebody would have asked me to turn it down. You would have thought anyway. I only wish.

The moving car immediately moved back into our view. The searchlight zeroed in on my loud ringing phone. It also zeroed in on three people doing their best to shut the damn thing off.

"Shut the damn thing off!" Dempsey cried.

"Where the hell is the off button?" Gail fumbled at the phone in my hand.

"Throw it!" Of course, football player Dempsey would try to solve my problem by throwing it away.

"Like hell! It cost me three-hundred bucks!" I yanked the phone out of his reach.

Gail pointed. "I think you hit the speaker phone."

"Three-hundred? Bugs, you got ripped off. I got the same phone for two. I also got a free—"

"Stay where you are! Hands up!" Harvey's voice sounded way too close for comfort. "Run!" Gail yelled. So we ran.

The trail separated us from the trees, allowing the moonlight to guide us. Finally, we could see where we were going. I started thinking of Lourdes. Of all places and times why now? I wondered. I could see her face, her hands, her hair. Immediately I missed her. I imagined her curled up in her favorite chair. The dark blue one that always sat next to the window, her favorite music playing softly nearby. Why was I thinking of something so pleasant while running down a trail chased by Ma and Pa ganga-dealers armed with shotguns through the woods in the middle of the night?

I came to a stop at the end of the hill. The night had caught up to me and in that moment, I couldn't tell if I was winded from the long curvy trail or exhausted from the strange bullet-ridden evening. Dempsey ran ahead while Gail slowed to join me. We rested with our hands on our knees, taking a moment to catch our breath. No one was coming. Were we in the clear?

I panted and took another gulp of air. "That was a good one. I haven't done that in a while."

"You're kidding?" Gail sounded as winded as me as her voice moaned for more air. "You could have fooled me. You weren't slowing down a bit."

"I haven't had a lot of practice and when I do, it's kind of boring to go at it alone." I turned and looked behind me, positive I could hear faint music.

"I like it by myself. It gives me time to think." Gail turned as well, as if hearing the same music, but turned back and took another breath.

Dempsey's Grill

I was starting to feel energized. "We need to do this again. You have no idea how long it's been."

I opened my mouth to add a final thought when the music returned. This time it was obvious it wasn't my imagination. As we stood and looked around, Gail slowly turned in my direction.

"I trusted you, Gibson! Why do you break my heart?"

It took me a moment to realize Gail wasn't doing the talking. For reasons I'll never know, I looked up and followed the trees under the moonlight, convinced they had learned to talk. I paused, believing that if one tree talked another was sure to follow.

"Who's the whore, Gibson?"

Gail, wide-eyed, gently took my phone and turned off the speaker. She bit her lip as she politely laid it in my hand. I watched helplessly as she ran ahead before disappearing into the darkness. I stood for what seemed like the longest time until I slowly pressed the phone to my ear.

"Hi, Lourdes." Her silence to my greeting as I made my way toward Gail and Dempsey told me all I needed to know. I tried to laugh. "This isn't what you think. In fact, you're going to crack up when you hear what's happened to me tonight."

"Answer my question, Gibson. Who's the whore? I'm waiting..."

I wasn't sure how to answer her. I had never been in this type of situation before. Aside from the fear of being chased by gun happy drug dealers with a weight problem, I was in the middle of enjoying my first and only feeling of being in control of this dying relationship. I had a bonafide happy moment, if you can believe that.

"Gibson!"

Her voice was loud, demanding and as usual, demeaning.

"Lourdes, this is really a bad time, can I call you back?"

"Oh, I'll bet it's a bad time. Who is she?"

"Uh, Lourdes, I'm sorry but I'm kind of in the middle of something...Can we—"

"I trusted you, Gibson. I gave you my heart and this is the thanks I get? How you pay for my affection? Who are you? What have you become? And again, I'll ask this one more time... *Who's the fucking whore?*"

"Lourdes, it isn't what you think. I'm not with a prostitute. Let me explain. See we're out in Spring—" I stopped running. They'd found us.

"Gibson?"

"I have to go."

"Gibson?"

Two police officers stood at the end of the trail with their guns drawn. Dempsey and Gail knelt in front of them, hands locked behind their heads. I placed the phone in my pocket, cutting off Lourdes in mid-sentence. Slowly I walked to my friends, my hands extended in the air.

Our night was over.

Chapter Thirty-One

TMI

    For the second time in under a week my two friends and I stood single file with our hands held high in the air. Actually, I need to make one small correction: In this particular incident, we rested on our knees, our hands clamped tightly behind our heads. Unlike our experience with Harvey and Lou, we were now in the company of Springfield's Finest.

    If there is one thing that I've learned as my twenties came crashing to an end was the ability to know when to talk and when to shut the hell up. A key example would be the situation I had described above. In that moment of confusion, I am proud to say I chose the path of righteous.

    Sadly, Dempsey missed that memo.

    "I don't have a gun! I swear!" Dempsey shifted from one knee to another. Fortunately, he kept his hands locked. I only wish he had done the same with his mouth.

"I mean, I do have a gun, but it's at my house. I really have two. Okay, I have three...but they're empty, I swear! They look really cool."

"Dempsey." Gail looked straight ahead while calmly saying his name. We didn't know it at the time, but a slow rage was boiling inside of her.

"I got the guns to impress a girl, okay?"

I had no idea where he was going with this, but I was curious.

"She liked guns and I thought it would increase the odds. Guns really turned her on."

I let out a sigh of relief figuring he was through. I was wrong.

"It worked. We did it three times, but I got tired and couldn't do it again, which is really weird, my magic number is five, and when I couldn't hit the five count I got to thinking maybe I should go see a doctor."

"Dempsey, you need to shut up now."

I detected an odd tone in Gail's voice. At first I thought it leaned on the shaky and desperate side but as Dempsey continued to open his mouth, I realized I was wrong.

"I have pot!" I couldn't tell if the officers were interested or bored. It was too dark to see their faces well. "It's in my car up on the hill. You can't miss it. I mean the car, not the pot. You probably know what pot looks like. It's in the glove compartment and I think it's old stuff. I was trying to hook up with a girl who likes pot."

"Please shut the hell up." Gail was no longer whispering.

"This wasn't the gun-girl, this was a different one. Turns out I didn't need the pot to get laid. I hit my magic number with that one. I think I have a problem with gun girls. You wouldn't think that would be a big deal. I remember once I hooked up with a girl who liked candy canes. You will not believe the shit she did with—"

"I'm going to kill you!"

Gail broke the line of defense knocking Dempsey on his face. I sat frozen watching all of this out of the corner of my eye. Dempsey had a good eighty pounds on Gail, give or take, but on that particular night, you would have thought wrong.

"Why can't you just shut the fuck up?"

Dempsey's Grill

It took both officers to pull her off him. Every time they thought they succeeded Gail found a way to jump the poor guy again. I was kind of bummed. I wanted to hear more about the candy cane girl. I decided not to tell Gail that one. Thankfully, the cops had brought multiple cars. I was grateful that Dempsey and I rode together. Gail needed a serious cooling off period.

Chapter Thirty-Two

Of Cops and Corndogs

Jail.

The walls echoed. If you listened close enough you could hear the lonely calls of inmates from the past. Their horrors and their cries bounced from wall to wall. How many innocent people lined these walls, their calls for help ignored? How many were like us, simply at the wrong place at the wrong time. We sat on the cold floor. Lost, alone and frightened.

"Wow, we're in jail. This is it, Bugs. This is really it."

Dempsey leaned his head against the cold, hard, glossily painted wall. His words expressed those repeated a thousand times before in this place.

"There was so much I wanted to do."

"We're so young," I added. My eyes stared straight ahead, watching my world crash to a fiery ending.

We sat together, a team, our heads and bodies supported by the same hard wall. Reality was setting in, working its way into our hearts.

Dempsey's Grill

"We are young," he agreed. "Thirty isn't old. Thirty is the beginning. It's the decade where adulthood begins."

"Used to begin," I corrected.

"You grow up..."

"Put the pieces together..."

"Figure things out."

I sighed. "We'll get through this. It's not always going to be this way. We may think of it as the end and, even if it is, what do you do when you're at the bottom?"

We looked at one another and smiled weakly.

"Climb to the top," he said, smiling a little.

We gave each other a man-size fist bump. Our future in despair, our hopes surprisingly golden but in reality our dreams were dashed.

"You guys are kidding, right?"

Gail sat across the room, relaxing in an oversized leather chair, a speck of mustard on her lips as she finished off the last of her corndog.

"You guys sound like you're on your way to death row." She paused in her observation, taking a sip of her large drink while finishing off the remainder of her onion rings. "Can I get you two a priest to say a little something before the Big Ugly chokes away your final breath?"

"Stop trying to be funny, Gail," Dempsey ordered. "Our lives are over. You have no idea how I feel at this moment."

"Let me guess," she pondered. "Full? You downed a triple cheeseburger and a large milkshake in ten minutes."

Silence.

It was one of those moments where anything was possible. The fighting, the kicking, the biting; it had been a long night. We were dirty, bruised, and exhausted. Not to mention our nerves slightly rattled from being shot at.

Gail and Dempsey locked eyes. I waited. Dempsey leaned forward and Gail copied. I watched with candid curiosity, my back hugging the cold wall.

Dempsey cracked first.

"Shithead," he said with a smirk.

"Bigger shithead," Gail said, smiling.

They laughed and so did I.

It felt good. Perfect. Relaxing. In fact, it was the best laugh I ever had. Well, maybe not ever, but it was still pretty good. It felt good because this was a good time. It was real and crazy and who cares if it didn't last forever.

Dempsey ruffled my hair, reached for my arm and yanked me to my feet. He placed his long arm around my shoulder. Gail yelled, "Group hug!" and wrapped her arms around us. We danced and laughed at 1:44 am in the Springfield police station. It was a time when three soon-to-be thirty-year-olds could count happy days on one hand. This was a digit worth remembering.

The cops had arrested Harvey and Lou on charges of growing and distributing marijuana. A tip led them to the area. A night-raid had already been planned, the gun shots simply speed things along. The car with the bright lights following us was a police car. At first they thought we were the grower's helpers, but they knew who we were by a description. They were simply following us to see where we were going. The reason they had their guns out was because Harvey and Lou had been shooting prior to their arrest.

Inspector Eric Walker gave us the rundown on the entire story. We wouldn't be charged with a crime.

"Unless being in the wrong place at the wrong time is illegal." Walker chuckled. I didn't appreciate his attempt at humor.

Aside from Dempsey's car having two bullet holes in the windshield, no other damage occurred.

"All three of you are very lucky," Walker concluded.

Dempsey and Gail repeatedly thanked Inspector Walker for his courtesy and information.

"Thank you, Eric. You've been amazing." Gail smiled sweetly, her eyes as bright as Venus at midnight, her voice as soft as an early morning lullaby.

"Anytime, Gail," he smiled back, his eyes slowly tracing down to the broken buttons on her shirt.

"The next time you come to the bar it's on the house. We can't thank you enough."

Walker smiled lecherously. "I'll take you up on that."

Dempsey's Grill

Bastard.

I did everything to ignore Eric the Inspector. His perfectly combed blond hair, his dazzling blue eyes, and his all-American Boy Scout tan. I also ignored his full-time job, which probably required an above average intelligence. But most of all, I ignored the absence of a wedding ring.

Double Bastard.

I got a call from Lourdes tonight. True, the timing was really bad, I get that, but how could she know? She might want me back. Maybe our break was worth it. Eugene, Oregon has served its purpose. I did all I could, but I belong in Seattle. That's where the action is.

Just keep saying that, I tried convincing myself.

"You know Gail, I'm taking my boat out next week. There's plenty of room." Walker leaned back in his chair, his detective biceps bulging on display.

"That is so tempting."

I watched the all-American Boy Scout undress her with his eyes. The next step was sailing off into the sunset full of orange and blue. I was tempted to add a heavily large school of hungry sharks, but Gail was on board. A mere two hours earlier she'd been lying on top of me, shirt unbutton, loosely fitted bra, and happy hands below my belt.

"What do you say guys?" Gail turned her head looking directly at Dempsey and me. "Could be fun."

Dempsey was oblivious to the detective's motive, which explains his enthusiastic response.

"Hell yes!"

"Sorry, fellas. There's only room for one." The inspector slipped another smile in Gail's direction, this time missing her eyes but landing perfectly on her breasts and navel.

I tried going another round with thoughts of Lourdes, Seattle, and her sushi-eating friends. I ordered my mind to take me back to my weekends of the past full of endless hours in basket and carpet stores, fine wine sipping in galleries, and creative poetry rainbow designs, but it was no use. My mind was busy with other things, primarily Inspector Eric and his attempts to use telepathy to remove Gail's underwear.

He smiled. "I'll give you a call. Leave your number on the way out."

We were going to have sex! We should have had sex!

"Thank you, Eric, but I think I'll pass. I don't date cops."

Fourteen years after our first and only time. The odds of it being a whole lot better the second time around were off the charts.

Why the hell did Dempsey have to show up? Twenty minutes was all we needed. Fifteen! Ten!

Detective Eric frowned and rose from his comfy chair. For a moment I thought he was going to storm out, but instead he greeted an unannounced guest.

"Gail, gentlemen, I want you to meet the person who tipped us off this evening. Without her help, I'm afraid to even guess what might have happened to all of you."

Chapter Thirty-Three

New Blood

Hope stood in the doorway, an embarrassed smile on her face, followed by a polite wave in our direction.

"Please join us," Eric said. "Have a seat."

Hope and I locked eyes. Eric offered Hope the cushy leather chair. As she sat, he stood in front of her and explained.

It turned out Lou and the Harvey had been under the microscope for months. It all started when the owner of the property died leaving his kids to liquidate his estate. They had little interest in managing property, but they did have interest in the money it was worth. Hell, who doesn't? One day they drove by and were stunned at the trash pit that Lou and Harvey had created on their father's land. They wanted the place cleaned up now and not after the lease ran out. Who wants that kind of work? This is where Hope came in. Since she was the Old Man's realtor, the first thing his kids did was call her. They knew her reputation and realized it would be a quick fix by sending her in. Turns out it wasn't as quick of a fix as they had planned but it did get things rolling.

Hope knew right away something strange was going on. Lou and Harvey's paranoia were running deep the moment she showed up. They would only allow her to walk around in certain areas and the second she tried to push her way through, they tried their intimidation routine. Need I describe again what we went through? You get the idea. These goobers were cutting into her 'pride and reputation' – her words, by the way – and she would be damned if that was going to happen. She determined to get them evicted without breaking a nail and still have time for an ice cream treat by the afternoon. While Lou and Harvey laughed, Hope was busy speed-dialing the romance artist, Inspector Walker. Within the hour he had all the info he needed; it was just a matter of time until a raid was set up.

Hope stood and attempted to leave as Eric's story concluded. She saved us that night, but it didn't matter. At least, to her it didn't. I'll never know if she was scared for all of us, for me, or just plain angry at our carelessness. This is Hope we're talking about, where emotions are kept in check 24/7.

I watched as she stood and walked to the door, hoping to disappear into the night. Maybe later, months later, I would be allowed to bring it up but only in private, preferably in a soundproof car on a freeway.

Hope's goal of a peaceful getaway turned into a pipe dream as Gail leaped out of her chair and threw her arms around her neck. Hope stood like a statue, her arms to her side, her eyes focused straight ahead. It didn't matter. Gail hugged the person who may have prevented some really bad stuff and damnit, this hug was for her.

After Gail's monster hug, Dempsey followed by picking Hope up and holding her in his arms. Hope's arms moved around his neck, a slight smile easing the corners of her mouth. I couldn't believe she was allowing this.

Dempsey lowered her to the floor, but the hugging didn't stop there. He held her a little longer and whispered something in her ear. She never told me what he said but for the longest time she smiled. I was surprised to see her hands reach up and hold him as well. For a moment, they looked like a couple but when Dempsey released Hope, she immediately transformed into the strait-laced, uptight wasp of a sister I knew. She straightened her hair, readjusted her shirt, and returned to the stoic stature I had grown accustomed to.

Gail walked over to me and placed her arms around my waist. We ended with another group hug. This time Hope was included.

For the remainder of the night my mind refused to wander. I would not think about the grill being out of reach or our dreams of running a business over. All those things would come later. Probably the next day, I figured. It's true, isn't it? Bad thoughts, bad realities, always knocking on your door. Sometimes they arrive out of nowhere, other times by appointment only.

My memories of that night after Hope arrived are dim. Sure, I was back to square one. Lourdes's phone call might have been the final straw, Gail and I almost had sex, unemployment with zero career ambition hadn't changed, and my worries of accomplishing something before time ran out were sitting on the threshold. But for now, none of it mattered. I was a part of something and that's all that mattered.

Hope drove us home. Dempsey sat up front while Gail and I sat in the back. I reached over and held her hand. We smiled. None of us talked, except for Hope.

"Fresh blood is the foundation of growth." I couldn't understand why she sounded so enthusiastic, but I was in no mood to ask. "Never forget that. Downtown Eugene is stagnant. They are begging for someone new to come in."

I wasn't paying much attention. Although, I must admit, I hadn't seen her this excited since she closed on the half a million home in the South Hills. Dempsey was the opposite of Hope's current mood, which is rare, I might add. He didn't move, he didn't say a word. All he did was stare out into the darkness like the rest of us. Sure, he was happy as a clam to get out of the police station without a scratch, but now what? On the other hand, the last time I saw Hope talk at such a feverish rate was at our cousin's wedding. I'm pretty sure that was the night she discovered gin.

"Investment!" she shouted. "Do you hear me? Every city needs investments, but right now Eugene is moribund."

I felt bad for her. Clearly, she was the only one excited. Not only with her voice and ideas but with her right hand.

"I understand you are down at this moment." She turned her head and whispered Dempsey's way. "But that doesn't mean your dream has died."

She laid her hand on top of Dempsey's and gave it a gentle pat. Physical contact not being one of her calling cards, I must admit I was a bit surprised, but given the night we had I figured anything was possible.

"Do you know how many times my dreams have died?" She waited patiently for a reply. Unfortunately, she'd have better luck getting a response from one of the seatbelts than from us.

"Actually, that was a rhetorical question," she continued. "I have succeeded in everything, but you're young. All of you. So what if the grill is gone and your dream is dead? Focus on something else."

Hope grabbed Dempsey's hand and raised it in the air. I wasn't sure where she was going with this but whatever it was, he was in no mood and within seconds his hand crashed into his lap. Later, when I had time to think I realized I may have just witnessed the only time Dempsey didn't make a move after a girl touched him. True, it was Hope, but still...old habits and all.

Dempsey's Grill

I took a deep breath and realized it was over. And to think not too long ago all I wanted was to be alone, but not anymore. Hope parked in front of Dempsey's house. He practically oozed out of the car into a puddle of depression. I was hoping for words of encouragement or maybe Plan B. I thought everyone with a Plan A had a Plan B. But not tonight.

"See you two around," he said. "We'll do something."

My heart sank. It wasn't the words he said but the way they sounded...alone and defeated. He turned and left before I could say anything.

I watched the city sleep as Hope drove us home. A town I grew up in, a town I kept pushing away, but like a stubborn adversary, it refused to oblige. My fate continued to enter my thoughts no matter how hard I tried to push them away. Would the town strangle me, or would it nurture me like a favorite son? If it did have control over what I would become then what direction would it take and how kind would it be?

"Now what do we do?" Gail asked.

I didn't answer.

Gail leaned over and kissed me, our promising smiles holding tight. We had a moment, not a future, and we both knew that moment would only happen once. Hope parked in front of Gail's house. She squeezed my hand a final time, thanked Hope and faded into the night. Loss and rejection quickly turned into acceptance. Soon she would disappear from my life and this night would fade from our memories. Gail was engaged to be married and I was teetering on a breakup. Okay, not teetering, but trying to reverse it. We were two adults; we had a history and our history came close to repeating itself tonight.

I knew my mind would play games in the coming weeks. It would remind me of the what-ifs and could-have-beens. Why fight it, I resigned. Let's face it, whenever my phone rings, I would think of Gail instead of Lourdes and when it wasn't her, I would hurt. Sometimes it was good to be honest with yourself, but generally I tried not to be *too* honest.

I do this shit all the time. Falling hard is my way, I guess. My favorite road seems to be the one full of potholes and land mines. I avoided the smoothly paved paths in the good part of town. Don't fight it, I told myself. Let it happen. Do you hear me Gibson? Gibson?

"...Gibson? Gibson?"

"Huh?"

"I said, do you hear me?"

"Yes."

Hope turned around with her familiar impatient glare. The lost little girl I saw in the police station was all grown up.

"I'm not your limo driver. Crawl up front."

I did.

Hope glanced at me with calm eyes. Maybe it was the early morning hours. Maybe not.

"Let it happen," she said.

"What?"

She smiled.

"Work it out of your system. Whatever happened tonight needs to happen again in that brain of yours."

"You mean getting shot at?"

"No," she laughed. "I'm talking about the hickey on your neck."

I touched my neck. I forgot it was there. This was the first time I noticed it was sore.

"Oh...that," I said.

"The last time I saw that look in your eye was the day Gail moved away."

"I was just a kid."

"It doesn't matter how old you are, it always hurts."

"But it doesn't seem to hurt you. Why?" I asked.

She slowed the car down and looked at me. The lost little girl suddenly appeared again.

"I'm the queen of layers, little brother. I'm always covering something up. Sometimes I hardly recognize myself."

"Why do you do that?"

Dempsey's Grill

She looked at me with defeated eyes and shrugged. "Habit. Besides, if I don't keep all this mess together, who will? Todd?" She snorted. "You?"

We drove home in silence. I watched the dark houses as we passed, wondering what dreams were being played out inside each. Did the dreamers wake with a smile or were they scared and wondered why? Hope pulled up behind Dad's truck. I climbed the steps to my parent's front door, too tired to think.

"Gibson," she called as I placed the key in the lock. "Come here."

Puzzled, I walked down the steps.

"Why did that grill mean so much to all of you?" she asked.

I gave myself a moment to think. It was a tough question but when the answer came it was easy.

"Hope," I said.

"What?"

"No," I smiled. "Not you, the word."

"Hope," she repeated, then nodded. "Good night, Gibson."

"Good night, Hope."

Chapter Thirty-Four

Happiness is an Empty House

It was ten o'clock on a Friday night, five days after escaping the shootout with Dempsey and Gail. My parents were attending a fundraiser, a warm summer breeze was slipping its way through the screen door, and I was enjoying a late evening combo of a movie and a turkey meat pie. For the first time in my life, I was worried about gaining weight. Would I be one of those thirty-year-old's walking around with a gut hanging over their belts?

My worry ended when the oven dinged, signaling my meat pie was ready. As I sat comfortably in my favorite chair and enjoying my quiet evening, my phone interrupted the silence. It was Dempsey.

I answered the phone on the final ring, inches away from voice mail. A part of my mind was happy he called but the hungry side wanted the meat pie.

"Hey, Dempsey." I pushed the fork into the crust allowing the mouthwatering scent to escape.

"Hey, man. Um...how are you, Bugs?"

Dempsey's Grill

It was rich and savory and ready to please.

"I'm good." I slowly sunk the fork to the bottom.

"That's good, man. That's good. I just...um...I just wanted to say hi."

The crust was flaky, the turkey moist, my taste buds waiting and willing.

"How's your new job?"

I plunged the fork deep into my mouth. Tiny pieces of heaven danced on the edges of my tongue playing gospel to my taste buds delight.

"Bugs, you there?"

"Sorry, Dempsey." I laid the fork down and took a quick drink of my ice-cold milk. "I'm glad you called," I lied as my taste buds called for more. "I'm off tomorrow. I'll come over."

"Can't, man. Gotta work."

I lifted the fork and pushed away the outer crust. I watched as it floated like a raft surrounded by baby peas and carrots. I plunged the crust deep into the gravy watching it disappear into the mouthwatering sea.

"How's Hope? I haven't seen her around in a while."

"Same old. You know how sisters are."

Peas and carrots floated to the top covering the tasty raft below. My fork plunged deep stabbing the turkey as it carried gravy, peas and carrots to the top.

"I guess Gail is back at the bar, huh? Looks like we're all back to doing what we use to do."

Turkey and gravy filled my mouth. Each helping heartier than the last. When I reached the bottom and tasted the final bite an empty feeling washed over me, causing me to suddenly feel oddly lonely.

"Well, Bugs, I'll let you get back to doing what you were doing. I miss—"

I drank the last of the milk. Suddenly my thoughts cleared. Was it just me or was this more than a social call?

"I'm sorry, Dempsey, I didn't hear what you said."

A long silence made me wonder if I was talking to air but soon, I heard a clearing of his voice followed by his final words.

"Nothing, man. See you around."

Dempsey's Grill

Chapter Thirty-Five

Smelly with Disgusting Hair

I couldn't get that the phone call with Dempsey out of my head. It seemed incomplete. I didn't know if it was the sound of his voice that bugged me or his lack of words. Either way, I set out to pay him a visit. I knew he was working but I've hung out with him before on the job, so I didn't see a problem. But another problem took priority; I missed Gail, which might explain why I bypassed Dempsey and paid her a visit instead.

She was standing in the middle of the bar taking orders from four guys. Three were talking to her breasts and one to her ass. They didn't seem to mind that the conversation was one-sided. Gail saw me the moment I walked in. She rolled her eyes and motioned me to follow her. I walked in the back where I was greeted rather testily.

"Our new hire didn't show, the boss is sick, Garcia is my only help, and good luck talking English to him. I haven't sat down for six fucking hours and my hair smells like beer."

"May I suggest sex?"

I was hoping to lighten the mood.

"Trust me, you don't want any of this right now. On the other hand, a little lay might relax the tension in my neck."

"Little?"

She ignored me.

I glanced Garcia's way and saw him smile. I had a feeling he spoke a lot more English than he let on.

"Deliver this pitcher to those tongue wagging college boys and help me clean up the place."

I delivered the pitcher to the boys and smiled as they thanked my chest and ass before realizing who was doing the delivery. I cleared off six tables, took three orders, rolled an empty keg to the back, hooked up a new one and delivered two more orders.

"Thanks," Gail said as she wiped the sweat off her forehead.

Her face was drawn. The way someone looks who desperately needs sleep. I forced her to sit down and, to my surprise, she didn't argue.

"You're worn out."

"You think?"

I was getting worried. I wondered when she'd last ate or had anything to drink. I had Garcia make her a grilled cheese sandwich and told her not to move until it was gone. She ate two of them.

During this time I cleared off two more tables, said goodbye to the horny college boys, and was able to contact the new hire and the owner. The owner was on his way and the new hire thought she started tomorrow, not today. I walked back to where Gail was. She looked better but I was still worried. I explained to her the news on the new hire and said the owner was on his way. She smiled and motioned me over.

"Come here. You deserve a kiss from a smelly girl with disgusting hair."

She grabbed my face and pulled me down to her level. She didn't have to work all that hard. She gave me a long kiss and smiled. She could have smelled like a sewer drum for all I cared.

"Where have you been all my life?" I smiled.

"Living here and loving it." Her voice reeked of sarcasm.

Dempsey's Grill

"How many hours are you putting in?"

"I don't know. Ten, maybe twelve hours a day. I haven't had a day off in six days."

"Why?"

"One moved away, one was fired, the new hire doesn't know how to read, the boss is fishing, and the owner doesn't give a shit. Take your pick."

I stayed another hour, long enough for the new hire and the owner to arrive. The owner thanked me and offered me pay but I passed. Gail gave me a long hug before I left. I could tell she wanted to talk but the words weren't there.

We promised to call each other but I knew that wouldn't happen. I don't know why I felt that way, but things were different now. She was back to waiting for her phone call, Dempsey was surviving, and I had settled into a routine. I turned to wave but it was too late. Her attention was now on the new hire.

The next day I went back to work. I remembered what my boss said: *In a blink of an eye you meet a nice girl, settle in, pay your bills and forget the dream you use to have.*

I started to think of my dad. Sometimes I would see a small grin on his face next to his dead eyes. Does that explain the silence? Was he thinking of his past and what could have been, and if so, how long before that is me?

Chapter Thirty-Six

A Polite Kidnapping

It was a Tuesday, a week after I'd helped Gail out at the bar. Partly cloudy, mid 80's with a light summer breeze. In other words, it was an average summer day in the Willamette Valley. I offered to fill in for an employee on vacation and asked to be trained for other jobs. I was beginning to settle in. Now all I needed was to meet a nice girl and knock her up. I know...too much.

Two things stood out that day. The first was an unfamiliar calm that had washed over me; a combination of confidence and ease. With each passing day, routine had taken the place of fear, something I had lacked as a teacher. When I was teaching I had a routine, but uncertainty and fright took center stage. A question mark hung over my head reminding others I was a joke. I could see it in the students' eyes. They smelled fear. They knew I was little more than an overgrown babysitter as my worries about the possibility of getting fired took priority over teaching geometry. Every day, I knew my job was a joke. Every day, the joke flooded over the weakened dikes like an out-of-control river. Soon it would expand and destroy every town in sight. I was surprised I lasted as long as I did.

The other thing that I remember on that partly cloudy, slightly breezy summer day was Hope. As I walked to my car enjoying my unfamiliar calm and confidence, a single question stopped me in my tracks.

Why was Hope sitting on the hood of my car?

She smiled and looked comfortable. The thought of Hope sitting on a dusty, slightly dented hood of a car, or anything other than a proper wooden chair of her choice, made about as much sense as a spider and fly performing a beautiful song and dance routine on your kitchen counter.

But here she was.

"Get in," she ordered, motioning to the car behind mine.

"Get in?"

"Please?" she asked, her face producing a forced smile.

Her car sat a few feet away from mine and looking closer I saw two heads in the back seat. I lowered my head to get a closer look. At the same time, Hope released her familiar disappointed sigh before sliding off the hood and pushing me to her car.

"One day I would like you to do what I say without questioning me."

She grabbed me by the wrist and pulled me to the passenger side. Her grip on my wrist fell into the same league as an eagle clutching a fish. She opened the door and shoved me inside as Gail and Dempsey sat calmly in the back seat. They each produced a polite wave and smile. I would not have been surprised if they were handcuffed and gagged.

I tried to ask what this was about, what's going on, where are we going...you know...typical stock questions anyone would ask when their sister shoves them into a car without warning, but silence was my only friend.

Dempsey looked away the moment I tried to make eye contact. He investigated the length of his hands, the texture of the car's ceiling, the floor design, anything to avoid me. Realizing Dempsey was a lost cause, I gave Gail a try. She helped by pressing her index finger to her lips.

Silence followed.

We drove through the University district which followed the main bus routes and side streets. Without warning, Hope stopped. Did I mention driving was not one of her top fives? I lunged forward and quickly snapped back. Seat belts do a fantastic job, by the way. Her car rested in front of a giant white house on the corner of a busy street. A ten-minute walk from campus, a street or two from the sororities and fraternities, and other fun stuff.

It was like every other house on every other street. A house that an average guy like me wouldn't look at twice. Thinking back, the house would have failed as a marker to remember a street by. Its average look made it nearly invisible.

Except for one more thing: a large "For Sale" sign in front.

I was dragged from the car in record speed, Gail and Dempsey grabbing and pulling an arm, my shirt, anything that would or could be used to force me to follow.

As Hope opened the front door, it kicked and moaned in a comical squeak. Walking inside our footsteps echoed, bouncing from wall to wall. A large stained glass window stood surprisingly beautiful near the ceiling. Spacious rooms complete with endless wooden floors greeted us. Dempsey laid his hand on my shoulder as I soaked it all in.

"I'm in a shit jam, Bugs," he whispered.

I wasn't surprised.

Chapter Thirty-Seven

I'm In

"Lourdes, I can't talk right now."

Her familiar silence said hello as I listened to the empty echoes. I was in no mood. Lourdes had called just as Dempsey opened his mouth to explain my kidnapping and the adventure of the empty run-down house. I opened my mouth to say goodbye. I didn't know it at the time, but things were starting to change. Maybe that's why her words carried different meanings.

"Let me guess." She paused. I heard a clicking in the background. Her fingernails, I guessed, clicking on a nearby table. "You're with your loser friend and one of his whores. What is wrong with you, Gibson?"

"Lourdes."

An unfamiliar anger in me said hello. I couldn't remember the last time the sound of her voice made me feel that way. One guess was never.

"Do not address me in that tone, Gibson. Remember who you're talking to."

"Lourdes, this is a bad time."

"I'll bet it is!"

I raised my hand to my temple and gave it a gentle rub. A small ache had found its way between my ears. It now had company with the anger boiling in my veins.

"I know you're spending time with that loser. You will say goodbye to him. You will go home, and you will wait for my decision. I am this close to reconciling. Don't disappointment me, Gibson. Goodbye."

I put the phone in my pocket. Her words were nothing new. Whore, loser, piece of shit. After a while it was nothing more than background noise. Elevator music. But this time it was different. In the past her words were always directed at me, but this time they were aimed at my friends. I looked at Dempsey, Gail, and my sister. I realized for the first time I would be more than happy to succeed or fail with these people than spend a lifetime listening to Lourdes' petty insults and put-downs. It didn't matter. They believed in me. We believed in each other. And who's to say we're going to fail? Was there ever a doubt? No, there wasn't. We knew what we were capable of. Between the three of us and with Hope on our side, I'd say the odds were pretty damn good.

"I'm in," I smiled as I returned to the waiting trio.

Chapter Thirty-Eight

Claire

    Our first interview was scheduled on a Friday morning at ten. We picked out our best clothes, wore our best shoes, and constantly checked our breath. Dempsey and Gail were big on spearmint. I could not get the taste out of my mouth for a month.
    Her name was Claire. A nineteen-year-old sophomore business major from the University. A local kid in need of some pocket change. At least, that's what we thought. You have no idea how wrong we were.
    Gail kept the job listing as simple as possible: Wait Staff & Host/Hostess - 20/25 hours a week max. Minimum wage to start.
    Short and to the point.
    Dempsey had some concerns. "Maybe we should look further out. You know, not hire locals."
    Gail shrugged. "It's not like we can fly people in to work for us. What's the problem with local kids?"

Dempsey cleared his throat. "Not kids, just girls." He rubbed the back of his neck. "I have...history with a lot of local girls. Would be weird to be their boss, ya know?"

Gail sighed. "Well, we'll try not to hire any of your old flames. Just keep it in your pants around our employees so we don't get sued, Casanova."

We were a little nervous. Hell, let's be honest, a lot. At no time in our lives had we been in a situation like this. We tried to pretend it was no big deal, just an interview with a possible employee for a business we were trying to create that we had no business attempting. Only a complete moron would dream of such a thing, let alone follow another moron to his icy hole of death. Yes, too much, but you get the point.

"Stop making this so hard, we don't need to sit!"

Dempsey stood in the entryway attempting to win an argument. According to Dempsey it made perfect sense to perform the interview in entryway. I could picture it now. A nice little chat while walking her to her car. Dempsey's hand politely on her back, slowly moving southbound, offering to buy her another drink.

Seeing sexual harassment on the horizon, I opened my mouth. Gail beat me to the punch. "We're sitting at a table. You, me, and Gibson on one side, and," she checked the email confirmation for the interview, "Claire on the other. This is not your Friday night pick-up girl, Dempsey."

I figured we'd be there a while. Dempsey holding strong on his end while Gail stomped his opinion into the ground like yesterday's caterpillar. But I was wrong.

"Okay." He turned and disappeared with the look of a child missing out on All-You-Can-Eat candy day.

"He's nervous," I said with a hopeless grin.

We settled ourselves at a long folding table and reviewed our questions.

We chose the center of the building with lots of windows. Since the electricity was turned off we all agreed it was a great idea. The only problem was the waiting. Dempsey rearranged some chairs while I replaced our pens with new ones. I even straightened out the table, although nothing on it needed straightening. Gail curled up on a nearby windowsill reading a book. How she could be so calm at a time like this puzzled the hell out of me.

A car drove up and parked. The door slammed. Footsteps coming toward us. The bell rang.

"Fuck!" Dempsey sat down, stood up, took two steps toward the door, then came back and sat down again. I had never seen him so nervous and yes, that includes all the big games in school. "I'm not cut out for this! You guys do it. I don't know what the hell to say. What if I do something stupid? What if she recognizes me? I might have hooked up with her or her sister or her mom! I could really screw this up. This was a stupid idea."

The bell continued to ring. I was about to call it off when Gail did the unthinkable.

She motioned for me to get the door. As if in a dream – and not a good one – I trance-walked to the door and opened it. Was I smiling? I hoped so. I couldn't tell because my face was numb.

When it comes to observation I suck. I would have been the one asking why the play had abruptly ended on the night Lincoln was shot and I would have wondered if they were going to finish it long after the funeral passed. So, I guess you could say it should come as no surprise that I noticed little of Claire's appearance when she walked by. Thankfully, Gail did.

Claire walked past me with the confidence of a matador seconds after a fresh kill. For a second I swore I heard the crowd's approval as she stepped over the imaginary dead bull.

According to Gail her hair was dyed blonde. It was pinned in a relaxed bun with a few strands around her temples and ears. Her makeup was perfectly cats-eye eyeliner with dusky blue eye shadow. Gail admitted how she loved Claire's vintage eyeglasses along with her lipstick—fuchsia with just a hint of sparkly gloss. What I do remember is her scent tickling the air long after she left. Gail was quick to detect Dior perfume.

As for clothes, I do remember some, but it was Dempsey who remembered it all. He loved her suit jacket and silk blouse, but he was particularly interested in her pencil skirt and nude nylons. If he had to choose a favorite, he later admitted, it would have been her sensible black pumps. I stared at him for the longest time after that. Sensible? Who knew he had a thing for sensible shoes?

Gail concluded with her observation, along with a confession of how jealous she was of Claire's pearl earrings and matching pearl necklace. Overall, I'd have to say the one thing that stayed with me was Dempsey and Gail's argument over the brand name of Claire's wristwatch. Dempsey won. A tasteful, but small Burberry.

"Thank you for inviting me." Claire smiled as we took our seats at the interview table. "I'd like to start off with some questions."

I glanced at Gail, she glanced at Dempsey, he in turn glanced at me. Weren't we supposed to be asking the questions? But since none of us knew what the hell we were doing we pretended we were old pros and agreed.

At first Claire focused on Gail a positive vibe. A sort of 'We girls need to stick together' attitude. But the vibe blew away like a hummingbird in a hurricane once she understood Dempsey's importance. As for me, there was something about her I just couldn't place. It was as if we had met before even though the name and face didn't register.

"So, this is a joint venture, I take it, or is there a main proprietor?"

"Me?" Dempsey sounded like he was trying to BS his way through a pop quiz he hadn't studied for.

"Our proposed name is 'Dempsey's Grill'," Gail explained.

Claire focused on Dempsey, leaning slightly forward and smiling like a cat eyeing its favorite birdy.

"What a cute name...Dempsey. Is that Irish?" she asked.

For once, Dempsey was strangely quiet, off his game to say, which added to the odd sense that Claire was ready to pounce. He just nodded and blinked at her.

"How many years have you worked in the restaurant business?"

"Umm...nine?" Dempsey waited for us to correct him, but our eyes were focused on Claire. I had never seen anyone so confident in an interview.

"Wonderful!" Claire reached across the table and lightly touched his hand. "That's a huge advantage over your competitors."

Dempsey's Grill

Dempsey's smile widened as Claire turned to her right. "And Gail?" Gail jumped to the sound of her voice, causing Claire's grin to widen. I suddenly thought of sharks and baby seal pups. "I did some research on you, too."

"Of course." Gail flashed a confused smile, pretending to be calm. Trust me, she wasn't.

"You've worked a variety of jobs in the last ten years. Attempted business school, which I applaud, but dropped out. You've always fallen back into bars and truck stops. I'm not sure how to read into that."

Gail raised her eyebrows and slowly looked my way. I looked at her with a questioning grin. I wasn't sure how to read that either.

I had a feeling I was next.

"And Gibson." Yep, I was next. "A former substitute teacher in the King county area of Seattle." I opened my mouth to agree but Claire had no interest in my response. "They released you from your contract," she concluded.

Claire slowly folded her hands on her lap and gave us a measured stare. Suddenly, it was us looking for a job and she held the cards. I could feel myself beginning to sweat, hoping I'd get the gig.

"The courage to create a business and convince people that your place is better than others takes...guts," Claire said delicately as she slowly removed her glasses and focused her eyes on Dempsey. She whispered. "Correct?"

"Uh-huh."

I wasn't sure if Dempsey was in love or scared shitless.

"Um, Claire." Gale leaned forward and waited for eye contact. I swear I was about to watch a steel cage match. The hell with the interview. "I think we need to get back to our questions." She held up the printed pages we hadn't even looked at yet for the interview. Gail waited for Claire to turn into the interviewee, but it was not happening.

"What is your long-term goal, Dempsey?" I'm pretty sure he tried to answer but she didn't care. "Whatever it is, be the one that others fear."

He nodded. "Okay."

"Two things, Dempsey. Look sharp and look busy."

"Um, Claire," Gail's voice reached an annoyed tone. "Let's focus on—"

"Do you know your customers?"

Gail dropped her pen and glared at Dempsey, but it was no use. Claire owned him.

"Now is the time, Dempsey! You want to place this amazing idea of yours inside their minds long before those doors ever open." I followed her finger as it pointed to the door. "You need to walk downtown, stand on the street corner, and tell them your story. Agreed?"

"Fuck yes!" Dempsey grinned. His eyes way off into some imaginary, bizarre sunset.

I once saw a video of Hope doing some kind of inspirational speech at a Real Estate seminar. I was getting a feeling of déjà vu.

"This interview is over." Gail waited for Dempsey to agree but it was clear his attention belonged to only one person.

"Do you have an opening date?" Claire asked, unmoved by Gail.

"Um...kind of?"

"Kind of?" she echoed. "May I suggest you get one and never waver?"

"Never waver," Dempsey repeated.

"Waver my ass!" Gail rose to her feet. I tried pulling her back but she's really strong.

"Looking at it must cause panic, determination and passion! Do you feel it?"

Claire pulled Dempsey's hands dangerously close to her breasts.

"Okay, we'll call you later. Thanks. Goodbye." Gail was now standing at the end of the table. The following day she said she was surprised I didn't back her up. I wanted to but I was too caught up in the train wreck in front of me.

"I feel it!" Dempsey shouted. He probably would have joined a cult had Claire asked him to.

"Call me when this circus is over. I'm going home." Gail stalked out.

Dempsey's Grill

I wanted to follow her, I really did, but I couldn't leave Dempsey alone with Claire. Who knew what he'd agree to?

Claire slowly released Dempsey's hands and relaxed in her seat. If she would have excused us and told us to leave, I'm pretty sure we would have obeyed. I only knew one other person who had that kind of power over us mortals.

"Are you a closer? You're selling an idea. You need to close the deal, and this is your deal." She nodded as she spoke, and Dempsey's head bobbed along with hers.

A long silence drifted between us making me guess that this weird ass interview was over.

"Are you a nice guy, Dempsey?"

I guess it wasn't over.

"I... umm..."

"I don't want a nice guy."

"I can be a bad guy."

"Nice guys do minimum work. Every day you need to offer more than your competition."

I watched with a combination of fear and flashbacks of being lectured by Hope as Claire slowly rose from her seat.

"One last thing." She waited for Dempsey to respond like a dog on a leash. When he did, I swear she tossed him a treat.

Claire reached across the table and gently laid her hand on his cheek. "Swim to success," she whispered. "Here's my card. I'll be in touch."

For the longest time we sat and stared at the table. Finally, Dempsey spoke.

"Oh, I like her."

Chapter Thirty-Nine

Hope Saves the Day

Gail and I needed time to think. We both agreed we had to get away, but unfortunately Hawaii wasn't an option. Instead, I knocked on her door.

Gail opened the door with a mixture of anger and worry. I really wish she hadn't done that...now I was feeling it. We sat in her small but extremely tidy kitchen. Her house was orderly and smelled nice, like cinnamon, unlike Dempsey's where the smell of sex and nightclub lingered in the breeze.

On any other occasion we would have laughed about Dempsey and how easily Claire had bewitched him. At least Gail would have. To be honest I would have faked it while worrying Dempsey would let Claire distract him. Gail and I would get left with all the responsibility for the restaurant. But who was I kidding? I can't fake anything in front of Gail. No matter how hard I tried she picked up everything. I was only in Eugene for a little while, we both knew that.

Dempsey's Grill

Seattle's up the road. Lourdes will miss me one of these days, it's bound to happen, and deep down I miss her, or at least some part of me does. I tell myself I still miss Lourdes, that the night in the car with Gail was just hormones. It's not like we have any kind of future. It's not like this whole crazy restaurant business is bound to amount to anything. It's not like—

"Gibson!"

I looked up from Gail's slightly scratched kitchen table and saw an impatient expression in her eyes. I had a feeling I had just missed out on a small part of a conversation.

"I've been talking to you for five minutes."

Check that: All the conversation.

"Can you please stop doing whatever the hell it is that you're doing up there?" She gave me a frustrated stare while pointing to her head.

"Sure." I wasn't positive she bought my assurance.

"I'm not buying it." She paused and gave me a good long stare. "Forget it. Let's get down to business."

"Absolutely." I was pretty sure my voice cracked.

Speaking of business, how long before she realizes this restaurant thing isn't going to work out with Mister Bad Boy? I mean, he's way more fun to hang out with. Everyone else thinks so. I guess it's only fair that Gail join the pack. Let's be honest, I was just a toy anyway. But why is that? Why am I always the toy? Why can't I be the one doing the operating? I can be the operator just as good as anyone, right? I really need to get out of here. I have no business being part of anything. I am a fucking mess, aren't I?

"Gibson!"

I looked up into Gail's face. Her chin rested gently in her palms, her elbows on the table. A sly smile creased her lips while those eyes that I secretly loved stared into mine with a promise they would never tell.

"It was a terrible idea to have him be part of the interview. Knowing what I know now we should have let him walk. We could have handled Claire on our own."

"Speaking of Claire." I tried to focus on our current problem.

For the past two days Claire was all Dempsey had talked about. To make matters worse, she had sent him a laminated printout of all her ideas. Who the hell does that?

"Here's my concern." Gail removed her chin from her palms and placed her hands in front of me. Her knuckles were white. "What if she changes his focus?"

"He just met her. I doubt it could happen that quickly." I was trying to reassure myself as much as her.

"Think about it. You've known him longer than me. How many young, attractive women have changed his focus in a matter of seconds?"

"Oh shit."

"Yes," she agreed. "Oh shit."

This was a ticking time bomb with the mother of all explosions waiting in the wings.

"What do we do?" I asked. I was getting a headache.

"Nothing we can do. We didn't sign a contract."

"Oh shit." I laid my elbows on the table and collapsed my face into the palm of my hands. Why is it every time a good thing comes my way it gets blown to shit? What are the odds a nineteen-year-old business genius would swoop in for the kill? As my mind took me down the familiar road of disappointment my phone buzzed.

It was Dempsey but I decided not to tell Gail. I raised the phone to my ear, said hello, and listened.

Sometimes you win the lottery. Other times you win the toy surprise. Some of us find a dollar bill in a landfill while others find hope. Gail and I found hope.

"What?"

"How could she do that to me, Bugs?" Dempsey moaned.

"What?" I repeated. Gail leaned closer and I tipped the phone so she could hear.

"Hope. She hired Claire. One minute I was telling her all about our dynamite new employee and she goes, 'Fascinating. I'll call you later.' But you know who she called first?"

"Who?" I tried to keep the growing grin on my face from creeping into my voice.

Dempsey's Grill

Gail's smile turned to laughter causing her to gag. This was followed by a coughing fit forcing her to stick her mouth under her faucet. I covered the phone while she collected herself.

"Claire. She called her and she hired her. Just like that. We saw her first!"

"She's not a dessert. You don't get to call dibs," Gail said.

"Oh, great. Gail's with you?" Dempsey grumbled. "I hope you're happy."

"Yep." Gail did a little hop and waved her hands like a cheerleader. It was cute and sexy.

"Um, Dempsey, I'll call you later."

"No, Bugs, don't you dare—"

I hung up.

I swear I have never seen Gail so happy. "That's it. Claire is gone."

"Yes. Hope saved the day." I couldn't believe I was actually saying that.

"Let's go." Gail grabbed my arm and pulled.

"Where?"

"Dempsey's. We're drawing up a contract."

Chapter Forty

Risk Takers

With the Claire debacle behind us, we were able to concentrate on the important stuff and trust me when I say, it scared the hell out of me.

"Wow, this is actually happening." Gail looked at me and smiled. "We're really doing this."

"The inspectors are coming tomorrow." I tried to ignore her. This was really happening and if I thought about it too much the mother of all anxiety attacks would explode. "They're going to look at the structure, the plumbing, you name it."

"And don't forget about the carpeting," she added. "You don't want carpets in a restaurant."

"Why?"

"Are you kidding? Vacuuming, wear and tear, the smell. Once you spill something it never goes away."

I never thought of that.

"That's true. I was wondering about that," I lied.

Dempsey's Grill

She could be the manager, I thought. She's stable, mature, has as an eye for all the little things I never thought of and if I could see it, Dempsey could too.

"If this turns into something, maybe I'll quit my job," I told her. "For now, I'll do both. Too risky."

"Same here. But I must admit, getting out of that rats' nest is tempting."

I was surprised she was still working at the bar. Rats' nest was too kind of a description. It was more like a fire hazard, disease center, and shortened life span command control center. But I wasn't going to tell her what to do.

Standing on outside Dempsey's door last night, Gail had taken my hand. "I feel like we're buying a lottery ticket."

I nodded. "Yeah, but we just might win."

Dempsey opened the door and, I don't know about Gail, but for me it the look in Dempsey's eyes sealed the deal. Those sad puppy dog eyes, slumped shoulders, and feeling of being let down. "Before you say anything, just listen," he burst out. "I know we don't have Claire's business savvy, but we can make this work. I've got the money for the initial investment. Had to take out a little loan, but guys, guy and Gail, we can do this. We can."

And we bought it, again. Even as we sat in the office going over paperwork and plans, Gail shook her head. "He has no doubt this will work." She sounded amazed at his confidence.

"I know." I flipped through a pile of papers. "I couldn't take that kind of risk."

"I can't see how anybody would want to start something like this. I'd be micro-managing the shit out of it." Gail stood up and stretched. "Speaking of which, we need to go over menu items. We never agreed what we were serving, and we need to start hiring."

"Dempsey said he's on it." That was a lie. He was still pissed we lost Claire.

"Stop it."

"Huh?"

"You're covering for him. He can't interview. Let's brainstorm what we're looking for and send it out. I'll set up interviews this week." Her confidence was growing like a backyard weed. "Tomorrow you, me, and Dempsey will finalize the menu. That's a priority."

Chapter Forty-One

Eager to Help

Gail and I drove to the restaurant the following morning. When we arrived, we were greeted by a seemingly endless line of construction workers, plumbers, painters, and an old fat guy with a clipboard. Yes, clipboards still exist.

"That's Hope's job," I added.

"Hope?" Gail introduced herself to the clipboard guy as I followed. She scanned the list and questioned a few items.

"I know. She's really eager to help. I can't figure it out either. On a normal day she takes over and by night you're forgotten. She even wants to bring in her ice cream as a side dish."

The clipboard guy stood at attention as Gail circled a few items. He gave me a strange look when I talked. Maybe I was supposed to stand at attention, too.

"I think the ice cream is a nice touch." Gail returned the clipboard and smiled. "It gives her an excuse."

"Huh?"

Gail ignored my question and walked ahead. Old lighting fixtures were being replaced with new ones along with new floors and windows. But that wasn't what I noticed. To be honest, I'm surprised I saw that much. No, what I saw was a part owner scanning the place and making sure it was done to her liking.

"Wait! Who ordered those frames?"

She stood by the giant window with the best view. If successful, this would be the top spot for our customers to sit. The thought made me smile. Our own top spot. Cool.

"What the hell was he thinking? We want light frames not dark. This entire area cannot be dark."

The carpenter didn't put up much of an argument. He gave me a call for help but all I could do was smile and shrug my shoulders. She made sense. The dining area was way too dark.

"When is Hope bringing in the ice cream?"

She walked past me and found an open counter. A notebook she had been carrying was spread out with notes and pens and a checklist. A checklist?

"She didn't say."

"I don't have her number. I'll need it." She took her pen and marked off a few items. I was curious what was on the list but figured I'd wait till later to ask. "When Hope gets here, I want to talk to her. She recognizes talent. Maybe we can bring her in."

Bring Hope in. The words hung in the air like a balloon in a comic strip.

"Relax. Hope is fine." Gail patted my arm. "High strung, sure, but I think Dempsey has a... calming influence on her." An odd smile curved her lips. What did she mean 'a calming influence'?

I was about to ask what she was talking about when she said, "It'll give her other excuses to come in."

She flashed another bemused smile. Knowing full well I had no clue what was going on in her head, she squeezed my arm and led me to the front door.

"Hope hates restaurants," I said. "She says their full of bugs and illegal aliens."

Dempsey's Grill

We walked past the construction crew, past the painters, and through the open space that would someday be the door. It was at that moment that it hit me. This was no longer a dream. We were now sitting at the grownups table. Gail and I stopped. We stood in the center of it all while the painters, the carpenters and the clipboard guy walked around us. We looked at each other.

"I'll set up interviews this week," Gail said. "Tomorrow you, me, and Dempsey will finalize the menu. That's a priority."

We walked outside and glanced back. Before we went our separate ways, Gail kissed me on the cheek and gave me a slow smile. I stood in place for the longest time wondering what I valued more. Her kiss or our place. Before I decided I knew there was one thing I had to do.

The following day I gave my two weeks' notices.

"I don't get it," he argued. "You're throwing away security for a pipe dream."

"Wrong," I said. He gave me a puzzled look and walked away.

It's funny, but at that moment I had expressed a level of confidence I never knew existed.

Chapter Forty-Two

Palaver at Picalo's

It wasn't long after the Claire debacle that I came up with an idea. Hope had lots of connections in and around the valley. Hell, the whole state if you want to get technical and because of those connections, I thought she might be a good fit for our team.

I handed the idea to Gail. I knew Dempsey would be an easy sell, but Gail might not. Given their questionable past I was prepared for a battle. I was wrong.

"I like it," she said with conviction. "We need all the help we can get."

"Great." I smiled.

I set up a lunch date with Hope and the team. My concern was Hope taking over. I knew Gail would have none of it and our meeting would end in an ugly food fight or a trip to the emergency room. To avoid this, I chose a place in Hope's comfort zone—Picalo's. "The greatest restaurant ever." Hope's words, not mine.

Dempsey's Grill

Picalo's was a high-priced restaurant down by the river, surrounded by fancy houses near the golf course. If you're not a surgeon, lawyer, or their analyst, forget about it. On the other hand, if you're their realtor, you're in. Enter Hope.

"Over here!"

We walked past the "Reserved" sign and ignored the disappointed stares from the wait staff. Apparently, our particular dress wasn't up to the unwritten dress code of the place.

Hope nodded to the waiter nearby who immediately ran to the back room. We joined Hope in a comfy circular table where Dempsey smiled and immediately shoved a cloth napkin halfway down his shirt. Gail, on the other hand, rolled her eyes and whispered something that sounded like corn dogs and onion rings.

"Tully, place the entrees in the center and bring us another pitcher of mineral water. I asked for lemon slices and I see none. I'm disappointed," Hope remarked without making eye contact with the nearby waiter as he deposited plate after plate of strange food on the table. To us she said, "I hope you don't mind, I ordered for us."

Gail and I leaned forward, examining the oddities in front of us. Picalo's was far from a burger joint and to be honest, I'm not sure what I would call it.

"Is that radicchio with tahini dressing?"

We slowly turned our heads in Dempsey's direction and watched with fascination as he took bite after bite of what looked like shredded red cabbage with yogurt on it. "Bugs, you've got to try this."

My mind rushed for excuses as Dempsey waited for me to join in. Thankfully, he saw something shiny.

"Cooked collard greens in olive oil? Hope, this is incredible." Dempsey waved at us to join in. Gail and I smiled and pretended to play along, but who were we kidding?

Hope smiled. "I'm glad you like it, but you need to try the roasted squash and cauliflower."

"Are those anchovies?" he whispered.

"And tuna," she whisper-replied.

I had no idea why they were whispering.

Gail nudged me in the ribs. I knew she wanted to get down to business. My biggest concern was prying Dempsey away from his meal. How did I know he would treat radicchio and tahini with the same excitement he treated twins in a hot tub?

I figured it was now or never. "Umm...Hope."

"Hold your thoughts, little brother." Hope nodded to the waiter and within minutes another dish was served.

"Tully, the double bacon cheeseburger goes here," she pointed at me. "And the corndogs are for her," pointing at Gail. "Place the onion rings between them."

"Oh, wow!" Gail and I both said.

"Hope, I..." For once Gail was at a loss for words. "Thank you."

"No thanks needed. The chef and I go way back." Hope smiled tightly. "And in a way you and I do, too. Now, bon appetite."

We finished our lunch in record time. I had a weird feeling Picalo's had never seen the likes of burgers, corn dogs and onion rings in its lifetime.

As Tully cleared our plates, Hope cut to the chase. "I hear you want me to join your team. Very flattering." A tiny smile creased her lips.

"Oh." Gail paused. "You already knew."

"Yes, dear. Gibson gave me a heads up. I hate coming to meetings unprepared."

"I'm sure you do." Gale smiled and poked my thigh under the table. Hard. I had a bruise later.

"I would love to be a part of the team," Hope said. "When do we start?"

"Well..." Gail never had a chance.

"I'll handle all the scheduling," Hope continued. "It's important to set expectations in the beginning of the endeavor. We will be at the mercy of our employees, so it's imperative they respect the sanctity of the schedule. Any unexplained absences will be fired immediately."

"Hope," Gail waited for Hope's eyes to meet hers. "We're dealing with workers who might have other jobs, families, school commitments. We can't just fire them for one absence. I'll do the scheduling."

"You?" Hopes eyes narrowed "Remember, you came to me for help, or was I mistaken?"

"No, there are no mistakes," Gail explained. "But we're partners. We'll listen to your advice but at the end of the day, we'll make our own decisions. You are an outside consultant. Understand?"

"And if I disagree?" Hope asked.

"Then we're done here and thank you for your time." Gail half-rose from her seat.

"But you would be a very valued consultant." Dempsey blurted out.

Hope's frown softened as she looked at Dempsey. "Fine, I respect your boundaries. That's a necessary ingredient in a relationship, especially a business one. Looks like we're partners."

Dempsey made it official by us all shaking hands. I have to be honest, it felt a little weird shaking hands with my sister.

Chapter Forty-Three

Life Coach

"I have eleven clients as of today and I have interviews with four more. At this rate, I'll have twenty by the end of the month. It's wonderful being a life coach, Gibson. So many people need me to steer them in the proper direction. It's not only rewarding, but exciting. Just the other day I spent two hours with a young lady who is only twenty-six and recently divorced. Her entire world was surrounded by yellow. She cried when I explained that if she moved on to, let's say, lavender or baby blue, well, that subtle change would signal strength and prosperity and who knows, a new love in her future."

I tried to pay attention, but I was having trouble summoning up any interest in some lady's color scheme issues.

"I was so happy when I left her home. Because of me, her life is about to take an amazing turn. Why, just before I left, I'll never forget this for as long as I live. She took me by the hand and told me the sweetest thing I have ever heard in my life."

My phone buzzed. An incoming call. Oh, thank God!

"Lourdes? Sorry. Hold that thought, I have another call."

My right ear throbbed, but not as bad as my left ear. I also had a headache coming on. Lourdes was ankle deep in her new career and for the past thirty minutes I was given the pleasure – word used loosely by the way – of hearing every fucking detail.

"Dempsey," I answered with relief. "Please let this be an emergency."

"We're fucked, Bugs! Completely fucked. Why the hell are we doing this? I am the stupidest dumb shit in town!"

"Calm down. Take a breath."

Whatever the problem was, I welcomed it with open arms. Lourdes had finally decided to speak to me again and now her marathon narrations on her experiences and joys of life-coaching had turned from nauseating to suicidal.

"What happened?" I calmly asked.

"Our supplier is screwing us. You're not going to believe the shit that just went down."

"Hope," I calmly stated.

"Listen, this piece of shit thinks he can get away with—"

"Hope."

"Just because we're new at this doesn't mean...Hope?"

"Hope."

"What the hell are you talking about?"

"She can handle the supply chain, right?" I explained, "She has all the connections we need. She can do in an hour what would take you or me all day."

"I'm not cut out for this, Bugs." He was out of breath. I could tell he was bending over, trying to control himself.

"You thought this was going to be easy? Wait 'til we open," I reminded him.

"Oh shit. What have I done?"

I gave him time to think about it. With Dempsey, the less you say the better.

"Do I call Hope or you?"

"You call Hope," I said.

"Oh." His voice had a plaintive, child-like quality. This was new to all of us, but I knew he'd take care of it.

"Hi Lourdes, I'm back. Sorry. I had an emergency."

There was no noise on her end. No music, jewelry jingling, background voices...zip. I was about to give up when a small cough gave notice of her existence.

"Lourdes?"

I waited for a response. A sign of life. A hiccup. Anything. Maybe the noise I'd heard wasn't a cough. A glitch in the software, maybe, or a mysterious rasp of another kind; the kind where the phone is dying because I am too damn cheap to upgrade. But why should I upgrade? Aren't we paying enough for these things? And I don't mean money. Sure, money is the bottom line in everything, but society is paying a huge price. Welcome to the new addiction. All of us are slaves to these little miracles that rest comfortably in the palm of our hands. Palm watching. Sure, laugh, but think about it. How many people in your town are transfixed by their little palm-miracle while paying little to no attention to the people they pass by? Yes, I realize I sound like an old man, but let's face it, what we're doing is strange. You want a world full of robots—

"Gibson?"

...the generation I'm in now...

"Gibson?"

...and the ones to follow are officially, unequivocally...

"GIBSON!"

...screwed.

"*Answer me!*"

"Lourdes?"

I wasn't sure how long she was there but when I heard her voice, a strange feeling swept over me.

"Don't you ever put me on hold again!"

Lunacy.

"I am not one of your little friends, Gibson! I am not sure you fully understand who you are talking to."

I didn't answer.

Dempsey's Grill

"You put me on *hold*. Why don't you just slap me in the face? It would at least be honest. I can't believe you would diss me like that. Seriously? I thought you were working on your respect issues."

My voice was low. Almost a whisper. "I apologize, Lourdes, it wasn't meant to degrade you."

"Degrade? Is that your new word? Congratulations, Gibson, your little town has taught you to replace respect with degrade!"

"It wasn't—"

"Hush, Gibson!" Her voice trembled, sadly her words did not. They just kept coming. "What are you doing, Gibson? Today, right now, what are you doing?"

For once, she asked about me. I was almost too stunned to reply, but I didn't want her to think I was ignoring her, so I blurted out, "I quit my job. Dempsey is opening a restaurant. I signed on as part owner. Our friend, Gail, signed on, too. The building needs a facelift but once that's complete, we'll decorate it, organize it, and open. My sister's helping out. Even my parents offered to pitch in."

A long silence separated us. But unlike the silence before, this time I knew she was there.

"Dempsey?" she asked.

I didn't answer. I knew there was more to come.

"That tall pervy guy with the shaggy black hair? The one who undresses me with his eyes? The one who I told you never to talk to again?"

"I don't think that's what he was doing."

That was a lie. He told me he did that with every girl he thought he had a chance with.

"Oh, stop it," she snapped. "He's a horrible example for you to follow. He's probably a heroin addict."

"Lourdes, he doesn't do—"

"Hush, Gibson!"

"Drugs."

"Oh, I know all about the drug culture in Oregon. It begins in Portland and works its way to Eugene. Those filthy towns are filled to the brim with corrupt, spineless, cold-hearted people and my biggest fear is coming true. Gibson, you're becoming one of them. Putting me on hold is just the beginning."

"Lourdes?"

"Hush, Gibson! And that...that girl..."

"Who?"

"That *girl*."

"Girl?"

"The woman!"

"Woman?"

"Gail! Stop it, Gibson!"

When she mentioned Gail, a protective guarded feeling washed over me. My hand gripped the phone. My back stiffened in anger.

"What is she, one of Dempsey's chickies? How long before she's all over you? Is that what Dempsey has done to you? Are you almost there or have you arrived?"

I didn't answer.

"Gibson." Her voice broke. "I told you never to talk to them again. Why would you ignore me? Are you trying to kill our relationship, and over what? A stupid diner waitress?"

Now it was my turn for the long silence. I waited long enough until the words were just right.

"Lourdes, you need to stop talking about Gail."

"*Women who work in bars are below you!*" she shrieked.

"That's her job," I explained. "Survival. Do you even know what survival is?"

"I'm losing you," she cried. "You would never have spoken to me like this before. This is what happens when you allow filth into your life."

I started to think, which was unusual for me when it came to Lourdes. I always reacted. It was never a question to act any other way. Not once did she ask me to come back. She never said come home. What exactly *is* home? Is it a place where you pay rent, or is it a place where you belong?

She said more but to be honest, I didn't listen. I didn't argue either. I guess what I did most was learn. When she finished, I welcomed the silence. I used it as a blanket.

"Talk to me," she demanded.

"I'd rather listen," I said.

"Fine. Just tell me three things. Whatever you say, I will believe you. Do you have a drinking problem?"

"No."

"Drugs?"

"No."

"Are you having sex with Gail?"

"No."

"Liar!"

I stared at the dead phone in my hand. This wasn't the first time in our relationship she had hung up on me and it wasn't the first time she had called me a liar when I was telling her the truth. But unlike the previous times before where panic, fear, and endless apologies escaped me, this moment was different. I found myself relaxing to an odd little emotion that we sometimes take for granted.

Hello, Calm. Plan on staying a while?

I smiled and waited for an answer. It didn't have a lot to say but I could tell it was nesting. A few minutes later I reached for my phone and brought it back to life.

"Hey, Dempsey! What did Hope say about the new supplier?"

Chapter Forty-Four

The Great Escape

    The three men walked out of the front door, the satisfaction of their work complete. They smiled at Dempsey and me but gave Gail an uncomfortable stare. So did I. Was she always this detailed? When did this happen? Did I miss something when we were kids?
    I watched curiously as Gail studied her notes. Drawings and scribbles were everywhere. Remarks on the layout, square footage, plumbing, and ideas for future additions took up an entire page. I was not only amazed at the detail, but the artwork involved. With nothing more than her chewed up pencil, she had created an exact replica of our building, inside and out. She glanced at me and smiled. It was easily the most confident smile I'd ever seen.
    I stood in the middle of the large, empty room. It would sit a hundred and seventy people, according to the local fire code. My shoes echoed off the shiny floor and my voice bounced off the freshly painted walls. This is really happening, my mind panicked. Run, damn you. Run! I shook off a panic attack and asked if it could delay its plans

until later. Understanding the situation at hand, it obliged and allowed life to go on. You're welcome, it said.

The building already had a layout we liked, so most of the work upgrading and refinishing. The only add-on we created was a vestibule—Gail's idea.

The first thing the customer should see when they walk in, she noted, were pictures of the crew and the menu neatly framed on the walls in the well-lit vestibule. The menu items would show pictures of tasty burgers and fries and thirst-quenching drinks.

Eight steps later – trust me, she measured – they would stand in front of the large door. Inside was the wide-open space of the dining room where tables for two, four, and six waited. The grill stood center stage where people could see, hear, and smell their orders being made. A host would greet and seat them. They would order and pay at their table. None of that lining up at the register crap. No, we were a classy burger joint.

A wall separated the cooking area from the back room. Two doors stood at opposite ends of the wall, allowing workers to enter or exit. A window in the upper center of each door helped prevent collisions. The back room contained the prep area, the dishwasher, a walk-in cooler, and the freezer. We elected to use patties that were not frozen. Hope arranged for us to buy local and keep a limited supply. As for utensils, we avoided plastic. Every glass and dish were the real thing.

Expensive? Yes. But in any business image is the key and you only get one chance to prove yourself.

A freezer was already in place. At first we had worried it was too big since we only had a few items that had to be frozen, but Hope offered her German ice cream as a side dish and had plenty to freeze. We promised her we would add more flavors if the first go-round succeeded. She actually liked the idea.

We chose hardwood floors over carpeting. Gail came up with the idea to add tiny foam cushions on the bottom of the chair legs so they could slide. I thought that was the best idea of them all. With a good shove and some practice, a chair could slide a good twenty feet.

There was one door leading to the upstairs offices. Dempsey had called dibs on the big comfy office complete with window and central lighting long ago, leaving Gail and I cramped in the smaller office with no window and no built-in light. I guessed it was once a storage room and smelled of mothballs.

The door leading up to the offices had an automatic lock and could only be opened by a key card. Yes, another expensive item, but Dempsey thought it looked cool and when you think about it, with all the money and stuff upstairs, it was actually a pretty good idea.

As evening fell, Gail and I huddled in our tiny office going over our notes and lists.

"We open in about a month," I said. "Did we forget anything?"

We were waiting for Dempsey to join us like he usually did after we'd spent the day at the restaurant. This was the time we'd generally hash over ideas and concerns or changes, but tonight the room remained silent.

I looked over my shoulder, all around, and finally at Gail. "Where is he?"

"I thought he was here," she said.

I yelled up the stairs. No reply. I stood up and looked around.

"Maybe he went out the front door," Gail suggested.

"No," I said.

The door to the vestibule was a step or two away. We would have heard Dempsey open the main door.

"It's hardwood floors," she said, now clearly annoyed. "We would have heard something."

I stood in the center of the restaurant and yelled. "Dempsey!"

I took another step and was about to try again.

"Wait." Gail grabbed my arm and pulled me towards the end of the hall leading to the bathrooms. "Have you noticed anything odd about him today?" Her voice lowered to a whisper, her eyes darting from the bathroom doors than back to me.

"He's odd every day," I answered.

"I'm serious."

I *was* serious.

"Peeing," she whispered.

Dempsey's Grill

"Peeing," I repeated. Now it was my turn to look at the bathroom doors.

"He's been peeing all day," she continued. "I swear every fifteen minutes."

"He's nervous," I guessed.

"I get that, but after a while the well runs dry."

I don't know why I was suddenly nervous, but I was. I looked behind me to the open room. I felt trapped at the end of the long hallway. Dempsey tricked us, of course. Now it all makes sense. An elaborate hoax created by the town ax murderer. How could I have been so naive?

"I'll check the bathroom," Gail said.

"What if he's peeing again?"

"Then I'll see something nearly every woman in Eugene between eighteen and eighty-three has already seen." Her words had entered the sarcastic on-ramp. "What's a girl to do?" she added.

She opened the damn door just enough to peek inside.

"Empty?" I asked.

"Empty."

Gail walked ahead of me as we both entered and stood next to the urinal. "Empty," she repeated.

She began to argue that a person could not disappear into thin air. That was soon followed by the obvious question ... Why? Why was it so important to disappear?

I opened my mouth to agree but stopped when I noticed the window above the sink. It was our next project, but it was a week away from completion. We all agreed a window large enough for someone to crawl out of or into was bad news.

"He crawled out the window," I pointed.

"He must have taken his shoes off to sneak past us," she added. "Gibson, have you ever seen Dempsey cry?"

Bryan Fagan

Chapter Forty-Five

Walk with Me

    Earlier that day, Gail had gone to put an additional touch or two on our office. I was fine with the desk and two chairs and four blank walls, but Gail insisted that nesting was key to creativity. Realizing it was an argument already lost, I stepped aside. As she entered our office with her arms full of pictures and full of ideas, a muffled noise could be heard down the hall. Dempsey's office was ten feet from ours and the bathroom separated the two. The floor was carpeted, so no echoing of footsteps to be heard.

    Gail explained, "I was afraid he might be entertaining some aspiring waitress, so I was hesitant to go in, but still curious. I peeked around the corner, prepared to quickly look away but he was alone, sitting in his chair looking at a picture."

    "And he was crying?" I'm being set up for a joke, I figured.

    "Yes. I couldn't see the picture, but he was crying and saying something."

    "What?"

Dempsey's Grill

"I don't know. He was whispering at it. Is there anything you can think of that would make him cry?"

I started to think, and the answer was clear. Nick.

I sighed. "Yes." Dempsey was the type who was fearless with his honesty. Trust me, throughout our friendship I heard more truths than I could ask for but let's face it, we all have that private side, don't we? Those secrets that are too painful or too embarrassing to be shared. Most of us keep them safely hidden in a cold, dark cellar, while others smash them to bits leaving only dust and memories. I had a feeling Dempsey had found the key to unlock his own cellar. We all have one and when on those days we choose to enter it, that first step is always the most slippery. Sometimes we fall.

"Walk with me," I said.

We left the restaurant and headed west. I wasn't sure if I should tell her everything or bits and pieces. I chose the bits and pieces.

"I know where he is."

"Where?" She gave me a puzzled look and slowed her steps.

"We always went to this one spot if things got out of hand or if we needed to think about things"

"Okay, I'm up for anything." Her steps quickened.

I only hoped she didn't ask more questions.

Chapter Forty-Six

Our Rock

We walked down a long walk leading to a lookout. The view of the river was peaceful. It was calm and steady; welcoming. It was a warm summer night. Fall was coming and so were 20,000 college kids. By October, the city's heart would be pumping at full speed. Duck football, leaves crunching underfoot, blue sky hanging on to its final days, students preparing for their first exams and, hopefully, a packed house at Dempsey's Grill.

"Why the hell did he disappear?"

I wanted to tell her everything. Dempsey may seem like an open book with nice big fat letters and lots of pictures, but there was a secret page only a few of us knew about. Occasionally, those closest to him were allowed to read it. Maybe catch a picture or two. As we got closer to the Rock I wondered if Gail had entered that circle.

"There he is!" Gail grabbed my arm and pulled, her free hand pointing in Dempsey's direction. "Good guess. How did you know he was here?"

Dempsey's Grill

I didn't answer.

Dempsey stopped when he saw us walking to him. I could tell he was nervous and uncomfortable when he saw Gail with me. It wouldn't have surprised me if he turned and ran but he didn't.

He sat down and waited for us to join him. How many times had we sat on this rock buzzed on a beer, dreaming of a girl or questioning our future? The answers were simple back then, but of course every answer is simple when you think of the past. It's the ones you have to answer today that are hard and sometimes there are no answers.

The moonlight danced across the water, painting a welcome home party. *Where have you been?* the Rock asked. *Come on over and have a seat. I have all the answers. Who's the girl?*

Gail sat next to Dempsey and smiled. I stood a few feet away. I couldn't shake the feeling that something bad was happening. We couldn't see it or touch it, but it was there. It was all around us. Something was wrong and if left alone nothing would be the same again. Maybe this was worse than I thought. Sometimes when we dig too deep and the water we discover drowns us.

I sat next to Gail and waited. The hard part was over, or at least I thought it was. Do I talk? Does Gail? Or, do we sit and wait and if we do, are we helping or hurting?

We sat in silence for the longest time. The friendly sounds of people laughing, bicyclists speeding past and little kids giggling filled the night air. The river and its cool breeze had everyone in a good mood.

Almost everyone, that is.

I suddenly wished I had brought beer. Gail looked at me and smiled, so I smiled too. Did she feel as helpless as I did? What do we say or do? Is there a standard manual for something like this?

I opened my mouth to say anything. I must do something to break up the deafening sound of silence, damn it! I figured if I downshifted to small talk things might improve. I was tempted to ask an easy question, the most likely coming to mind would be why a person of his size would choose to crawl out of a bathroom window while a cramp-free oversized door stood a few feet away. That was the only question that came to mind. Unfortunately, it was the one question I felt was best to avoid at the time.

I pounded my memory bank for easy questions. I would talk in a low voice, I promised. Steady, calm, and understanding. We were best friends and with friendship came trust and all that other stuff. Plus, I was a teacher. Well...sort of. True, while I was a teacher the students' problems seemed pointless and ridiculous most of the time and maybe I was out of line by suggesting they climb the monkey bars until they were too tired or bored to care about their pointless and ridiculous troubles, but Dempsey was not a student and I was no longer a teacher. And let's be honest, this was the real world with real problems. No monkey bars allowed.

My good friend was experiencing a problem that required a delicate ear, a voice of understanding, and a foundation of trust. True, he wasn't saying a damn thing and to be honest, the silence was beginning to piss me off, but here I was, a trooper in all my glory. I was his best friend, his only friend, and let's face it, Dempsey might be friendly enough to score one-night stands, but he was crap at long-term relationships.

Why the hell didn't I bring beer?

Chapter Forty-Seven

Unavoidable

When Dempsey finally spoke it nearly threw me off the rock. Luckily, I hung on to Gail. Unfortunately, I came close to taking her in with me.

"Sorry, Dempsey," I said as I repositioned myself on the rock. "Could you repeat that?"

Gail glared at me as I did my best to appear unflustered.

"I said we need to change the name." His voice was soft and defeated with no signs of energy.

"What name would you like?" Gail's voice, on the other hand, was soft, calm, and encouraging.

Dempsey didn't answer as he raised his knees up to his chin and clenched his fingers around them. Gail gently placed her arm over his shoulders. I waited and watched. It had been a long time since we talked about him.

"What name would you like?" Gail repeated.

When Dempsey answered, his voice was so low I couldn't hear. His head rested on his hands, his face on his knees. I waited patiently until he was ready to say more.

"It's all right," Gail whispered. "We're listening. We have all night. You can tell us anything."

She was right, he could tell us anything. I started to understand how much trust we had in each other. I saw his face clearly for the first time. The rising moon's light reflection in the river water displayed stains of tears on his cheeks, pieces of hair stuck up here and there as teardrops fell off his chin. I knew him well enough to understand this wasn't about the business he created or the stress of being shot at while buying the grill. It wasn't about an ex-girlfriend or an angry ex-boss, either. It wasn't about any of that. Let's face it, whenever we cry, it comes from a deeper place, a place where the only footsteps to be seen are our own.

Gail moved his matted hair away from his face while gently laying her hand on the back of his neck. I moved to the other side blocking his escape. This wasn't about beer or girls. I almost wished it was. But Dempsey had moved on to other things and I suddenly became aware that I might not be ready for this.

"Nicky," he said.

Gail looked at me. Her eyes full of questions. Nick. Of course. I should have seen this, but I was blinded by all the other stuff. He was ready to talk.

"It's okay," I said. "Tell her about him."

"All the girls called him Nicky. The boys called him Nick and Mom called him Nicholas." The tears came back, but now Dempsey managed a smile. The name lit up his face. I caught myself smiling as well.

"He was my older brother." Dempsey cleared his throat and ran his hands through his hair. Gail handed him a tissue to wipe off the tears, but he passed.

"You never mentioned a brother," she said.

"I'm sorry, Gail." His voice was tired but strong. "It's something I've always avoided."

"You don't have to avoid it anymore," Gail said.

Dempsey's Grill

Dempsey smiled again and launched into his story. "He was born in Sacramento six years before I came along. He took after my dad. He was the leader in everything he did. He played shortstop his freshmen year and quarterback sophomore. One summer, he hurt his knee racing motorcycles and he had to quit sports, but he didn't care. Nothing bothered him. He always had a Plan B. Mom said he was born smiling.

"Dinner time was always my favorite part of the day. Nick and Dad would tell us about their day. They liked to argue over facts and details. When dinner was over, we'd all be laughing. Damn, Mom and Dad loved him. Everyone did." Dempsey picked up a pebble and rolled it back and forth in his hands.

"He got sick when I was thirteen. For about a year it looked like he was going to make it, but then it came back. Fucking leukemia. When it came back, he promised Mom he'd beat it for good. She believed him but Dad didn't. Myself, I didn't know who to believe. I blocked a lot of it out. What I do remember is getting in fights at school, getting suspended, and not giving a shit about anything."

Dempsey paused, drew a sharp, ragged breath. He whipped his arm around sending the rock skipping around the rippling moon path on the water.

"I came home one day with a cut lip and a bloody nose. By then Mom had put a hospital bed in the front room. She didn't want Nick out of her sight. She told me years later it was Nick's idea. He wanted to die at home. Nick took one look at me and asked what the other kid looked like. We started laughing. It was the first time I'd felt good in a while.

"He made me sit down on the bed. I hated that bed. The look and smell made me want to run, but I did what he said. Nick had lost a lot of weight. It was so bad that I was actually bigger than him. He told me that life and sports were all the same. Some win and some lose. It's all about playing by the rules, but regardless of the outcome, make sure you play hard. That's why he loved baseball. There was nothing better than playing shortstop. Me against the batter, he said. Sometimes I won and sometimes he won, but I never wanted the ball to go anywhere else. And that's how I want you to face life. There's no other way. 'Always play hard,' he said."

Dempsey shook his head, his eyes focused on distant memories.

"Where do you want to be, little brother? Do you want to be part of the box score or the one reading it? You might live to be a hundred or you might die young like me, you don't have a lot of control over that but what you do have, is a choice in how hard you want to play.

"He died a month later. Dad moved out by the end of the year, Mom filed for divorce, and that summer we moved here. I'm sorry to unload all of this on you, Gail, but I guess I'm doing exactly what he wanted me to do and it made me think about him. I promise this will be the last time you see me like this."

Gail gave him the longest hug I think any girl had ever given him. They could have eloped, and I wouldn't have cared. Just as long as he was happy. That's all that mattered to me.

Dempsey rarely talked about Nick again. I think that night on the rock was enough. Damn, can you blame him? Every now and then he would say things that Gail and I guessed were his brother's words and every so often I would catch him in deep thought.

At first, he wanted to name the restaurant Nicky's, but after a day of thinking it over he decided against it. He figured too many people would want to meet Nick and the thought of having to repeat over and over, 'He's dead' was too depressing. Plus, Gail pointed out, girls will be impressed when they found out Dempsey was the owner.

After that night a lot of things changed for the three of us. The fear of what we were doing seemed to go away and we didn't fight any more. It seemed like the closer we got to opening day, the more confidant we became. Maybe the answer to solving problems is to sit on a rock by the river on a summer night and spill your guts out to your best friends.

Is it really that easy?

I wish I'd met Nick but in a way, maybe I have. We're all a blend of the people who made us and the people we admired in our lives. We're a mix bag of fruits and veggies and steaks and fries. Some of us have more fries than fruit, and others are all fruit. I guess what I'm trying to say is we're not who we are by chance. A lot of people helped

Dempsey's Grill

create who we are today and that's something special when you really think about it.

Chapter Forty-Eight

Cold Ice Cream and Hot Housewives

"You understand, right? This is the design I'm looking for and if you don't have it, I need to know now." Dempsey waited as the door salesman looked over his inventory. He had six different designs to choose from but none of them were to his liking.

"The closest I can match would be at a warehouse in Medford. That's six hours round trip. The ones I have on hand are in town. What's the big deal?" The door salesman looked defeated. He knew he would walk away empty-handed.

"You've got 'til the end of the day," Dempsey said. "Call me either way."

Dempsey closed the door and walked to the center of the dining area. That area would be his biggest challenge. Space would be an issue but with luck, by arranging the tables correctly, it could be less of an issue. He took out his notepad and added designs and figures to his other examples. With a renewed commitment to making the

Dempsey's Grill

restaurant work after our night at the rock, Dempsey had taken to emulating Gail's habit of going around, checklist in hand.

As the door salesman left in a hurry, Hope arrived with her delicious selections of German ice cream. Each carton, written in German, contained the yummy creations of chocolate walnut, strawberry, vanilla, and so on. Hope attempted, and to her surprise, failed, to add her favorite, hazelnut torte to the menu. Dempsey passed.

"Simplicity," he explained. "None of this German language stuff. If the customer can't pronounce it, they won't order it."

I sat at a nearby table concentrating on the upcoming interviews Dempsey and I had planned. I looked up and smiled as he stood firm against Hope's suggestion. I say suggestions loosely. Let's be honest: Hope fully expected to have her way but Dempsey was different on this particular morning. His decisions were quick. His mind unusually sharp. It was odd to see him this way. Not once did he panic or seek answers from Gail or I or run to a nearby club for some serious soul searching.

It seemed like his mind had turned into a sharp fancy knife; the kind found only on a lonely late-night infomercial. From the time we arrived that morning he had sliced through details, slashed pesky problems, and diced into remission any and all worries of the day. So, as I watched the drama unfold in front of me, I watched with enthused curiosity as the infomercial knife – yours for only $19.99, a $79.99 value – took on the challenge of jackhammer, otherwise known as Hope.

My sister meticulously laid the ice cream on the table. Each sample lay inside a cozy four-ounce cup complete with its very own spoon and lid. Dempsey was on a tight schedule. He had a list of priorities that he was determined to keep. The way he was rolling I had no doubt the tasks at hand would be complete. As he turned his attention from Hope's ice cream back to his checklist, my curiosity heightened. Hope didn't like to be ignored.

She scooped out a nearby chocolate walnut, tapped Dempsey on the shoulder and smiling as he turned shoved it into his mouth.

There are a few things I have never seen in my life: A T-Rex interrupting a Super Bowl halftime show, Jesse Owens giving Hitler a piggyback ride in the 100-meter dash, and Hope feeding an adult.

"What's wrong with you?" Gail stood by my side with a list of venders she had been working on. My mouth resembled that of a hungry baby pelican waiting for a bag of worms. I slowly closed my mouth as Hope removed the spoon from the chocolate walnut and dipped it like a pro into the vanilla-strawberry swirl. Meanwhile, Dempsey found his own spoon and randomly did his own dipping into the chocolate mint cup. I, unfortunately, had a bizarre flashback of my first porn clip involving a lonely housewife and an ice cream vender.

I was shocked, dismayed, and for no reason at all, had suddenly come down with a mild case of the hiccups. As the show continued, I watched as Hope dabbed a drip from Dempsey's chin and slowly fed him with her finger. The porn clip continued.

"Well, that's interesting."

I had forgotten Gail was there and to be honest, I had pretty much forgotten everything else. This was Hope. I was pretty sure the conception of her children resulted from an orderly, well-timed, textbook style session of passionless Republican intercourse. Complete with study guide, proper rhythm technique and months of non-physical planning. All, I might add, in the most secure and private setting, courtesy of a triple bolt, military-issued lock system.

"She's dipping the strawberry spoon into the chocolate walnut." I had resorted to pointing and whisper-shouting.

Gail gave me a good long look, the kind one would give a friend on an acid trip. I ignored her.

"That's nice, honey," she whispered with the patience and care a mental hospital orderly.

I responded with a shush. Hope had something to say and I had a front row ticket.

"The raspberry crème is an excellent choice. Do you agree?"

Hope's tongue poked out and captured a wayward dap of ice cream from her lips. Dempsey was silent with only a smile to tell his story. I'd heard that story from him a lot and I knew the ending. But with Hope? With my sister? No. I must be imagining...no, she was smiling and touching his shoulder.

I'm pretty sure Hope got around to other flavors. Maybe she and Dempsey discussed the dessert menu with a promise of rotating other flavors. While at it, of course, Dempsey probably figured in the cost and time spent on Hope's part ending with a promise of a limited partnership if current business succeeded. But until that fateful day I watched with utter confusion as Hope gently placed the recently licked raspberry crème onto the corners of Dempsey's lips.

"Let's go upstairs, shall we?" Gail dragged me off the stool at the same time Dempsey and Hope graduated from cup to spoon sampling to finger licking.

"What the hell is going on?" I felt like a parent catching their teenager in the act.

"You never saw this coming?" Gail smirked as she peeked over her shoulder for a last look into the dining area.

"Saw what coming?" I tried to look around her, but she rolled her eyes and dragged me upstairs. I waited for an answer.

"She's having a little fun." Gail closed the door to our office firmly.

How the hell could she be so calm?

"But—"

"It's harmless. They're adults and they deserve it."

"Gail..."

I stopped and waited for her to turn around.

"This isn't an adult, this is Hope."

I stood helpless in the middle of the room. I probably looked like the average four-year-old if he'd been told that in order to get candy, he must pass calculus. Gail gave up and flopped into her chair. We didn't talk about the ice cream moment again. Maybe Hope was having a little fun. Let's face it, her marriage was on the rocks, but this was Hope. And Dempsey!

I blinked the image out of my mind and found my way into my chair. Gail was working on menu items. The only item I could think of was ice cream and lonely housewives.

Chapter Forty-Nine

A Promise Kept

Gail and I took the night off.

"What do you say we act like grownups for a night?" Her words were music to my ears.

We took a walk downtown. Fall was knocking on the door, but summer refused to answer. A cool breeze gently nipped at the warm summer air. The life of a college town was about to awake from its long summer nap. Rested and healed, the town was once again prepared for a mix of new and familiar faces. A giant swarm of energy was about to invade the valley.

"So, tell me," Gail asked as her arm nested cozily around mine. "How many of them lose their virginity in the first month?"

"Who cares?" I said. "We got them beat."

"Really? I didn't know it was a contest." We held hands as we walked past stores and restaurants. I doubt either of us realized what we were doing. It was natural; it was how things were supposed to be. We chatted along the way, just small talk, inconsequential stuff. It didn't matter. We were happy with each other's company. We found a tasty restaurant and shared a large drink of something cool and munched on a plate of chicken wings. Half spicy, half regular. Gail refused the regular.

"I can't believe you still eat things plain," she said, rolling her eyes.

"Why? If you have to add a bunch of stuff to it then it's probably not any good."

"Please," she argued. "A little spice in your life gets the heart pumping."

I watched with admiration as she devoured a chicken wing in one bite. Two tiny bones barely survived the ordeal. With her face smeared in sauce, her fingertips red and sticky and her lack of concern that her current state closely resembled that of a hungry two-year-old, it occurred to me in that moment that I had never stopped loving her.

The amount of time I spent on wasted thoughts and worry for a call that never came had lessened. I no longer spent my entire day wondering where I had gone wrong or thinking that Lourdes was right, that somehow I would have to change. That infamous fright of dying alone we all hold heavy in our hip pocket seemed lighter to the touch. I realized the fear would always be there, but its priority had moved down to the bottom of the ladder.

My time with Lourdes seemed to fade. The memories of her were taking their own walk to places I haven't seen, possibly enjoying summer's last hold as much as I did. We were taking our strolls in different directions and for the first time, we had finally found the separate paths that were meant for us. How long would this go on, I wondered. How long before I—

"Stop it," Gail ordered.

My thoughts crumbled like an icicle. Winter had suddenly thawed into a hot summer day. I glanced to the surrounding tables, sheepishly grinning as those sitting next to us watched with curiosity and concern. Is he dangerous or is this just a boring lover's spat, their faces wondered?

"What?"

"Wherever you are right now I want you to put on the brakes, turn around, and come back."

"Huh?"

She finished off the last wing and attempted to wipe off the goo from her hands. She leaned forward and smiled. "You do realize you take a little reality break every now and then."

I could feel the back of my neck tightening. "Damn. Was it that obvious?"

"Of course, it's obvious," she said while picking pieces of chicken from her teeth. "We all do it but you, my love, do it more than others."

"Did you just say, 'My Love'?"

She missed a spot on the side of her face. I kept it a secret, hoping it would last as long as possible. It was strangely adorable, innocent, and hungry at the same time.

"Yes, I just called you 'my love.'" She smiled. "And the reason why I said it is because you *are* my love."

She reached across the table with her freshly cleaned hands and cupped them into mine. My mind had finally caught up to reality. I could get use to these U-turns.

"Every now and then I want you to stop thinking about the past, the future, and all those questions that you just can't seem to answer." She paused until I looked up into her eyes. "Look around and soak in all of the good stuff you have at this moment."

I allowed the silence to drift between us. Finally, I said the only thing that was right. "I suck at it, don't I?"

"Yes honey, you do." She squeezed my hands in a sorrowful way while acceptance and protection filled her eyes. "But you've always done that, and I don't believe in taking away a calling card."

"But there's a time and a place, right?"

What is wrong with me?

"There's nothing wrong with you," she promised. "You've made a lot of headway since you moved back."

She was right. So many things could have been worse.

"The one thing I've noticed is how little you check your phone and I don't hear her name as much."

Dempsey's Grill

"We've had a great summer. We nearly got shot, we got arrested, Hope fed Dempsey ice cream..."

"Still think it was kinda weird," she noted.

"And we found his grill."

"I'll drink to that," she said, laughing.

"Imagine the possibilities."

We walked back to our cars. The night was getting cold as the warm summer air was losing its grip to a fresh cool breeze. I placed my arm around her, and she wrapped her arms around my waist. We walked the rest of the way in silence.

Maybe it was her turn to break from reality. I wasn't the only one with questions that night. There were decisions and choices she too would have to face, but for now we were happy with the moment we were in. Why worry about tomorrow?

"I'm going to say something, but I want you to promise me you will not say a word. Promise?"

"Promise," I said.

We stopped and stood near our cars. She turned and faced me, a tiny smile dancing on her lips.

"I'm going to get into my car and drive to my house. I would like you to follow me. I think two twenty-nine-year-olds making love is far better than two bumbling fifteen-year-olds. If you feel my invitation is too much, or if you already have plans, I promise there will be no hard feelings. When I see you tomorrow at the restaurant I will smile and say good morning, but I would like to say that to you in my bed, first."

Gail turned and walked to her car. As promised, I kept my mouth shut. Not once did she turn around. I watched her drive away, her lights slowly fading into the night. My mind didn't race to conclusions. For once I did not analyze the situation. Facts, numbers, weights, and equations were all left on the cutting room floor.

My hand dipped into my pocket, searching desperately for the damn car keys. At first, I panicked. I lost them. Somehow, they fell out. I turned around, hoping for a minor miracle. Maybe they were lying a few feet away. I took a step and another and another. Three, four, six, twenty! How many steps until they're in my hands?

But wait!

As if it had a mind of its own, my left hand calmly leapt into action and plunged deeply into my left pants pocket. Like a deep-sea diver rising to the surface holding a pot of gold, my hand triumphantly lifted the car keys high into the air. I ignored the strangers walking by as they mumbled and giggled and quickly walked by. I jumped in my car and raced to Gail's house.

I pulled in next to her car. I didn't think, I didn't wait, and maybe for the first time in my life, I didn't worry.

When Gail opened the door, I picked her up and carried her inside.

I kicked the door shut in the way only a movie star could. But unlike the movies where reality is far away, Gail made me put her down so she could lock the door and pull the blinds.

When we woke the following day, she smiled and said good morning. It was the best promise she ever kept.

Chapter Fifty

The Only Sport in Town

Countdown to Grand Opening: 20 Days

The tension was thick. One of those butter knife moments. It was so thick we were all pretending it wasn't there, but who were we kidding? We were going bat shit crazy. Every day was a preview of what was to come. We were reminded that a business, especially a restaurant business, was doomed to failure. Even the best run, most well-organized plan can fail.

Do not say the word FAIL. A motto we lived by. If you say it the word will breed. Little failure seeds will imbed their tiny claws into every crevasse, crack and curve they find. Every dog, kitten and baby will be infected. The idea of reaching for the stars of success will crash before the first blueprint is drawn.

"What's that, Daddy?"
"Failure, son. Success doesn't exist."
"Why?"
"Because I said so, you. Now get the hell out of here."

See what I mean?

Our crew was almost complete. We still had a hire or two left, at least Dempsey and I thought so.

Gail disagreed. "It's best to be understaffed. That way if business drops off we're better prepared."

Dempsey leaned against my desk. "Nah, if we approach it with the attitude of success and prepare that way, the employees and the customers will feed off it."

Gail looked at me. I didn't want to tell her, but I agreed with Dempsey. We had to be aggressive. I mumbled something like, "Have to be aggressive."

Gail frowned. "Fine," she said in that tone that means it's anything but 'fine', but she didn't argue further, so I guess Dempsey and I got a win on that one.

Dempsey had sold his place to raise money and rented a small apartment a few blocks from the restaurant. It was a lot different than the place he used to live. A worn-out mattress, an equally worn-out recliner, and a wobbly table filled the necessities of his tiny home. Since it was an efficiency, a tiny kitchen and an equally small living room gave way to the bedroom. The only privacy was the bathroom, but even that spared little room for the imagination as it too lay close to the other activities.

Gail, Dempsey, and I sat on his living room floor, eating pizza. Our goal that night was simple: Examine every inch of the menu. Was it easy to read, were there typos, were the items we want to sell most up front and center and finally, did it look professional?

We were open for discussion, ready to argue and fight for changes or demand things stay the same. If it took from sundown to sunup, so be it. We were business owners and that's what we do.

Who are we kidding?

Our conversations touched on everything *but* the menu. And opening day? Zip. Why go there if it only made us nervous?

Gail came up with a great looking design for the menu. In fact, it was far better than anything Dempsey or I had thought of. A giant fancy letter D with a cool looking grill in the middle. I loved it. We had

Dempsey's Grill

been prepared for weeks; we had five run-throughs with only a handful of mistakes.

We ate our pizza in silence. Our nervous energy wrapped us in a firm grip. I was glad we ordered two large and one medium, even if the medium was spicy sausage with double onion, Gail's favorite. I was prepared to eat an entire pizza if given the chance. For the past week I could not eat enough and that night in Dempsey's apartment was no different.

And then there was Gail.

It had been five days since our night together. Five days, eleven hours and forty-three minutes, if any of you are curious. I'd made her a promise I would not analyze anything from that night and my promise held true. My mind formed a brick wall or better yet, a six-inch steel vault. Every so often a part of my brain would attempt the combination and thankfully fail. Maybe I was finally getting good at this. Maybe I could actually enjoy a night of stress relieving sex. Nothing more than the two of us taking care of our built-up energy that was begging to be tapped. It was a perfect night meant only for what it was. My emotions were kept in check. No bridge between us. An endless body of water, not caring where the current would take us. Love, happiness, need, and guilt all washed away. Sex was the only sport in town. Let's move on people, nothing to see here. On to the next show.

Chapter Fifty-One

Falling Apart in the Rain

Our silence was interrupted by a soft knock on the door. None of us were expecting any company, which would explain the puzzled stares. Dempsey opened the door a crack, his hand guarding against the back. The apartment complex was good if you rated it on a lousy to excellent scale. A bit shady—more than a few meth heads who would break into your car or apartment to steal ten dollars' worth of CDs they could sell for five. Other than that, it seemed like a nice place.

Hope stood on the other side of the door, soaking wet with an apologetic smile trembled on her lips. I couldn't figure out why she was wet since the apartment was walking distance to the parking lot and there was a rain protector above the door, a new feature that the management was really proud of, I might add. Dempsey invited her in, turned and gave me a puzzled look. I think he was thinking the same as me.

Dempsey's Grill

Hope held the folder close to her body and stood protectively by the door. In case she needed a quick getaway. "I forgot to give you your copies for the lease."

The one thing I will always love about Gail is her ability to figure stuff out long before anyone else. This was one of those times.

"Hope, would you care to join us?" Gail rose to her feet and softly walked up to her. Gail later admitted there was something in Hope's eyes calling for help the moment Dempsey opened the door. I just thought she needed a towel.

"I should go. It looks like you're busy."

But it was her voice that gave me the first clue. The same voice I heard in the garage that day. I gave her a long stare and began to understand.

Gail caught something in my look and slowly looked in Hope's direction. Unlike Hope, who seemed content to stare at the apartment's worn-out, late '80's tile, Gail had ideas of her own. Through all this Dempsey somehow figured out what Gail and I already knew. Weeks later he told me he'd had a premonition Hope would come to his place that night. He claimed not to know why he'd thought that. My mind wondered back to the ice cream moment. Sure, Gail convinced me it was nothing more than innocent fun and after a while I agreed, but as I watched Hope create a puddle on the tile, I realized her heart was breaking and all she wanted was to be held.

"I'll get you a towel. You're soaked." Dempsey headed to the bathroom while Gail motioned Hope in. I still sat by the pizzas until Gail gave me the signal to join her. It's funny how the little things can become a life-changing event. At the moment, it's just stuff. Looking back, I wonder how things would have turned out had I not moved.

Twice in my lifetime I have seen Hope cry. The first came on the night Clinton defeated Bush for the presidency. The second came on the day Clinton was caught with his pants down. But I don't think those two count when compared to this.

The dam broke the moment I stood. Hope covered her face with her hands and began to shake. By the time I realized what was happening Gail had taken control. Hope collapsed on Gail's shoulder. The sound was awful. Let's face it, who really wants to hear anybody cry, especially your sister who's usually stoic and mean?

The tears drenched Gail's shirt at an alarming rate. Gail didn't seem to mind as she held Hope tight in her arms. Dempsey appeared with the towel and gently laid it over Hope's shoulders. The three of us traded confused stares while Gail patted Hopes back and helped her dry off. Dempsey located a wobbly chair and I held Hope's hands. For once she didn't pull away.

I didn't know what to say or do. In the books and movies there's always that one line that clears everything up, but I just stood, holding my sister's hands and trying not to move. Thankfully, Gail had it all figured out.

"Hope, what happened? You're with friends. You can tell us anything." Gail's voice was soft and safe, like a mother promising her child that tomorrow will be a better day. I lowered myself to Hope's level and looked into her eyes. Dempsey did the same. So, there we were, the three of us bent down to our knees, huddled around my crying sister whose only history of crying that I knew of centered around Bill Clinton.

I figured she'd find an excuse and retreat to her privacy and pretend none of this happened, but a funny thing happened that night—Privacy and Pretending took the night off.

"The son of a bitch left me! He took our savings, grabbed my favorite suitcase, and stole our matching umbrellas!"

It took a moment to figure it all out.

I tried to ask about my niece and nephew, but she wasn't finished. "Hope, where are your—"

"He even had the balls to take my favorite solar equinox power nap blanket, and it's not technically a blanket! It's a display!"

Gail looked at me for help. Right then all I could do was think of the power nap blanket. It was the only gift from me that she ever liked. That son of a bitch!

"Um...Hope...so, Todd?"

Dempsey's Grill

It occurred to me in that moment that after the row over Gail's affair with Mr. Young Republican, she might be cautious of giving Hope any relationship advice.

"Yeah, Todd," I explained. "Her soon to be ex-husband."

"You're single?"

"Dempsey!" Gail turned her glare away from Dempsey and focused on Hope. "Okay." She smiled as she slowly collected her thoughts. "So, Todd left you. Maybe it's for the best..."

"She's his twenty-two-year-old intern!" Another round of tears flooded the already flooded valley as Hope gave details of Todd's newfound flame. "Perky tits. Bouncy ass. Pouty lips. Pick your poison!"

On any other day this would have been the perfect time for Dempsey to ask specifics on the perky, bouncy, pouty intern. Mostly her name, address and phone number, but things were different that night and he stayed silent, his eyes glued to Hope's tears.

"I knew he was messing around." Her voice lowered to a tired tone. "Late night meetings, conference calls, endless apologizes. I forced myself to believe his flimsy excuses as the truth."

The room grew silent as Hope's tears slowed to a drip. I was afraid I'd say something stupid and make it all about me or worse, think of something positive to say about Todd. But I locked the door to all that stuff and kept Lourdes and everything else that tried to pay a visit away. Todd hurt her. He created this mess. I could picture his smug smile as he and his intern flew off into the sunset, leaving my sister and their children behind.

Dempsey broke the silence with a soft voice of his own. We were all full of surprises that night, so I guess it made sense for him not to disappoint.

"Hey, I've got an idea. How about you and I take a walk? I've got an umbrella to keep us dry and some wine at the restaurant. We'll bring it back."

"Dempsey, she probably..." I was hoping to cushion the blow to his kindness. It's not every day he gets to do a good deed, but attempted kindness and Hope went together about as good as—

Hope rose to her feet and smiled. "That's a wonderful idea."

"We won't be long," Dempsey promised as they walked out the door.

I stood up as they left and was about to remind them to take their time, but I didn't get a chance. Without warning, Hope turned to me. She threw her arms tight around my neck and held on. It might have been the first real hug we'd ever had. I felt the emotions of her day and the wreck of her life tremble through me. I held her tight and promised myself she would never feel this kind of pain again.

"Fight for it," she whispered. She pulled away from me and placed my face in her hands. "Promise me," she said.

"I promise."

I wasn't sure what I was fighting for, but I figured now was not the time to ask. She walked out the door with Dempsey following. Little did I realize her words had predicted my future.

Dempsey's Grill

Chapter Fifty-Two

Burning Desire

How long had they been gone? An hour? Two? I didn't understand. Gail and I were alone for a long time and that only meant one thing—Lots of zoning. I can zone a long, long time, did you know that? Hours, days, an entire month. Okay, too far. If I panic, I zone on zoning. Soon it becomes layers. A giant concrete slab so thick that the dirt that started it all never sees the light of day. That still doesn't answer my question: Did they make it to the restaurant?

I should have walked with them. Better yet, I should have been the one that walked with Hope. My own sister came needing my help and what did I do? I sat around and discussed future children that would never exist. I ate pizza and complained about the spices.

Is this it? Is this what I do? It's all about me, isn't it? Ignoring my sister when she needs me the most. At least Dempsey came around and did the right thing.

"We should go check on them, don't you think?" I finally asked.

Gail pulled on a sweater and opened the door. "Way ahead of you."

I don't remember if I locked the door. Probably not. The meth heads must have decided to give us a pass that night.

The restaurant was almost a mile away. After about ten minutes, I started to shiver. The night was suddenly cold, and I hadn't brought a jacket. Why didn't I bring a jacket? With fall on its way it gets cooler at night. I'd grown up in Eugene and lived in Seattle. I should have known better. It's the Northwest, you dummy! Cool and damp was our motto, our religion and blood, and all that other shit rolled up into one, giant mud patty. Every born and bred Northwesterner comes prepared, even in the middle of July.

Gail was watching me...really, really watching me. Was I that obvious? Did I zone too deep? It's the guilt. I'm ravaged with guilt, aren't I?

"She's fine, Gibson. The walk will do her good." Her voice was soft and understanding. Her words weren't aimed at Hope, we both knew that. Their purpose was to calm me. She could feel it; she could see it. This was the downside of being with someone whom you've known since the first grade.

"Breathe."

Next time I'll walk with a stranger.

"Gibson?"

And there's always a next time, isn't there? And when that happens, I'll handle this a whole lot better.

"This has nothing to do with you."

Why were we stopping? Why was she holding my shoulders? She stood in front of me. Wait, we weren't there yet. Why do I always fuck things up? She just kissed me. Not a tiny peck on the cheek. No. This was the good kind. Nice and long and loving. The kind that kicks all the bad stuff out of you and replaces it with everything that feels good. The kind that makes you really love life for a while. That kind of kiss.

"Hi," she said, smiling. "Remember me?"

I smiled back. Yes, I do, my smile said.

Dempsey's Grill

"Calm down and focus," she ordered. "Slow down that crazy mind of yours. Hope had a bad night but it's not the end of everything. Got it?"

"Got it." I wasn't all that convinced, but I said it anyway. "She's just having a bad night," I echoed.

"Of course," Gail agreed. "Hope's strong-minded and we'll get through this together."

"Yes," I promised.

We started to walk again. The night air wasn't so cold after all. I was getting warmer as I walked faster. Why weren't we running? I panicked. We could have there already if we had run from the start. I was the one controlling all of this. If I ran Gail would run, and if I didn't, we didn't. So, where's the problem?

We ran. Really, really, fast. See? No problem.

"Slow the hell down! I'm going to fall on my face!"

For a minute I gave in and slowed down to a trot. Watching Gail face plant on a night like this and having it be my fault would simply add another layer of guilt to the evening. I looked at my watch. I was surprised we hadn't met them on the way. I looked at it again. At first I checked it every minute and then every thirty seconds. Gail watched all of this and smiled. Her eyes were cautious and calm and to my surprise, no worry. She didn't ask questions, but I answered them anyway.

"I should have taken her," I shouted. I wasn't talking to anyone. The words were being tossed up into the air. I didn't care who caught them.

"She would have talked to me. I'm her brother. My job is to listen. I'm supposed to be there when she needs me. Of course, this is Hope I'm talking about. When did she ever need to be taken care of? One word comes to mind—Never. But tonight was the exception...the one lone exception. Somehow in this town she managed to locate the tiny rat hole apartment I was in and I allowed her to leave without me."

I stopped and listened to what I'd just said. I was an idiot. "She came to me crying. She'd never done that before."

I blew it. I was still a kid. That's it, wasn't it? I was a decade behind. I stared at the streetlights, or was it the stars? Whatever they were, I could feel them looking down at me in disgust. The stars that is. Streetlights don't have eyes.

Gail took my hand and squeezed. We started to walk again. Faster and fasterer and fastiest...I know, goofy words.

We ran, is what I'm trying to say.

We ran up the street, past the post office, past the bookstore, past people and cars, rickety old newspaper stands and phone booths... Yes, they still make them.

And then we saw it.

That perfect old house in the perfect part of town. High visibility, low crime, surprisingly good parking, and ready to serve your every hunger need.

We stopped.

We stood in front of the house, The Building, as we always called it. The Building. Funny, now that I think of it, we never called it what it was, a plain old two-story house.

Gail pointed. The dining area was lit up. "The lights are on."

"I smell something," I said.

I walked up the steps and tried the door.

Gail took the ramp. "My ankle hurts from all the running."

I reached in my pocket for the key and opened the door. For a moment I stood there, afraid to walk in. I don't know why fear had suddenly decided to pay a visit, but it did. Maybe this was the first time I had seen Hope at her worst and let's face it, having her husband run off the way he did would ruin anybody's shiny day. I guess I was afraid for her and afraid for myself. Now it was up to me. I had to be the grown-up. Imagine that.

Gail grabbed me by the arm and shoved me inside.

Silence.

A lone dining light hovered warmly above an intimate table set for two, a chilled unopened bottle of wine sat in the middle. It was the table we'd labeled 'the dating table.' It had a nice corner view with a window overlooking parts of the river and downtown. In the center of the table, a small, empty vase awaited a single rose. On the other side

Dempsey's Grill

of the room two burgers sizzled. Burned, that is. The silence rose to an insane level. I flipped the burgers off the grill and moved them to the side. I was too full to eat, so was Gail. I turned off the grill and listened. Why was it so quiet?

"Looks like they went elsewhere for dessert. Let's put this to use." Gail opened the bottle and took a swig. I raised my hand to say no but grabbed the bottle by the neck instead. It went down smooth.

"Wonder where they went?" she asked. "Did your mom and dad call? What happened?"

"Maybe there in the back." I brought the wine with us as we walked through the kitchen where we were greeted by more silence.

"Her kids," Gail burst out as if she had suddenly remembered. "Of course! She had to pick up her kids. The camp must have called."

"Explain the burgers?" I asked.

"Emergency," she guessed. "You know how kids are."

Gail gave me a doubtful look. I smiled and did the same. I took another drink and looked around. A comfortable wine buzz had settled in nicely. Not enough to be annoying, but just enough not to be ignored. I could tell by Gail's face her buzz had equaled mine. It was nice to have a partner on this little journey.

"Either way, we really should clean the grill," I noted while taking another sip. "It'll be hell to scrub tomorrow if this stuff bakes on."

I stared at the grill for the longest time. We both knew my idea was just talk. She took the bottle out of my hand and took a sip of her own. We leaned over the grill, turned to each other and giggled.

"It's bad already," Gail noted. "Really burnt to shit. We should get right on that."

She took another sip, her body inching closer to mine.

"This could take a while," I said. Our eyes locked on to each other's. Her free hand rested on my chest. "Hours," I added.

"Hours," she repeated. The bottle was half empty.

"Lots and lots of rubbing," I noted.

"You mean scrubbing," she corrected.

"And rubbing," I added.

I took the wine bottle from her hand. We stood close to one another, no space in between. I took another sip, and another. She took the bottle and finished it off. We'd need another bottle, but not now.

"We really should clean that grill," I reiterated. "It's getting crusty and..."

Her lips were on my neck, then her teeth grazed my chin. Her hands moved down.

"Hard...crusty and hard," I mumbled. My train of thought would have stayed on track if her lips had not moved on to mine. It also didn't help that our hands began to explore each other's bodies with a determined destination. No, that type of action pretty much wiped out all kinds of deep adult thought processes.

But a part of my mind still worked. None of this made sense. Hope was in the middle of a breakdown. Why would she disappear when it was clear she needed people around her? I get it, this could happen to anyone. Look at what I went through. But still, where was she?

I wanted another drink.

Chapter Fifty-Three

Stairs to Heaven

My shirt lay on the floor next to Gail's bra and beautiful white summer button down blouse. I'd broken two buttons getting the damn thing off; we found one later while cleaning under the grill. Gail didn't seem to mind. She took the bra off herself. She didn't trust me after the shirt. I promised myself there would be no zoning. Aside from my thoughts drifting away to Hope, I did a pretty good job. A lot of it had to do with Gail's hands tangled in my hair and me kissing the lower part of her neck. The lack of zoning was also attributed to how our bodies rubbed and rolled against one another while we made our way out of the kitchen and into the dining room.

"Pick a table. Any table," she moaned.

"Probably not the singles," I said.

"You think?" Her body moved faster against mine, her voice out of breath.

"The floor," I said.

"Yes! No!"

We paused. Which one? Make up your mind!

"The curtains are really thin, and the damn moon is shining through."

Good point.

"And the floor is really hard," I added. Neither of us would want to be on the bottom.

"Upstairs!"

"Huh?" I was still thinking of the floor and the damn moon. No zoning. Focus! Dempsey had put a mattress in the spare room in case we needed a nap. "The nap room!"

"What the hell are we doing down here?"

Gail didn't give me time to answer. She grabbed me by the neck and jumped into my arms, her long legs wrapped tight around my waist.

"Hurry!"

The stairs were endless. Miles and miles. Two, three miles, at least.

Gail held a freshly opened bottle of wine with one hand while her other hand clung around my neck. She managed to drink while I took us upstairs. I was really impressed by her dexterity. My legs ached. My body screamed. Damn it, are we there yet? I've got a half-naked woman wrapped around me. Will somebody cut these stairs in half?

Gail moved her tongue over my ear and whispered, "Hurry." She told me what she wanted and promised to return the favor.

Are we getting closer? Are the stairs playing a wicked game? Am I the victim of a terrible dream?

Gail's legs tightened. My ribs ached. She pressed her lips against my neck and groaned. A possible mind-numbing orgasm on the stairway. News at eleven. Chopper team on the way. Video of the aftermath. Warning to small children.

"Stay with me! Oh God," she screamed as her body rocked against mine. Her legs tightened. Her teeth clenched.

Almost there. So close. Her nipples against my chest, her legs loosening, my ribs bursting, my legs numb.

Climax!

The stairway — If only it could talk.

Dempsey's Grill

We reached the top. I paused for a moment as Gail handed me the bottle. My legs stopped aching, but other parts continued. We giggled and kissed. Her first stair orgasm.

I carried her down the hall and opened the door. We'd spend the night in the nap room and later – much, much later – we'd dip into the inventory for an early morning nightcap.

"Turn on the lights," she whispered. "I don't want you tripping over anything."

I turned on the lights and immediately realized my mistake. Both of our two office tables were lined up in our cramped little space, our laptops resting in the far corners, our chairs balanced between spaces, and the narrow walkway where one wrong move and you fall over everything. This isn't the nap room; this is our office.

But if I did fall at this particular moment, I would find myself in the middle of a very naked Hope and an equally naked Dempsey.

Gail screamed.

Chapter Fifty-Four

Table Your Remorse

"You fucked on our table!" Gail immediately crossed her arms over her naked breasts. "Why did you fuck on our table?"

Her face bloomed with confusion and anger. Her point was well taken. Why did they fuck on our table?

"The nap room," she yelled. "It has a mattress. Napping is optional, you son of a bitch!"

Most of that moment was a blur to me. I'm pretty sure my mind hit the delete button a few times. Maybe it was the panic switch. You get the idea. I do remember Dempsey looking for his pants and Hope wondering out loud if her bra sprouted legs and walked away.

Gail refused to budge as I tried to tug her away. Her disbelief and anger seemed to be at an all-time high. Apparently, anyone having sex on her office table caused immediate, heat-activated rage.

"A room and a mattress just down the hall," she continued, her face red and hot to the touch. "Are you really that stupid?"

Dempsey's Grill

I saw my sister naked and I don't mean examination room naked. Here miss, lie on this shiny thing and don't move. This'll be cold.

No, this was far worse. This was porn naked.

All these years later, just seeing the words "porn" and Hope on the same page still gives my stomach a bad rumble.

Dempsey fell over everything trying to find his pants. Once he found them, he fell into everything else. Hope somehow managed to dress herself in an unheard-of record time. Her shirt and pants remained wrinkle free and full of denial.

"Gail..." Hope smoothed her messy hair. "It was a misadventure and I take full blame. I had a moment of weakness."

"Weakness? Shit. You fucked on my desk. Fuck!"

"And I promise," Hope continued, her voice as soothing as a baby's touch, "we'll replace your desk with a new, improved model. All of this out of my pocket, of course."

Hope's voice was strangely calm. Relaxed even. Satisfied, came to mind.

"Let's find our bras, shall we?" Hope added with a smile. Gail still clasped her hands over her naked chest. She growled.

I leaned against the wall. Only one question came to mind: How did I not see this coming? The day at Hope's house, the ice cream episode, and pretty much every time I mentioned Hope's name to Dempsey. Of course, why the hell didn't I see this? But Gail saw it, which explains pretty much everything.

Gail's voice echoed in the hall. "They were nice tables. New and shiny and no sex stains. Shit."

"I know, I know. And the new tables will be just as nice." Hope's voice sounded like a psychologist talking down a suicide victim. I stood near the stairway, soaking in the aftermath.

"We're switching offices," Dempsey promised. He had managed to find his pants, but his socks and shirt were still AWOL. "I'll switch everything around tonight. I should have done this in the beginning. That was really rude of me."

Dempsey was being incredibly kind and patient through all of this. It had yet to sink in that he had sex with my sister. My mind would have to deal with that later. But how bad could it be? Four adults. Two couples. A little wine. A little sex. It happens.

I walked back to the office and stood, observing them. Hope, freshly dressed, minus shoes and socks. A rather odd glow on her face. 'Sexually satisfied' sadly entered my brain. Dempsey looked like a character straight out of Woodstock. Or was it the Manson Murders? Long shaggy hair messed in all directions. No shirt. Pants unzipped revealing purple striped underwear. Yes, purple stripes.

Moving on to Gail. No shirt or bra, still looking for both and looking cold while doing so. All that was left to finish off the image was to set the three of them standing in the middle of an idyllic meadow. Two words came to mind: Album and Cover.

"I suppose I came here intending to give in to my urges. I've been frustrated for a long time and I suspected that Dempsey would be happy to help me confront my..." Hope paused, "liberal demons"

Hope covered her mouth. A look of fright washed over her eyes. I waited for the song and dance number to follow.

"I gave in," she finished. "I allowed my knees to weaken for a man consumed with sexual lust."

Dempsey opened his mouth to protest. He later told me he was a tad hurt with the 'sexual lust' comment. For the first time in his life he had a vague understanding what it was like to be fucked and forgotten. But in that moment, his complaints would stay a mystery. A phone buzzed during all this mess causing each of us to pat our pockets and purses for our own.

I stopped searching when I recognized it was Gail's. It had survived the journey in her hip pocket. I think I was just as surprised as her. At first she didn't answer but when she glanced at the screen, I knew. Don't ask me how, but I knew.

Gail covered herself with her left arm and turned away, edging past me towards Dempsey's office. Her eyes wide with guilt and confusion. "No, I'm not busy. Not busy at all." She mouthed, *I'm sorry* to me. "Yes, of course. I miss you too."

Dempsey's Grill

Hope and Dempsey stood behind me. Dempsey tugged my arm while Hope tugged the other. They motioned me downstairs, but I didn't move.

"That's nice. I can't wait."

Gail's eyes filled with tears as she quickly looked away. She reached out one bare foot and kicked the door mostly closed, but I could still hear her side of the conversation.

Hope whispered in my ear. I'm pretty sure Dempsey did the same, but I didn't catch a word. I was way too busy staring at the empty space.

"Come on, Hope. He needs to be alone," Dempsey whispered.

I stood alone in the hallway, my shirt in my right hand. I waited for someone to tell me what just happened, but no answers were needed. I turned and left.

Chapter Fifty-Five

A Dream of Waking

I can't remember how I got home. A mixture of wine, Bruce's phone call and, of course, my sister riding my best friend like a carnival Shetland pony, pretty much evaporated any chance of intelligent thought for the remainder of the night.

I never found my shirt, but I did have a weird dream. Not surprisingly, it involved a naked Hope and an equally naked Dempsey dancing around Gail, also naked, as she played a fiddle complete with mystery background vocals and drums.

I woke up hungry and cold to a ringing phone.

My left arm made the first move, cutting into the air hoping to find a blanket. Disappointed and empty-handed, it ended the search and returned to my side. My legs curled tight under my chin, my arms wrapped tight around them.

The ringing stopped.

I reached for my blanket as my dream began to fade. The real world slowly came into focus, separating the truth from the lies. My arms and legs held tight, fighting off the cold as the ringing began another round.

This time it sounded angry. It was out to get me, but why? What did I do? It came with a mission. It knew what it needed.

"What?" I said to the dead air.

I woke.

Chapter Fifty-Six

Enough Silence

    My eyes managed to focus. They told me I was in my room. Of course, I was. I was sitting in the middle of my bed. My pants were in a heap on the floor and my shirt was still MIA. The covers of my bed were keeping my pants company while the phone in my pants pocket stopped ringing. It gave up, foolish thing, with a sigh of relief or a grunt of disgust, I wasn't sure which.
    Silence.
    I woke up hungry. Really hungry. I grabbed my pants, found another shirt and checked my phone. My curiosity was stronger than my hunger.
    Lourdes.
    Three calls in twenty minutes. No messages.
    I sat down on my bed. My first wrinkle of the day. That didn't take long, I thought. We all get them but at different times, don't we? Do I call back, or do I ignore it, I wondered? The only thing to do at this moment, I guessed, was to carry on with my day. Scrambled eggs,

Dempsey's Grill

bacon and Mom's homemade bread. The choice was simple. Nine out of ten doctors advise it.

Who was I kidding?

My mind started replaying last night as I pressed the phone to my ear. What should have happened last night and what did happen came into focus. Suddenly I wasn't hungry anymore. I wasn't nervous or scared or any of that stuff as I sat in my cold room on that early fall morning.

My head hurt but not for the lack of caffeine. The world on the other end of my phone seemed different. How do I say...

Lourdes answered with silence.

I felt the familiar jolt, the panic and the fear knocking on the door. It was the same door I always answered. Come on in. Stay as long as you like. Don't worry about the mess, I'll clean it up...I always do. The knock grew louder and louder. The pounding increased; the door shook. Open up! Stop being a fool! You know we belong inside. We'll mess up your room and your life, and you know what's funny? You will clean up after we leave. Isn't that a kick? You always do. That is who you are. *Now open the fucking door!*

Not today.

The pounding stopped. Panic, fear and everyone's favorite, Mister Jolt, slithered away. I heard a rumor they took the last train out of town.

"Yes, Lourdes," I answered slowly. My voice lacking interest or energy. "You called?"

Her familiar long pause said 'Hi' for her, as it always did. My old friend had returned. Was there actually a time when I missed her silence?

Yes, I remembered. Long ago, it seemed.

"Goodbye, Lourdes," I sighed.

"You sound tired. What's wrong?" Her voice hadn't changed. Anger, impatience, and disappointment played bass to the same song and dance. But I could tell something was different. A different sound, as if someone new had joined the group.

"I'm fine," I said. My voice sharp and clear and surprisingly impatient.

"Why are you tired?" Her question had a ring of concern. Something new.

"I'm fine," I repeated.

"Why do you own a business?"

"I have reasons," I said. I was tempted to say more but I didn't feel like it.

"Um....uh...I am proud of you, Gibson. Owning a business takes a lot of courage."

"Thank you."

All four of us have courage, I thought.

"But I am scared for you, Gibson. I know you and sometimes you do things to forget. What are you trying to forget? Is it love? Is it me? Or perhaps both?"

I didn't answer.

"You need to fight, Gibson. When you find someone who changes your life, you fight for them."

"What if it doesn't matter?" I asked. I didn't care what she said. To be honest, I was asking myself.

"It does matter."

"Why?" I asked.

"Sometimes trying is enough. Have you ever tried, Gibson? Have you?"

It all made sense. Why does the world's most complicated question have the easiest answer?

Have I ever tried?

I saw Gail's face and I realized how different everything had become since that day I saw her in the bar. As I sat on my bed with the phone pressed to my ear, I realized what was missing. We should have woken up together. I wanted to wake up to her smile. That's all I really wanted and when I really thought about it, everything else is just stuff.

And isn't that how it should be?

I relaxed and smiled. A simple answer to the world's most complicated question. My first A in the classroom. I wasn't cold or hungry anymore. I had some place else I needed to be. No strings attached, she said. Just fooling around, stress relief, adult fun...

Dempsey's Grill

Bullshit. The string was a rope. It held us tight and Gail knew it. The rope grew into a steel cable. It started out as a tiny string in the first grade and now look at it. All grown up ready for the big show.

"I know how you feel," Lourdes continued. Her voice was hard, her tears loud. Now it was her turn to be cold. "Nobody knows you like I do. You're sad and lost. When will you stop being a little boy?"

I've only felt sadness and loss twice in my life. The day Gail moved away and now. I hadn't even felt this bad when Lourdes kicked me out. Sure, it was awful, but I had known that I would recover. What does that tell me?

"It takes a life-changing experience to open your eyes," Lourdes continued. "Are your eyes open, Gibson? Mine are and I know what I see."

Last night was not about Hope or Dempsey. It was a reminder that these past fifteen years were a joke, and the joke ends today.

"Yes, Lourdes, my eyes are open. Goodbye." And I hung up. I had never ended our conversation first before.

I ran downstairs and drove to Gail's house.

Chapter Fifty-Seven

Seattle Calling

Will someone answer the phone?

Here, I present to you this lovely little device. An invention, if you please. A miracle of miracles where a traveler can take this amazing, incredible, how-the-hell-did-I-live-without-it gadget and talk, text, play, porn on the go, giggle video device, and use it wherever. But, and this is a big but, if the party on the receiving end of said-device does not respond the damn phone, this miracle that I'm talking about becomes, how do I say, fucking useless.

I stood in front of Gail's door and knocked. No answer. I called her cell. No answer. I looked in the backyard. I looked in the neighbor's yard. She was gone. I gave up dialing and gave up looking. In that moment, it seemed everyone was gone. The whole world, except for one happy spider above her doorway had vanished. I called Dempsey. Dempsey's phone was on par with Gail's, of course. Why should anything operate in a normal way on a day when I made a huge decision? This left me with only one choice.

Dempsey's Grill

The restaurant.

For some reason I ran. I remember running to the end of the street before I realized I had my parent's car. The downtown area was especially busy on this particular morning, eliminating any chance of a perfect parking spot. Could I have parked behind the building? Of course. Was there a designated lot specifically for us owners and employees? Yes. Could I have parked in either one? Yes. Did I? No.

I parked on the street across from Dempsey's apartment, my spinning mind convincing me this would be my final destination. A quick knock on the door, then Dempsey answering, Hope and Gail finishing off the remainder of the veggie double onion dip and Gail saying everything I was going to say first. Where was that world? I wanted in.

I ran down the stairs, across the street, and straight to the restaurant. I kept the phone glued to my head. Gail's number was now on speed dial. Her recorded voice said she was away and to please leave a message. How the hell could her voice sound so pleasant in a moment like this?

My heart was beating at an alarming rate and not from all the running. The restaurant was in view. Opening day was in full view. I imagined her trapped in our tiny office making last minute decisions, convincing Dempsey to do it her way and throw away his. Her chances of achieving this goal were high. Dempsey couldn't run a business if you handed him the ultimate blueprint, and let's face it, Gail did most of the leg work. She was the brains behind all this, and we were fine with that.

Two people came into view as our restaurant grew near. Their faces and body shapes familiar. I suddenly had a strange feeling they were waiting for me. I slowed and walked.

Hope and Dempsey smiled as I slowed from a clumsy run to a curious walk. As their faces came into focus, so did their unease and nervous stare. My walking stiffened and my arms dropped to my side. I was entering dangerous territory, but I couldn't stop.

A nervous smile said hello as I stared into my sister's eyes. I had seen that smile before but for a moment I couldn't remember where or when. I slowed to a walk, curiosity and fear caught in my throat. Her odd smile stirred up memories long forgotten and settled.

"Bruce," she said. Her voice defeated, her eyes loving. "He's in Seattle. He told Gail to meet him there. Today."

Her words bounced off my head and crashed to the ground. They lay before my feet, dangerous and sharp. Dempsey stood behind her, his eyes watching and waiting for my response. Hope raised her hands to cover her mouth.

"Why?" It was the only thing I could think to say.

As other questions floated above my head, too far above to read, Hope began to cry. I should have reached out and calmed her, but I didn't. Let her be the one who cries instead of me, I thought. She cried on my shoulder, her tears soaking through to my skin. My conservative sister showing emotion and in public, of all places. My, how times have changed.

"I forgot about him," I said as my eyes stared off into a blank future. "I'm stupid. I am really stupid."

Dempsey stood beside us, placing his hands on our shoulders, his unusual silence growing by the second. They walked me inside. The restaurant was light and welcoming. It seemed to sense my mood and was doing its part.

"She went home to pack," Dempsey said, "and then she's headed straight to the bus station."

My head shook. Concrete fell. Lights shattered. Injuries. Overload. Too many questions and not enough answers but at least someone was telling me the truth.

"She was afraid to tell you," he continued. "It all happened so fast. One minute she's trying to find her shoes so she can chase you down and the next minute he's telling her to catch a bus."

I found a chair and sat.

"I told her she had to tell you," Hope said.

Dempsey nodded in agreement. "No shit, Bugs. Hope was ready to drive her over."

"It wasn't fair to keep you in the dark," Hope added. "But she wouldn't budge. She's been waiting to run off with someone her entire life."

"Her cowboy," Dempsey added. He shook his head in disgust.

"Into the sunset," Hope finished.

"Some fucking cowboy. Huh, Bugs?"

"And then my little brother comes along and spoils everything." Hope raised her hands to her face, her mouth trembling for the second time. "Isn't that the most romantic thing you've ever seen in your life?"

Bruce and Lourdes in the same town. Both on the phone to Eugene, Oregon. Imagine the Vegas odds on that one.

Dempsey lowered himself down to one knee. "Look at me, Bugs," he ordered.

I did.

"She's going to call you in five hours. That's her plan. She was crying half the night. She made us promise not to say anything. We lied and said yes."

I looked out the window. I wanted to run or find a corner to curl up in. Let's face it, I'm not good at stuff like this. I think I've gone out of my way to prove it. I stood and walked to the window. I had to think. Maybe I could figure something out.

I didn't get too far.

Hope came over to where I stood and hugged me. No tears. Her hug felt good. I've learned that when life sucks, really, really, sucks, you need people who understand and feel the same sadness you do.

"I know you love her," she whispered. "I saw it when you two were little. It was so real. I was always jealous. I wanted that kind of love too."

She held me tight, her words full of magic. Hope wasn't always cold and ruthless. I do have memories of kindness when we were kids. A time when I was little. A hurt knee or a bad day at school. Her love and promise of better days warming me like a blanket on the coldest of mornings. Maybe we were back to that time again.

"You'll get through this," she promised.

"No." I shook my head. I wouldn't 'get through' this. Gail wasn't someone you just got over, like the flu. I had to do something. I couldn't just give up on her, on us, if there was an *us*.

"Bugs?"

I looked up.
"Her bus leaves in twenty minutes. Take my car."
I did.

Chapter Fifty-Eight

The Rainy-Day Shirt

She's gone.

Was this a premonition or a guess? I wasn't there yet but somehow, I knew.

I sat at the red light with cars all around me. A mile deep, it seemed. Not really, but doesn't it seem that way on days like this? The huge Baptist church stood on my right, a nice cozy coffee house to my left. I watched a young couple at the window. The perfect window seat made only for them. Coffee and love. Love? How would I know, but let's pretend anyway.

I watched their smiles move to a rhythm of curious conversation. A young couple sharing a moment or planning a future or maybe two old friends meeting by chance. A perfect moment shared with a medium hazelnut coffee. Maybe if I—

The driver behind me laid on the horn. His free finger gestured the number of his choice. "It's green, jackoff!" he yelled through his open window.

I decided at that very moment – seconds after being called a jackoff, that is – to follow a rule and only date Baptist girls. Could the setting be any more perfect than this? Sunday morning spent in the giant church, ending with a pleasant stroll, arm and arm to the coffee house across the street. The scene was a perfect Hollywood ending, then driving fast into the sunset.

She's gone.

My mind turned a corner, avoided the perfect sunset and stopped in front of Reality Boulevard. I was just about to settle into a nice comfy fantasy of a pretty country girl, check that, pretty country, *Baptist* girl, and me. But the fantasy drew a blank. The only girl in my mind was real and let's be honest, when does religion really matter in any of this?

The bus station stood a block away from the coffee house. A quick turn to the left and there it was. I saw an empty space in front of the coffee house and parked. The young couple moved away from each other's eyes for a second to glance in my direction. They watched as I jumped out of Dempsey's car and ran. I wanted to tell them how lucky they were, scream: *You are where we all want to be!* I wanted to warn them to try and avoid being in my shoes at all costs. Don't ever find yourself driving your friend's car in a panic, wondering why you didn't say things when you had the chance. And most of all, don't think back to the summer when you had a night, a morning, and every day in between to tell her you loved her. You had it all, but now it may be too late.

In other words, avoid being me. It really sucks.

I stumbled around the corner. The bus station lay straight ahead. I tried to run, which makes a lot of sense when you're in a hurry, but my legs had other ideas. I could hear the buses growl their impatient rumblings and nervous energy, waiting for the signal to go. I walked slow. My heart raced. I'm not good at this. Let's get that out in the open. I have always avoided moments like this. What am I good at? I've been on this planet just a month shy of thirty years and I suck at everything.

Dempsey's Grill

I left Seattle without a fight. It was easy, wasn't it? Lourdes told me to get out, and I did. I hopped on a bus and slept in my parent's guest room that night. I did what I was told. Why? If you go against the grain, things get difficult, don't they? It's easy when you think about it. Just turn and leave. Who needs the mess?

I tried to stop, but my legs had other ideas. I tried to argue, I tried to reason. Fantasy is far better than reality, I tried telling them. You can control the dialog and ending. I suddenly realized my legs had taken me to the center where the buses were parked, their giant grills shaking, and their headlights masked like giant eyes daring me to stay. Laughing, was more like it. They knew the real me.

You don't belong here, kid. She's sneaking out the back door. Can you blame her? After a while they all leave you. So, what will it be, kid? Same old, same old, or something new?

"Get the hell out of the way!" The attendant dropped the bags in front of the compartment he was loading and followed me with his tired glare. "Inside or get out," he ordered.

I heard his words, but I didn't move. Gail was inside. She hadn't left. Yet. The moment had come. It was her and me and this was nothing like the movies. There was no music, no ticking clock, and no bad man to defeat. Damn, I hate real life.

"Hey, asshole! Inside or out?"

The attendant grabbed my arm. Every day same old shit, his eyes screamed.

"In," I said.

By the time the shock washed over me, I was pushed inside. It didn't take long to run into Gail.

Literally.

"Oh, I'm sorry," she said without looking. We bumped shoulders. Her coffee miraculously survived a spill, her free hand holding tight to her suitcase. She looked up and saw it was me. Her eyes looked exhausted and worried. I doubt she had slept all night.

For a moment we said nothing. Silence was our greeting. She was wearing her long sleeve blue shirt. Her rainy-day shirt, she called it. She wore it once during the summer when the rain came by for an unexpected visit. She would only wear it if the temperature dipped below 70. She wore it last week. A Tuesday.

Bruce knows nothing about that shirt, I thought. Who is this guy? Does he know her the way I do? Does he know she loves onions on everything? Does he care? Does he know she will only hang that shirt on the back hanger near the wall and away from the rest of her clothes? Does he know that every piece of clothing in her closet needs two inches of space to avoid wrinkles? She loves onions and hates wrinkles. Does he know that part of her? Why didn't I ask questions about him? Why did we avoid the topic?

"Umm...Hi," I mumbled.

"I hate Dempsey. I knew he would crack. Where is he?" She tossed her coffee into the nearest trashcan. Part of it splashed against the wall. She walked the other way. I wondered if she expected me to do the same.

"Hope told me," I said.

"Give me a break!" she yelled. "Hope wouldn't crack."

She continued to walk away from me, dragging her suitcase behind. Soon everything will fall into order, the world whispered. You will wait until she's out of sight. You will turn and disappear. She'll turn around and see that you're gone. It's all so easy and predictable isn't it? And why is that? Because that's how the world spins, Gibson. That's how I work...

"You can't leave!"

...or maybe not.

Several strangers turned and watched, while others pretended to ignore our little drama.

"You can't sneak away and pretend nothing happened!"

My voice was strong. I was calm. Determined. My mind clear. Something new.

"This is the ten-minute warning for the A-13 to Portland and Seattle," the overhead speakers called.

People stood and collected their belongings followed by the sounds of buses rumbling. Gail turned around and faced me. I saw the only eyes I've every loved and wondered: *Is this the last time I will see them?*

Dempsey's Grill

"Oh, honey." She tried to smile but not today. Tears gave away, landing on her long-sleeved wrinkled free shirt. "This wasn't supposed to happen. You have to go."

She took a step towards me and stopped. In her suitcase was her rain jacket and green umbrella, white mittens for cold morning walks and black boots just in case a mud puddle got in the way. Huddled around assorted pants, shirts, and underwear were three books: A mystery, a romance, and her favorite bird watching book. Someday we'll see them all, we promised. If I had told her all these things, she would have smiled and said, "You're right."

"I have to get in line," she begged. "Please go."

I could feel myself pulling away, my body leaning towards the exit sign. Just leave already! It's easy. You know how to do it. Old habits die hard, my friend. You've done it before, and you'll do it again. Turn and run and pretend the summer never happened. Old habits. Your best enemy. Oops...did I say enemy?

"NO!"

More people turned to watch. Some curious, others annoyed. I took Gail by the arm and pulled her outside. It felt powerful; it felt right.

"You're not leaving," I said. Anger and tears filled her eyes and it wasn't long before my eyes followed. "I'm not letting you go. This is a joke. You can't hop on a bus and pretend this isn't real."

For the first time in our lives, she didn't fight back. No snappy comeback, no threats. She didn't push me away. For a moment, I feared she was going to collapse.

"This has been the best summer of our lives," I told her. "Admit it. The spark is still there. It never died. I have always loved you and you can't tell me you don't feel the same."

I put my foot down. I stomped it to the ground. There, I said it. She's not going anywhere! Why would she want to? Everything is here. Her friends. Her dreams. Me.

She gently placed her hands on my arms, her eyes full of misery.

"You knew this was coming." Her voice stood its ground. Strong. Confident. "I told you about him and not once did you try to talk me out of it."

"I didn't know it would end up like this!"

That was a lie. I kept pushing it away. Pretending it wasn't there.

"I knew how it would end," she said. "I'm sorry, but I did."

"Then why didn't you tell me to get lost? That's a real shitty thing to do." I swiped angry tears away.

"Because I'm selfish, Gibson!" The look in her eyes returned. Gail the fighter was back. Her eyes were full of anger and determination. But she wasn't fooling anyone. She was scared and lost just like me. Sometimes those two old friends never leave, do they?

"Take a good hard look, Gibson. I'm the most selfish person in the world. My mom died. I was all alone working in a bar waiting for a phone call and one day, out of the blue, you and Dempsey appear. You dragged me into his pipedream world, that crazy grill that damn near got us killed and your crazy sister..."

For a second, we smiled. The memories catching up to us. Good times always had a way of following us. It was so easy, wasn't it?

"How could I say no to all that?" Tears fell down her face, but she didn't care. It was a good question. How could she say no?

"We were the perfect family," she whispered, her voice choked with restrained sobs.

"Then what are you doing here?" I whispered in a tired voice. "Don't go."

"I have to."

"Why? I don't get it."

She held my hands and squeezed. I squeezed back. She let go first and moved them up to my face. I was suddenly exhausted.

"This is what grownups do, sweetie. They make tough decisions. I've never made a tough decision in my life and it's time I start. I need to be a grown-up, and so do you."

I wanted to run but instead I panicked. "Hope needs you." I knew that was pushing it, but I didn't care. "If she's hooking up with Dempsey, she'll need someone to talk to."

"Hope is a big girl. She's going to be fine. She's got you. I don't think you realize how much she loves you."

Dempsey's Grill

I rubbed my hands through my hair, the feeling of loss running wild. I grabbed her hands and held on. I looked away and closed my eyes. I saw where this was going.

"Do you remember first grade?" She tugged her hands free and gently pulled my face to hers.

"Not really."

"I do. It was our first day. When lunchtime arrived one of our classmates knocked over my milk. I was so mad I started to cry. I stopped when you gave me yours. Every day we ate together and played together and that's when I started loving you."

And that's when I started loving you. Have I loved you that long?

I looked deep into her eyes. "I lied. I do remember that."

"I know," she smiled. "I can tell when you're lying."

"That was the year you drew a picture of me and you and your mom," I remembered. "You were holding hands with your mom and I was holding hands with you. I stole it from your bedroom just before you moved away. I probably still have it."

We paused, our memories dancing before our eyes. First grade monkey bars, second grade water fights, sixth grade dance, the day she moved away and the day I saw her again. Did it all happen in five seconds? Memories can do that, can't they?

"I have to go," she whispered.

I knew, but I still had to ask. "Why?"

"I've been playing it safe my whole life and now it's time to take a chance."

Gail put her arms around me and kissed me goodbye. It was the worst kiss I've ever had. I wanted to pick her up and run or hold her to the ground until her bus drove away. This stranger she was running off to would never see her the way I did and if he did, would it matter? I put my arms around her and held her tight. And then I said goodbye.

Why, you ask?

Because that is what you do when your best friend is hopping on a bus and you may never see her again. You say goodbye. Because you love her and that's what she needs you to do. To rip out your heart and let her go.

Gail turned away and walked inside and just like that, she was gone. My shirt was damp for the longest time. Her tears refused to dry.

Chapter Fifty-Nine

Here to Help

    I took a long drive that day. Where? Good question. To the moon and back, I guess. I didn't think of anything. I didn't zone, no weird stories danced inside my skull. A blissful blank.
    Dempsey and Hope left me alone. No calls. No texts. It was nice. When I came home it was dark. I sat on the porch and stared out at the sleepy neighborhood. I was tired, but I knew I wouldn't sleep. I needed to find my own place soon. My old boss had called a week earlier and offered my old job back if the restaurant business fell through. I thanked him and promised he'd be the first person I'd call if it did. Never burn your bridges, I was always told. Good advice.
    Losing Gail was different than losing Lourdes. With Lourdes it was all about a change in lifestyle. Looking back, it wasn't her I missed so much as it was Seattle. But this was different. This was a kick in the gut, to put it mildly.

I heard the front door open. My dad walked out. He joined me with his customary silent greeting. I returned it with silence of my own. For the first time the anxiety from his presence stayed away.

"Good day?" he asked taking a seat next to mine.

"No, Dad." My voice sounded tired and empty. "Not really."

He answered with a long pause. A silence that for once was welcoming.

"Good having you home," he said after a while. "It means a lot to your mom. She missed you. We all did."

"Thank you, Dad."

"You stay as long as you like and if you find a place of your own, we're here to help."

I didn't know what to say. I looked at him and smiled, hoping that was enough. He stood and walked inside but before he did, he paused and laid a hand on my shoulder.

"I'm proud of you, son. Always have been."

I never asked if he knew what happened that day. Maybe he just knew. Parents are like that, aren't they? Either way I had to say something before he disappeared.

"Dad," I called before he stepped inside. "I'm really glad I came home, and I want to thank you for letting me stay."

I waited for him to walk inside or give me a long stare before he walked away but something was different that night. Sure, it was one of the worst nights of my life, but on the other hand I saw a side of my dad that may have only been seen from my mom. Whatever it was I was glad.

"You're welcome." He smiled. "How about you and I go out for breakfast tomorrow. I'd like to hear how the restaurant is coming along."

I smiled in return. "I'd like that."

We went out for breakfast the following morning and it was nice. I wasn't anxious or wishing I was somewhere else. Sure, some of it had to do with being emotionally drained, but some of it had to do with Dad. He listened and he seemed to care. He asked questions and offered to help. Not once did he mention Gail but if he had, I'm pretty sure I would have told him everything. Maybe this was his way of

Dempsey's Grill

letting me know he was there. He was my safety net. That's why it was nice.

Chapter Sixty

Opening Night

I had never seen Dempsey so nervous in my life.

"This is a huge mistake, Bugs. This isn't going to work. We gotta bail. I'm going home."

Hope did her best to calm him. She reached up and straightened his tie. She removed a piece of lint from his shirt, she even lied and complimented his choice of colors: Green dress shirt with yellow tie complete with green ducks running north and south. She sounded convincing, but it did little in calming him down.

"I liked washing dishes," he mumbled.

She looked at me and shook her head, her mouth clenched tight, her teeth grinding. She did as promised. She held her comments in check. Silence, she'd promised, or better yet, reassurance and nothing else. This was a bad time for lectures or other realities. No, neither of

Dempsey's Grill

those things would be good right now. This was a time to embrace the madness. In other words, lie your ass off.

All is shiny and clean and cute as a kitten, I kept telling myself. This crazy idea of opening a burger joint when the town is already saturated with the burger joints will not fail! It's a great idea, damnit! I can't believe others haven't thought of it.

Oh God, what the hell were we thinking?

To my pleasant surprise, Hope followed my advice. Let everything run its course, I said. When Dempsey panics, and he will, do not stop him. Everything must play itself out. Allow everything to bleed out of his system.

Hope reached into her pocket and pulled out a comb. A wild hair had escaped from Dempsey's head. In one swift move she placed it back where it belonged. His freshly trimmed sideburns and clean-shaven face stilled.

Dempsey and I stood center stage and ground zero inside our new restaurant and ten feet from the front door. The vestibule was empty, the outer door locked. It was 6 p.m. on a Thursday night. It was the Grand Opening, and there was no turning back.

I glanced to my right where Gail should be standing and quickly looked away. Those thoughts would come later but not now.

It was Show Time.

"Ready?" Hope asked Dempsey. "Ready?" she asked me.

"Ready," we answered in unison.

Hope disappeared into the vestibule. I could hear the click as she unlocked the front door. We jumped at the sound and nervously smiled to one another. We turned and looked behind us. Our employees stood proud. Two cooks, four wait staff, a dishwasher, and a helper. We smiled and turned back to the door.

"Thanks for hanging in there, Bugs."

"Thanks for putting up with me."

"Like I had a choice."

We'd sent out fliers and mailers throughout the valley and the college campus announcing our grand opening. We had radio ads and local TV ads.

Buy Two Specials - Get One Free! Party of Four Gets Free Ice Cream!

Our plan was to give as much stuff away as possible without going broke. Give them a taste and with luck, maybe they would come back.

Dempsey took a step back. I pictured him escaping through the fire exit, never to be seen again, A vision so real I immediately grabbed his arm to stop him.

"Damn, Bugs, stop touching me."

Hope appeared from the vestibule. Her eyes were wide. A blank look crossed her face.

It was over.

Who cared about another burger joint? Dempsey was right. He's always right. At least I can get my old job back, but what about him? This could really push him over the edge. Maybe my old boss had room for one more. Dempsey was tall enough. He could reach the ceiling without a ladder. I looked over at him. He looked at me. Our shoulders slumped. Our eyes defeated. This crazy dream was dashed.

With a final look of despair, I glanced at Hope. I was about to thank her for all the hard work, but I stopped when I noticed a smile. My eyes widened as she opened the door and got the hell out of the way.

A mob of people appeared before us. The silence shattered. Soon we were surrounded by strangers begging to buy what we had to sell.

We were in business!

Chapter Sixty-One

The New Hope

The evening was a blur. A line of paying customers stretched from the cash register to the sidewalk. Dempsey and Hope served as hosts, seating everyone at the proper tables. We ran out of ice cream, we ran out of hamburger buns, and by the end of the evening, we ran out of hamburgers. By the time we closed, the only thing we had left were drinks and French fries, and even those were running low.

We sent the crew home and promised we'd have better organizational skills in the future. Our future began tomorrow at 11 a.m.

We collapsed in Dempsey's office. Our crew was experienced restaurant personnel, so they knew how to clean up far better than we did. In fact, we were in the way most of the time.

"We need a bigger crew," Dempsey said while leaning back in his office chair. "This is nuts."

"I'll make some calls and set up interviews tomorrow," I promised. "Maybe we can hire a couple more by Monday."

We were wrong about how many we would need. By the end of the month we'd hired six more and we were still short-handed.

As the month went on, we kept waiting for business to slow. We were told it would. We even had a chart full of projections preparing us for the weeks and months to follow. As a precaution, we kept our inventory low. Most of our staff were college kids and only able to work part time, but if things kept up the way they were going, we knew we'd be ready for full-timers pretty soon. No business can sustain a packed house every night, can it?

Yes, it can.

Hope's ice cream may have been a bigger hit than our burgers. She was constantly on the phone talking to her German supplier, working out details and asking about new flavors. Dempsey wasn't sure if we were ready to expand the menu, but I suggested we try using the new flavors as one-time offers.

As September turned to October it was clear—we were a hit. At least for now, we agreed.

I was exhausted, overwhelmed, and probably smelled like burgers most of the time, but for once I was confident and satisfied. I even moved out and found a place of my own. Mom cried and Dad tried to talk me out of it, but it was time to leave and deep down, they knew it too.

1053 square feet and it was all mine. My own bed. My clothes on the floor. My favorite chair. My 32-inch flat screen sitting on the kitchen counter. Why? Because it's my place. My rules. Even the ant colony living under the sink was mine.

I kept my mind off Gail as much as I could, but I wasn't always successful. Every now and then when the door opened and a customer walked in, I pretended it was her. I tried not to think about where she was or how she was doing but no matter how hard I tried, her memory was never far away. I knew I would never get over her, and I didn't want to.

If there is one thing a new business owner discover it's how little they know about anything and we were no exception. A month after opening night, Dempsey and I promoted one of our employees, Alicia,

Dempsey's Grill

to assistant manager. Business was booming but our energy level was not.

"I'm so damn tired, Bugs. The other day I gave a kid a beer and could not understand what the problem was."

When we finally added a full-time assistant, Dempsey and I took turns taking a day and a half off each week. After a month of busting my butt at the restaurant, being able to sleep in until the church bells rang high noon or being allowed to leave before the last guest had toasted the final drop of wine in the bottle was a simple but welcome indulgence. If business continued to boom, we'd eventually move her up to full manager status and give her an assistant of her own. Visions of two days off in a row danced in my mind, teasing me with the idea of a mini vacation.

My first full day off in a month was strange. The last thirty days had been a blur; a dream. A constant cloudy day, if you will. A bright beam of moonlight on a starless night...okay, I don't know what the hell that meant, either.

I wasn't sure what kind of day it would be and honestly, I was a little worried about it. With all the distractions, I hadn't had the time or the energy to think and I was glad. Gail would ambush my thoughts and quickly disappear. The responsibility of running a restaurant took everything out of me and allowed little time in my head for anything else, but now I had an actual full day all to myself. What kind of tricks would my mind play, I wondered? I could only imagine the games it would create or the cruel dreams they would become. Maybe a day off was a bad idea.

I soon discovered, on this first full day off, that it would not be spent alone, begging for distractions. In fact, it was spent at my sister's house sitting uncomfortably at her kitchen table. The constant tick-tock of her grandfather clock and the chill of her home tortured me and brutally passed through me as if it were trying to force this unwanted intruder out and away forever. But that didn't bother me. No, I was fine with that. In fact, I would have welcomed all of that if it had promised to stop the annoying racket of Hope's fingernails ricocheting across her shiny mahogany kitchen table.

She sat in a chair across from me, a determined and obviously fake grin smeared across her face. It was a week after the National Elections. The Republican hopeful lost to the incumbent. To my surprise, Hope was not suicidal. At first, I figured that's why I was here. I would sit and quietly listen as a flustered and flabbergasted Hope described how our country was going to hell. Check that...is in hell. Hope would then show me her passport and explain her plans of fleeing to Canada.

But none of that happened. Sadly, I was there for another purpose.

"We need to talk about love, little brother."

Hope sat relaxed in her chair, not her usual ramrod straight, school-marm perfect posture. Something had changed. The lost and sad little girl I had known nearly all our lives was gone. That secret side of her that only I could see had been replaced by a twinkle in her eyes and a sparkle in her voice. Today her will was strong. It was real. She was no longer hiding beneath those false layers. She was happy and excited, and I didn't care why. All I knew was someone or something had changed her. Little did I know I was inches away from finding who and why.

"Dempsey and I are getting into a serious relationship," she confessed. "I will admit, I'm a little scared, but it's incredibly exciting."

Hope paused, waiting for my reply. Or with a little luck, she had finished, allowing me to get the hell out of there. Before I could move, she continued.

"For years, I've been really..." she cleared her throat, "unsatisfied with Todd. In *that* way. Do you know what I mean?"

"Yes!" I nearly shouted. *Please don't go into detail. Please don't go into detail. Please...*

"I won't go into detail. Suffice to say, there's been no such issues with Dempsey." A smile curled the corners of her mouth. I swear a flush crept over the exposed skin of her neck and up to her cheeks. Even her eyes seemed brighter.

"Great. That's...um, great." I faked a smile so hard I could practically hear my cheeks creaking with the effort.

Dempsey's Grill

"After the first, shall we say, enthusiastic encounters, I assumed things would cool. Our mutual passions sated, we would go our separate ways."

And that we would never have to discuss my sister's sated passions again, I almost interjected.

"But that's not what happened."

Oh, dear God...

"I have to admit, I found a depth to Dempsey I had not expected in a purely carnal relationship. I began to see him as a man, not just as...well, a human..." she lowered her voice to a whisper, "vibrator."

Just kill me now!

"With Dempsey, I can be myself in a way I never could with any other man. He accepts me and encourages me to share every part of myself."

"I'm not Dempsey so stop sharing!"

But I didn't say that. I screamed it in my head.

"It's like a drug. I'm out of control. As you know, I prefer to plan things out. I'm quite proud of my organizational skills, but ever since Dempsey walked into my life, my daily planner has turned upside down."

She paused momentarily and took a deep breath. I was oddly curious and at the same time hoped she was finally finished.

"In the past three days I have been late for three appointments. I forgot another and I missed a PTA meeting."

"Aren't you head of the PTA?"

She is, by the way, and every teacher fears her.

"I was busy!" She quickly blushed. "But the thing is, Gibson, I don't care. Not once did I need my yoga meditation and I haven't been to my spiritual mountain in a week."

Yes, she has a spiritual mountain. It's actually a hill overlooking a pig farm. Todd once told me of a day she sat on an ant colony and demanded the entire hill be sprayed. I'd been there once. It smelled weird.

"And then there are the balls."

"Balls?" I weakly repeated, hoping to God they were of the bouncing variety.

"Not once have I had to use my stress balls. I couldn't even tell you where they are."

"Is that a good thing?" I didn't know what else to say. I found myself regretting saying anything.

"Of course it's a good thing." She flashed me an odd stare, then reached across the table and gently but firmly grabbed my chin. "Look at me, Gibson. We have a tyrant, socialist dictator sitting in the oval office ruining our beautiful country and I don't give a rat's ass."

She nodded her head and smiled. It was true. She didn't give a rat's ass. She was genuinely happy.

"I was wrong about Lourdes," she admitted.

It was my turn to smile.

"I was angry at the wrong person and I have asked you here to offer my apology. The best thing you ever did was come home. You made my life better. Thank you, Gibson. In fact, you made all our lives better. Dempsey said just the other day that without you, he never would have had the courage to open the restaurant."

Really?

"And Gail..."

My body stiffened. I didn't want to go there.

"Relax, Gibson. I know it hurts to hear her name, but you need to listen. She gave you love and a purpose and you will have that again. You deserve it just like I deserve it. In fact, every living soul deserves it."

She let go of my face. She was satisfied and confident but there was something else about her that I had never seen before. Dempsey had given her something Todd never could.

"Dempsey doesn't try to change who you are," I realized. "In fact, he loves your style and how you see the world and most of all, he understands your place in it. He wouldn't have it any other way. Am I right?"

The world's tiniest tear escaped from her eye and ran as fast as it could. Destination: Anywhere.

"Yes. You are correct, my little brother. Are you mad?"

Dempsey's Grill

I thought about it. On the surface Hope and Dempsey were wrong on every level. The math didn't add up. But since I suck at math, why worry about numbers if my sister was happy for once in her life?

"How could I be mad?" I reached out and squeezed her hand. "You deserve this. Both of you do. Maybe one day he'll let you cut his hair above his ears."

Hope returned the squeeze and smiled. It was one of those rare brother-sister love moments. Don't worry. I won't tell if you don't.

"Have you told the kids?"

"Not yet."

"Mom and Dad?"

"Are you kidding?"

"You'll have to. Plus, Mom and Dad love him. I'll bet your kids will too."

Hope released my hand and studied me. I was afraid she was about to give me Act Two of Mushy Romance TMI. Thankfully, she had something else in mind.

"Why don't you come over for dinner tonight?"

"Just you and me?" I asked.

"You, me, Ronny, and Laura. I think it's time we began to act like a normal family."

"Yes." I smiled. "So do I."

Chapter Sixty-Two

A Family Dinner

I thought I was nervous the day I came home but nothing compared to this. I was a stranger, an out-of-towner people whisper about. I came from a big city forced to be in their world and nothing more. Would I be the creepy uncle in their eyes? The one that sits in the lawn chair on the fourth of July, mumbling to himself after his third six-pack?

Look, Mommy. Uncle Gibson threw up on the grass!

Okay, that was reaching. But you get the idea.

My niece was six and my nephew was four. I had zero experience with people that short. I may have seen my niece a total of five days tops and that was when she was an infant. As far as my nephew, I hadn't a clue. Images of the little guy running to the far end of the house screaming, 'kitty killer!' danced on my disco memory floor while his mother admitted this was a terrible idea. How does one talk to a child if they have no experience? I guess it all comes down to that, doesn't it? Experience. I should have substituted at a kindergarten.

Dempsey's Grill

I hesitated as I always did on Hope's doorstep. For a brief second Gail was there, telling me I'd do just fine. She would have worn her best whatever and her smell would have been one step above lovely, but I put on the breaks and reminded myself now wasn't the time. I looked at the empty space where she no longer stood. This was a one-man show and the curtain was opening.

"He's here! He's here!"

The kids were glued to their bedroom window overlooking the neighborhood. They had been watching me the whole time.

Busted.

"How long can you stay?"

"Mom said he could see my room first!"

"No, she didn't!"

They stood in front of me. Their eyes big, their smiles amazing. I felt like a prize jumping out of their favorite cereal box. Ron touched my hand. Soon Laura followed. My lack of experience in scenes like this hopped on a bus and rode far away. I knew exactly what to do.

I knelt on one knee and smiled. Ron had the dark blue eyes of Dad's side of the family. So did I. Laura was Hope from years past, complete with the cowlick bangs.

"You must be Ron," I said. The boy's smile grew wide as he nodded yes.

"Ronnie," his sister corrected.

"Ronnie," I repeated. "And you must be Laura."

They moved a little closer. Their eyes full of curiosity and giggles.

"You're Uncle Gibson," Laura proudly noted as her voice filled with confidence. Her eyes dared anyone to argue. "You had a bad girlfriend. She told you to go home and that made Mom really happy because she really missed you."

"You weren't supposed to say that," Ronnie whispered.

A look of panic flashed in Laura's eyes as I bit my tongue fighting off a laugh.

"It'll be our secret," I whispered.

"Promise?" She hesitated, making sure I could be trusted.

"Promise."

They took me by the hand and pulled me inside. Within seconds, I was greeted by Hope with a hug of her own. She sent us upstairs until dinner was ready. The mystery of her home's upper floor was soon revealed. The kids showed me their toys, their drawings, their books and their smiles, but most of all they showed me their lives.

"My room first, Uncle Gibson!" Ronnie demanded.

"I'm the oldest so that means I go first," Laura reminded.

Laura's room was bright yellow, her favorite color, she explained. Her walls were lined with paintings and drawings and bookshelves on every corner. Her hardwood floor was decorated with a rug full of complex science and math symbols. I had a hunch they were memorized and understood.

Ronnie was the builder of the two. His room sparkled with emerald green. My favorite color, if you were curious. His floor was littered with clay castles, model cars and endless building blocks. I was about to compliment him on his detailed work when he whispered a confession. "My sister helps me."

"She did a great job," I whispered back.

"She said the next time I build something I'm on my own."

"I could help."

I cringed at my suggestion as a memory flooded in. I remembered Hope helping me when building anything from scratch. Before my eyes, history was repeating itself.

The kids sat me in the hallway across from their rooms. Laura was already the negotiator of the two and pointed out that the hallway would be the neutral spot.

"I'm sorry about Gail," Laura said as Ronnie laid a model car in my lap. "She's going to figure it out that she made a mistake and then she'll come back."

I looked deep into the promise of her eyes and wanted to believe. I began to wonder if every child was secretly brilliant.

Ronnie placed a drawing of trees and tigers and the moon in my lap as well. "What do you think?" His hands folded behind his back, waiting. I felt like a teacher again.

Dempsey's Grill

I gave him the stock answer every adult gives when handed a drawing from a child. "Wow. It's nice." I quickly realized our family did not allow stock answers.

"No, Uncle Gibson." Laura took the drawing from my hands and waited until she had my full attention. "He wants you to critique it. This is the first draft."

"Oh." I paused glancing at them both. "But it looks great." They weren't buying it. I was officially stumped. My first blunder.

"Mom says you have to hear the bad stuff as well as the good, otherwise you won't grow." Laura glanced at her brother, waiting for him to agree. "You won't hurt his feelings," she promised.

"Well, your mom is really smart." My illusions of my sister were slowly evaporating. Has she always been this way?

"Mom says you're smarter, but I'm not supposed to tell you," Ronnie whispered.

"Uh-huh." Laura agreed. "Mom says you've got an open mind. What does that mean, Uncle Gibson?"

Before I could answer, the dinner bell rang. Not literally, but you get the idea. We ran downstairs and ate at a table perfectly set for four. The house was warm, happy, and content. Anger and loneliness had packed their bags and traveled on. We talked about the good side of life and refused to flip the coin to the dark half. Sure, it was there. It will always be there. All coins have two sides, but not tonight.

I was teased over my second helping and third. I had no idea Hope was an amateur chef. We giggled and laughed and not once did the world stop spinning if a crumb found its way on her special tablecloth.

We played battleships during their bath and I ended up getting just as wet. Who cares? When the night ended, I read them a story and tucked them into bed and promised I'd see them again real soon. It was a promise I would never break.

"Thank you, Uncle Gibson for visiting us," Laura said. Her brother was already fast asleep. "I always wondered who you were and now I don't have to wonder anymore."

Laura wrapped her small, warm arms around my neck and squeezed all the bad stuff away. Is it possible for someone so little to make the world brighter and better? I think you know the answer to that.

When I came downstairs Hope and I talked. When I talked, she listened and when she talked, I did the same. This was far better than the talks we'd had when I'd first came home. We talked about Gail, Dempsey, and the restaurant. A future full of mystery. No more loneliness and longing, I promised. We get one crack at this, don't we? Yes, we do.

When the night ended and I said goodbye, I felt a part of me was different. Confident and a sense of belonging all mixed into one giant glazed doughnut rushed through my veins. I had no idea this special doughnut of mine was about to be put to the test.

Chapter Sixty-Three

The Lonely Stake Fry

Eugene, Oregon must be the bicycle capital of the world, or if it isn't then I can assure you it's in the top five. A light rain fell. It felt good as I maneuvered my bike in and out of traffic. I was getting the hang of it. Eugene is not for the rookie bicyclist and slowly I was becoming a pro. The heavy rains were on their way but for now they had the day off. The sun had burned away the morning fog and was beginning to settle in. Dempsey and I had to talk. He had been avoiding me since Hope came into the picture. Sure, we talked, but we never talked about the two of them. He had to understand I didn't mind.

I came in through the back door. The restaurant was equipped with a mudroom, perfect for days like this. I removed my wet jacket and shoes and placed my bike in the corner to dry. I ran upstairs where my official Dempsey's Grill attire waited. I dressed and ran downstairs.

Our work was becoming routine.

It was 9 a.m. and I would check inventory, add in last night's hourly intake, and today's estimate. I would help with the prep and fix anything that was broken. Mornings were the best. It was pre-game warm-ups before the big show. I planned on working and talking to Dempsey at the same time. For a little while it would just be us. I knew it wouldn't take much to get him to talk.

I heard voices as I walked downstairs. Our assistant, Alicia, wasn't due until eleven but sometimes she arrived early. I smiled. I was glad she was here. It would give me a chance to pull Dempsey away for our talk. He would resist until he understood I was on his side. Afterward, getting him to stop talking would be the chore. I walked out into full view of our restaurant. The grill area on my right, the dining area to my left. The place sparkled. The air was clean, and everything shined. Our night crew always did an amazing job. Too bad I sucked at it. Details were not my strength. I knew if Gail was here, she would have owned it and she would have made sure I owned it too. Partners do not suck at anything, she would have said. But enough about Gail. Hope warned me last night to turn the switch off when that happens. You must not take a step back, she advised. Don't worry I won't. Who was I kidding?

Dempsey stood in the middle of the dining room, his body blocking my view of Alicia. I found it odd they would be in the dining area when the back room was where the action was. He turned and made eye contact. I smiled. He didn't. I opened my mouth to talk but he shook his head no. I returned his 'No' with a curious look. Dempsey took a giant step to the left. His action reminded me of a curtain opening for the school play. As he did the star of the show was revealed.

A mind is a bizarre machine. If it encounters the impossible, the impossible becomes invisible. Reality turns into a dream or in some cases, a nightmare. Are we all like that?

"Gibson."

Yes, I believe we are.

"Look at me, Gibson."

I noticed a lonely steak fry resting quietly under a table.

"Are you happy to see me?"

Dempsey's Grill

A giant steak fry all by itself.

"Gibson? What are you looking at?"

How could our night crew miss it? On the other hand, maybe it wants to be alone. That I can understand. I slowly looked up into her eyes.

"Hi, Lourdes," I said.

Chapter Sixty-Four

An Overdue Farewell

Lourdes looked the same; same perfect hair, same fresh manicure, same chic clothes and expensive handbag. I didn't know if that was good or bad. Why would I expect anything else? She was the same person who had kicked me out in Seattle. Funny. Why does that seem so long ago?

"You look nice," I said.

Lourdes didn't answer. Lourdes didn't smile and she didn't frown. What she did was study me. I was now being analyzed inside and out. Same old Lourdes.

She hadn't changed much, but I knew I had. The tone of my voice, the color of my clothes, the length of my hair, all being observed and assessed. Could she see how much I had changed?

Dempsey stood between us, unsure what to do next. His body was tense, a polite smile polishing his face as he watched me, waiting for the next move.

"Gibson."

Dempsey's Grill

This is our place, Dempsey's eyes reminded me. Hard to believe, huh, Bugs? Lots of hard work but it came alive, didn't it? The burgers are great. We're all exhausted but who gives a shit?

"Gibson, look at me."

I'd played with my niece and nephew last night. I had enjoyed my sister's company. My parents are proud of me and I have my own place.

"You must have dozens of questions for me."

And I spent the summer with Gail.

Lourdes flicked a hand at Dempsey to dismiss him. "Thank you. You can leave."

Dempsey turned and started to walk away. I grabbed him by the arm and pulled him back. Lourdes looked at me, her eyebrows furrowed. I recognized that look. The look that used to make my stomach drop and have me scrambling to get 'I'm sorry' offerings.

Same old Lourdes.

"It's time to go, Gibson. I've decided to give you another chance."

She took a step forward and hugged me. I didn't hug back. Funny, this scene was the exact reverse not so long ago. She released me and took a step back, either unaware of our awkward moment or too involved in her next move.

"You'll have to sleep in the guest room until we have fully reconciled. You understand."

And for once, I did get it. For a long time, I hadn't, but now I did.

"You've changed." Lourdes eyes narrowed. "I'm sure I'll figure it out soon enough." She shrugged her shoulders and turned to Dempsey. She stared long enough until he looked away. She smiled.

"Get the door," she ordered. "You can have his things. Gibson, ten minutes. Say, your goodbyes."

When a mystery is solved, most of us shake our heads and laugh. It was so easy, I thought. The answer was right there, out in the open. Why didn't I see it earlier? Did my mind finally grow up, or did it take the people I surrounded myself with to help me understand?

Lourdes grabbed my arm and tugged me toward the door. "We're flying home. We'll eat in a real restaurant," she pressed. "You pick. You're favorite."

"My favorite?" I removed my arm from her grip. "What is my favorite, Lourdes?"

"Open the door," she snipped. "We're going home!"

Dempsey moved to the door. He later told me he had no control over his legs. She was forcing him, it seemed. A mental shove.

I smiled as I heard something click home. I got it.

Sometimes you have to be lucky, or in my case, you have to move away to see things. I read about this and I'm pretty sure I saw it in a movie. The mind snaps out of it, it kicks the fog in the ass and sees the real reason life is in the shitter.

"No," I said. My voice was calm and confident. I'm pretty sure this was the first time I'd ever said no to her. I wondered if this was a first anybody in her life had said no to her.

"Excuse me?" Lourdes eyes bulged wide.

Dempsey flinched.

"No," I repeated. My will was strong, my mind clear. "You wasted a trip. You should have called first."

"What did you say?"

Dempsey took another step to the door. He said the force of her voice passed right through him. We later agreed she would have made an excellent Marine drill sergeant.

Lourdes took a step towards me, and another, and another. We were now inches apart. Anger, surprise, and a tinge of hurt spread about her face. It's funny, a year ago I would have turned into a little boy, but now? Now I'm just a clumsy thirty-year-old. Imagine that.

"I should have called. I don't need your permission. I don't need you. You. Need. ME!"

After all these years, I can still see her face, her voice shrill, head low, eyes wide, unblinking. I still wonder how she did it.

"This...this filthy town has *poisoned* you," she whispered. She pressed her finger against my chest to make her point but quickly pulled it away. I wondered if she thought I was contagious. "We are having a long talk on the way home. No one has ever said *no* to me."

I was right. I was the first.

"Now, come on." She whirled and strode to the door, expecting me to follow.

Dempsey's Grill

I watched her walk away. The mere thought of following her gave me an uncomfortable dirty feeling. Was there a time when all I did was obey? Sadly yes, I'm afraid. Why had I been okay with that?

"No, Lourdes. I'm not going back to Seattle. In fact, I wouldn't walk across the street with you." The words came out calm and easy, almost humorous. The familiar knot in my chest had taken a leave of absence, replaced by a new friend. He went by the name, Mister Backbone.

I realized I was smiling.

Lourdes spun around. Her mouth puckered, her eyes narrowed in a steamy glare. I waited patiently as she collected herself. She pushed her hair back and came storming back like a running bull.

I, however, wasn't finished. "I owe you a huge amount of thanks," I continued, stopping her in her tracks. "If you hadn't kicked me out, I'd still be miserable. Did you know that I hated my job? I even hated our house – excuse me – your daddy's house. I ate your choice of food and only talked to your friends. I guess, what I'm trying to say is..."

How do I say this in a nice way?

"What the fuck was wrong with me?"

I knew this would take time to sink in, so I waited. When you have as many layers as Lourdes, it takes time for words to travel through the proper channels.

Lourdes shot a glare at Dempsey and turned back to me. He turned and looked at me. We smiled. She took a step forward. I held my ground. For the first time there were no sweaty palms, no rapid heartbeat, and no doubt.

"You have a lot of explaining to do." Lourdes's face had changed to a violent shade of red. Her voice growled in a low whisper. But to be honest, I hardly noticed. I was too busy remembering Gail's words the morning she left. 'I've been playing it safe my whole life. Now it's time to take a chance.'

Gail wasn't talking about herself. She was talking about us.

"*Do you know who you're talking to? I'm not one of your small-town hicks!*" Lourdes screamed. Her words didn't bounce off the wall or cut a hole through my mid-section. They were just words from a troubled woman who had once convinced me she was worth it.

"When we get home, I'm telling Daddy! I can only imagine what he'll have to say about—"

"Hush, Lourdes."

"...you" She took a step back and for the first time, I saw defeat in her eyes.

Dempsey opened the back door as the sun broke through the clouds. I think what I remember most about that day is how Lourdes never fought back. Maybe she decided in that moment that I wasn't up to her standards, or maybe she hated the town so much she had to get out, or maybe the sunlight cast a reflection of who she really was, and how she'll never change and that she blew it with a nice guy like me. That's how I like to think of it, anyway.

She walked out into the sunlight and stopped. I tried to turn away, but I couldn't. She started to turn in my direction, but Dempsey closed the door before I could see her face.

I never saw her again.

"Sorry, Bugs. Were you finished?"

I should have been finished years ago.

"Yes," I said.

"Good. Let's get to work."

We paused and smiled for a moment. We knew we would talk about this later, but not today. Priorities first. I went upstairs and worked on the books. Dempsey prepped the backroom and later we talked about Hope. A bump in the road repaired and paved over.

Our day had only begun.

Chapter Sixty-Five

Unexpected Homecoming

    Twelve hours later I went home. I worked the lunch crowd and dinner crowd. I prepped, I cleaned, and I cooked. Adrenalin is an amazing drug, isn't it?

    Dempsey tried to send me home earlier. Alicia tried. Our crew tried. All of them gave up. I was certain I'd work until closing, but the tank finally ran dry. Dempsey wasn't surprised by the day I put in.

    "That's what happens when you release a caged bird. You got your wings," he said. "Now fly your ass home."

    I did. As I pedaled, my thoughts began to float away like imaginary balloons. My mind had officially caught up with my body and was beginning to shut down for the night. I knew those balloons would be back. They always found their way back to their owner but tonight, they were free to dance the night away.

I knew I would drop the moment I walked inside. I hoped my mind wouldn't take me on too many adventures. I needed sleep and lots of it, but who was I kidding? This muscle locked between my ears has taken me on a non-stop rollercoaster ride since birth. Gail got a kick out of it, Lourdes hated it, and others like Dempsey accepted it. But Lourdes was right; I can't live off my dreams and fantasies forever. I must start facing the world that I live in. How many times today had I relived my conversation with Lourdes, my goodbye to Gail, and my pretend talks with stick figures?

I needed a doctor—the kind you see lying on a couch.

But what would a doctor do? Drugs? Counseling? A padded cell? Please, not the cell. I've seen the movies. I've read the books. It always turns out ugly. Maybe all those fantasies and dreams are healthy. It's the minds' way of dealing with unpleasant experiences. Maybe that's the cure for everyone. Instead of therapy or drugs or over the border sanitariums, let the mind play whatever game it has in store and in a month or two you're normal.

A final break with Lourdes. That life totally gone. I was entering uncharted waters. Not only was I part owner of a business, I also had zero social life. But I was glad I had no girlfriend. I didn't need a date to go to the movies or to dinner or long walks and talks. I was good at doing all those things by myself. Being single was new for me, but people do it every day. As they say, it's healthy to start over.

Right?

I'd said goodbye to the women in my life. One by choice and one without a choice. Thinking of the look on Lourdes's face brought satisfaction, relief and a defiant joy. Thinking of Gail...well that tied my stomach in knots. The color seemed to drain out of the world. I felt empty, lonely, stupid, and helpless. My emotional extremes knocked against each other. Maybe they'd find a balance between the happiness of no-Lourdes and the sadness of no-Gail.

Normally, when I arrived home I would have collapsed on my uncomfortable couch.

Not tonight.

My door was unlocked. My bedroom light on. Someone was inside making a lot of noise. I froze. I was fully awake.

Dempsey's Grill

What now?

The noise stopped as I slowly pushed the door open. This wasn't make-believe. My mind had run out of games to play. This was real. I closed the door and stood outside. It started to rain. Of course. Raining and apartment robbing is a perfect ending to an exhausting day.

Now what?

I had a key and the management had a key. The locks were new. Nearly burglar proof, the manager had told me. Nearly, he'd said. Never trust someone when they say 'nearly.' This was a good part of town where the odds of a thief taking their time robbing my place would be extremely low.

Did I lock the door this morning?

Think!

I thought.

Yes, I had locked the door. I lock everything that needs to be locked and I always check it twice. I'm sick that way. It's about as automatic for me as washing my hands after using the toilet.

A thud came from my bedroom.

I jumped.

Fear and caution took a step back. Anger was now in the lead. Who the hell breaks into my place?

Maybe it was the exhaustion or the confrontation with Lourdes or the new me. Whoever it was, I wanted them out. They were leaving. Now!

I pushed the door open and used the loudest, toughest, bravest voice I could find. "Who the hell are you? Show yourself!"

I stormed past the front room, the kitchen, and the bathroom. I followed the light. The bastards can't hide anymore! My legs slowed and tried to turn around. They weren't as tired as my head or as brave as my body. They still had an ounce of common sense and a pound of caution. They tried their best to leave. Call the manager, the police. They could have guns or knives. You'll die young. Protocol! Always follow protocol!

Too late. I had arrived.

I stumbled into the bedroom, my feet collapsing into each other. Instead of striding confidently into the bedroom ready to face the unwanted intruder, I stumbled and danced and found myself on the floor staring up at the ceiling and the intruder.

She stood over me. A box in her hand and a smile on her face. My mind surrendered. It was official. Stop the clock, call off the dogs. The game is over. This has now become the one and only weirdest day of my life.

"You have my drawing. Where is it?" Gail asked.

Chapter Sixty-Six

Breaking and Entering

Gail stood over me waiting for an answer, a box in her hand and another at her feet. I didn't move. What was the point?

"Huh?" It was the only word that came to mind.

"The drawing I made of me and you and my mom," she impatiently explained. "You stole it from my room. I don't like anyone stealing from me. Where is it?"

I didn't answer. I was too busy trying to figure out if this was real fantasy or fantastic reality.

Gail let out a disappointed sigh and dropped the box inches from my head. "I'm prepared to turn this place upside down. I want it now."

I cleared my throat and blinked. She was serious. She would tear my place down if she had to. I slowly got up and stood in front of her. She had cut her hair. It was a choppy bob, almost shoulder-length, the ends tickling her neck. I wished I was her hair. Gail wore a pale yellow and blue shirt I'd never seen before. I tried to push away the thoughts of her truck-driving man paying the bills.

"It's at Mom and Dad's house," I said. "It's probably in the attic. If you ask Mom, she'll know exactly where it is."

We stood silent, examining one another. I didn't know what else to say.

"Good." Gail frowned, pursing her lips. "I'll do that. She walked out of my room, past the kitchen and to the front door. She opened the door and stepped out into the rain. It suddenly occurred to me this was real. I had to do something and for once, my voice obeyed.

"Stop!"

She stopped. She didn't turn. Just waited with her hand on the door, the rain washing through her hair and down her back.

What now? Why had she come back? Was it only the picture? Don't be stupid. Of course it is.

Gail cleared her throat. She let her hand drop. She was going to leave. Say something!

"How did you get in?" Not the question I wanted to ask, but it would have to do.

Gail turned back to face me. She rolled her eyes, hands on her hips. "Please. Two paper clips, a tension wrench, and sixty seconds. It's not brain surgery, trust me."

"You carry a tension wrench?" Focus, Gibson!

She didn't answer.

"But..." I really wanted to know. "How?"

Gail shuffled her feet and ran her fingers through her wet hair. It was clear she didn't really want to talk about her lock picking skills, but she would indulge me. "This is a five-pin lock." She pointed to the door. "I steadied the lock with the tension wrench; I fish hooked a paper clip, jiggled the lock with the wrench, pushed the paper clip inside, raked it and pushed the pins up until they clicked. After that I turned the wrench to one side and presto, I was in."

It was official: I was in love with a thief.

"How did you," I paused, stumbling with my words, "learn all of this?"

"Well." It was her turn to pause. "I sort of did some time in juvie when I was a teenager. Not a big deal." Her eyes were full of guilt. Her pleading adorable.

"You were in juvenile detention?"

"Six months. Can we please forget the past?"

"Let me guess, breaking and entering?"

"Kind of." Gail fidgeted with the doorknob, like a child admitting she stole the last cookie. "After I broke and entered, I might have taken a few things. But I returned all of it!"

As I learned more and more about her and her crime-ridden past I was officially, without denial or doubt...aroused.

"Hate me?" she asked.

"Well..." Are you kidding? Did I mention I was aroused? "Surprised," I answered.

I looked at the door and back at her, a final question coming to mind. "This is a brand-new lock," I pointed out. "The manager told me it was top of the line, nearly break-in proof." I shrugged my shoulders, not knowing what to say next.

Gail shrugged her shoulders too and flashed the most beautiful guilty grin I've ever seen. "Looks like I made a liar out of him. If you're interested, I could recommend a better lock than this."

"Will it be break-in proof?"

"For me? Hardly."

I gave up, but there was another question I had to ask. "Your drawing," I took a deep breath. Time to stop dancing around the subject. Time to just ask, to face the truth no matter how ugly. I braced myself for another hollowing goodbye, but I had to ask: "Is that the only reason you're here?"

Gail didn't answer and for a moment and she didn't move. I expected a semi-truck to suddenly appear and for her to jump in it and wave goodbye.

That didn't happen.

Instead, she crossed her arms over her chest and walked inside. Her hair was dripping from the rain. She closed the door behind her.

"Mind if I sit down?" she asked.

We sat at my kitchen table. She took the chair with the wobbly legs but didn't seem to mind. As for me, I didn't care if she answered or not. I still couldn't believe she was here. I gave her a towel to dry off with and offered her coffee from my new machine. She passed. She'd once tasted my attempt at making coffee.

"Before I answer your question I have to tell you what happened after I...after the bus station." Gail tapped her fingers on the table. "I never saw him," she explained. "I had a lot of time to think and by the time I got to Seattle, I had pretty much thought of everything."

She never saw him.

"What did you think of?" I asked. Was it me? But I couldn't ask that.

Gail met my eyes. A small smile crept onto her face. Could she read my mind? Did she know how much I longed to jump across the table and wrap my arms around her, to never let her go again?

"My mom," she said. "I thought of my eighteenth birthday. Mom wanted to be eighteen again. She said if she could, she would have done things different. She never would have moved away with my dad. She and I would have stayed behind while Dad moved out and did his thing."

Gail shook her head. "My mom told me she made so many mistakes. Giving up her life to follow my dad was just one of the worst among many. She had to leave all her friends behind. That's where her world was. When she and Dad moved away she was positive she'd see that world again, but she didn't. She always put up a good front, but I knew. She was lonely. Sometimes she would talk about her friends. Her eyes would light up and we'd laugh. I'd catch myself being lonely, too. Her friends could have been my family. I never knew them, but I missed them anyway."

"Did she ever see them again?" I asked.

"No."

"What was your parent's marriage like?"

"Empty," she said without hesitation. "I never saw friendship or love or anything. They just sort of existed."

Gail smoothed back her rain damp hair. It was starting to curl in the warmth of my apartment. She continued. "When I arrived in Seattle, I realized I was copying her life. I was running away like she did. So, I asked myself if I loved him. Were we friends? What stories could we tell?"

Dempsey's Grill

She paused and looked away. "There are no stories or friends and when it came to friendship and love the answer was 'No.'"

She tried to fight off her tears. She lost. "I feel so stupid, Gibson. I loved the idea of being in love, but I wasn't in love, not with him anyway."

What was she saying? Was she in love with someone else? With me?

Don't make this about you, Gibson. Be supportive. If Gail needs a friend to listen to her, be there. Don't zone.

"How did you tell him?" I asked.

She sniffed and smiled. She wiped her cheeks. "He called. He was at some loading dock. He'd forgotten to pick me up. 'You can wait at the bus station,' he said. 'Or come meet me. It's only a couple miles.' My choice, like he didn't care whether I was with him or not. I told him I changed my mind and I wasn't coming. I told him it was over."

"Did he know you were in Seattle?"

"He didn't ask. In fact, he sounded relieved."

"You never saw him." This time I said it out loud. It wasn't a question. "Where have you been? It's been two months, Gail."

"Do you remember that little town in Northern Washington where my aunt lives?"

I remembered. "Sedro-Woolley."

"I called her from the bus station and told her I was stuck in Seattle with no place to go. The next thing I know I'm on a bus to go stay with her."

"Hurrah for Aunt..." I couldn't remember Gail's aunt's name and I really didn't care. The only thing that mattered was that she'd ditched the trucker.

"Penny. She's a single mom. Lives in a big white house with a big backyard surrounded by a white picket fence and everything. She runs a daycare out of her home and she's probably the most popular person in town. You'd love her."

I already did. She'd been there when Gail needed her.

"Aunt Penny put me to work. I rocked babies to sleep, I put Band-Aids on skinned knees, I dried tears, and I laughed and played. I felt like an aunt. The best part was telling her our stories. She laughed so hard she cried. She kept saying she wished she was there to see it. One night she saw me sitting in a chair staring out the window. She asked me why I didn't go back to the people who created those stories. I think she saw my mom's lonely eyes in me."

Gail rested her chin on her intertwined fingers. "She said, 'Do you know what I love most about being here in middle of nowhere?' and I shook my head. 'I live in a place where I feel alive, surrounded by people I love and who love me back. That's not nothing.'"

I stared at her. My heart was pounding so loud I barely heard my own voice as I whispered, "Do I make you feel alive?"

I had been miserable since she left. I desperately wanted her to say yes.

A tear slid down her cheek, but she smiled and reached across the table. It was the first time I had touched her since the day at the bus station. Her hands were cold that day but now they were warm and safe and a part of me. "Yes."

I clutched her hand like a tornado might come along and rip her away from me if I didn't hang on tight enough.

Gail pulled our hands up and kissed my fingers. She sniffed again. With my free hand, I handed her the roll of paper towels from the shelf behind me.

"Thanks." She blew her nose, cleared her throat. "All summer long, not once did I miss him. I waited for his call so I could leave because that is what I thought I was supposed to do, but deep down, I knew I didn't care if he never called. My life was just one big waiting game. With you, Dempsey, and Hope, it was happening. Everything moved so fast there was no time to wait and before I knew it, I started forgetting about that call."

Gail stroked the side of my face. "I love you." She smiled. "I should never have left. I was looking for a reason to stay and you were right there that day, right in front of me, but I didn't want to see it. I wanted love to be difficult and full of heartache. How messed up is that? I couldn't believe you loved me because you were so nice to me."

For once I didn't analyze. There was no delay while my mind raced to other adventures. I stood and pulled her up and hugged her close.

Dempsey's Grill

She was wet from the rain, but I didn't care. I kissed her hair and breathed in the smell of her, lemon and lilac and Gail.

"Making sure I'm real?" Her voice was muffled against my chest, her arms around my waist. She squeezed me tight.

"Yes," I said, "and I love you, too."

She was real.

"I still want my picture back," she reminded me. "You're not getting off that easy."

"Do you mind if we wait until tomorrow?" I asked. "Mom and Dad might be in bed."

"Fair enough."

"Oh," I remembered. "Dempsey has a check for you. You're still part owner you know, and Hope found your bra. Should I call them?"

I reached for my phone but was stopped as she said, "Mind if we wait till tomorrow? You and I have some catching up to do."

Epilogue

"Hi Emily."

"Hi Joe." Emily could tell he was nervous. People got nervous when they liked someone. That's what her grandma used to say, but why? Shouldn't you be calm and happy when you're around people you care about?

Weird. The whole world was weird.

Emily pushed off with the tips of her toes, setting the porch swing in motion.

Joe stood on the sidewalk as if afraid to join her. There was plenty of room on the swing, but he didn't move an inch.

If I ordered him to leave, he would and if I told him to sit, he'd ask where. Why do I have to do everything? Emily wondered.

Joe rubbed his nose with the back of his hand. "I'm sorry about your grandpa." His voice was sincere and caring. He sounded almost as sad as she felt.

"Thanks." Emily wanted to say more but the energy wasn't there. Grandpa's death zapped everything out of her. 'That's a first', she could hear him say. It made her smile.

"I'm sorry I wasn't at his funeral."

Emily knew Joe was trying his best to say something, anything, just to stay a little longer when all he had to do was sit next to her and say nothing. Was it really that hard to figure these things out?

"I get really uncomfortable at funerals," he continued. "I guess it's a reminder that we're all going to die too. But I'm really sorry. I should have gone anyway."

It was odd to watch him try so hard, but it made her feel good that he wanted to stay and talk to her. 'Hang on to those who care,' Grandpa use to say.

"It made me uncomfortable, too," Emily agreed.

"Really?" Joe looked up.

"Yeah. Who wants to be around dead people?" She kicked the swing a little harder then caught it with her toe to slow it down so she could see Joe. "I guess the best funeral is your own. Then it doesn't really matter. You're too busy with your new journey."

Joe nodded. He walked slowly up the porch steps like he was creeping up on her and she might yell at him.

A new journey, she wondered. Is that what Grandpa's doing? That's what he'd said when her grandma died two years ago.

"It's all right, sweetheart. Grandma Gail's going on a new journey."

Emily caught the railing and held the swing still as Joe crossed the porch to stand next to her. "It seems like all I do is go to funerals," she continued. "First my grandma and then last spring, Uncle Dempsey and Aunt Hope."

"I'm really sorry." Joe shoved his hands in his pockets and made brief eye contact. His confidence must be growing. "I didn't know your aunt and uncle, but your grandpa sure was nice. He was funny. How are your mom and dad and brothers doing?"

"They're okay. My mom and her sisters are busy feeding half the town at the restaurant. Mom said it's what Grandpa would have wanted."

"Oh."

Emily had an urge to run. She wanted to get away from the sad porch and the sad swing that Grandpa would never sit in again. She wished she could fly. To the moon and back, she thought, and suddenly she knew just the place.

"Wanna go with me somewhere?"

"Yes!" Joe grinned.

Emily smiled. His enthusiasm was through the roof. He'd probably follow me to the sewage treatment plant and never plug his nose, she thought

"Where?"

She was glad he was here. She'd always liked Joe and seeing him here today, when no one else seemed to notice her, she realized, 'He's my best friend.'

"It's a big rock by the river. I always feel better when I go there. My grandpa, Uncle Dempsey, and I used to go there and skip rocks. Come on."

"Cool." Joe smiled.

"Let's go." Emily grabbed his hand.

As evening fell, the two ran like children down the street. Their feet sent puffs of fallen leaves flying into the air. Soon it would be winter, and the town would be quiet, waiting for spring to bring it to life again. And through the rains of fall, the snow and cold of winter, the restaurant Emily's grandparents had founded with her great aunt Hope and great uncle Dempsey would continue serving the best burgers in town.

THE END

About the Author

Bryan Fagan is a former Chevy Chevette owner, a culinary arts degree holder and a one-time journalist. Although he enjoys writing stories, he wasn't crazy writing about other people's adventures.

Bryan grew up in Burlington, Washington by his grandparents, Helen and Joe Fagan, where he became a diehard Husky fan from birth. His grandfather ran a steel mill in Skagit County while his grandmother took care of the home. She was the only person who could make his grandfather behave. As a young boy, Bryan enjoyed playing with his dog, Copper, improving his skills at lawn darts and waving at the caboose. Because everyone knows if you don't wave at the caboose, the train will be sad. Aunt Betty wouldn't lie.

He moved to Eugene, Oregon after graduating from Southern Oregon University in Ashland. It was there he met his wife of over twenty-five years. It was in Eugene where he dabbled in short stories and attempted a couple of failed novels. He credits his daughters and his wife for challenging him to write a book that people would enjoy. When he's not writing, he's watching football in the fall, eating pizza on Sundays, he loves them all, and exploring used bookstores.

His adventures in life have allowed him to create funny and loving characters that he hopes you will enjoy with his first novel, Dempsey's Grill.

He has plans for as many future novels, as he has fingers. He does possess all his digits.

More from Foundations Book Publishing

Paved with Good Intentions
Dick Denny

"Just as HILLARIOUS and ACTION-PACKED as the first!

Hold onto your scotch and taquitos, this one's another wild, supernatural ride…"When you do a job for Hell, Heaven expects the same.
When Archangel Gabrielle shows up at the door of Decker Investigations offering some kick-ass cars in exchange for a job, Nick takes it just to keep the peace.

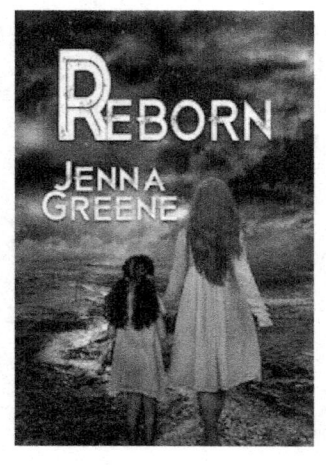

Reborn
Jenna Green

Those who bear marks on their skin are doomed to a life of slavery. Lexil has seven.

Sold into servitude, Lexil must deal with brutal punishments, back-breaking labor, and the loss of every freedom. When a young child she has befriended faces a horrible fate, she must intervene to protect her, no matter what the risk.

Foundations Book Publishing
Copyright 2016 © Foundations Book Publications Licensing
Brandon, Mississippi 39047
All Rights Reserved

10-9-8-7-6-5-4-3-2-1

Dempsey's Grill
Bryan Fagan
Copyright 2019 © Bryan J. Fagan
All Rights Reserved

No copy, electronic or otherwise, in whole or in part may be reproduced, copied, sold in physical or digital format without expressed written permission from the publisher, pursuant to legal statute 17 U.S.C. § 504 of the U.S. Code, punishable up to $250,000 in fines and/or five years imprisonment under 17 U.S.C. § 412. Not for sale if cover has been removed.

Made in the USA
Middletown, DE
16 August 2019